ARCTIC STORM

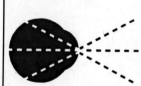

This Large Print Book carries the
Seal of Approval of N.A.V.H.

WATCH EYES TRILOGY, BOOK 1

ARCTIC STORM

JOANNE SUNDELL

WHEELER PUBLISHING
A part of Gale, Cengage Learning

GALE
CENGAGE Learning·

Farmington Hills, Mich • San Francisco • New York • Waterville, Maine
Meriden, Conn • Mason, Ohio • Chicago

GALE
CENGAGE Learning®

LIBRARY OF CONGRESS CATALOGING-IN-PUBLICATION DATA

Sundell, Joanne.
    Arctic storm / by Joanne Sundell. — Large print edition.
        pages cm — (Watch eyes trilogy ; book one)
    "Wheeler Publishing Large Print Western."
    ISBN 978-1-4104-8016-3 (softcover) — ISBN 1-4104-8016-X (softcover)
        1. Large type books. [1. Supernatural—Fiction. 2. Shamans—Fiction. 3. Adventure and adventurers—Fiction. 4. Survival—Fiction. 5. Chukchi—Fiction. 6. Siberian husky—Fiction. 7. Dogs—Fiction. 8. Ghosts—Fiction. 9. Arctic regions—History—20th century—Fiction. 10. Large type books.] I. Title.
    PZ7.S954645Arc 2015
    [Fic]—dc23   2015005904

Published in 2015 by arrangement with Joanne Sundell

Printed in the United States of America
1 2 3 4 5   19 18 17 16 15

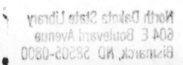

In loving memory of my loyal
Siberian sled dogs
Kraepelin ~ *Sigmund* ~ *Curie* ~ *Mesmer*
~ *Zeb* ~ *Zellie* ~ *Xander*

AUTHOR'S NOTE

The Chukchi people of northeast Siberia, over thousands of years, wisely bred and developed the Siberian husky we know today. This work of fiction is set in the context of real events that took place in northeast Siberia and on the Alaskan frontier in the early decades of the twentieth century.

PREFACE

Worlds ever brush past, both human and spirit. Good and Evil are born into each: some become master; some do not. Some suffer greatly; some do not. None from the spirit world can breach the world of humans, affecting anything in the mortal world. No mortal can breach the world of spirits, affecting anything in the spirit world . . . *unless* . . . their life force, whether created for good or for evil, whether born out of prophecy or fanaticism, naturally grows in power and strength, finally gaining enough momentum to crash through and leave a mark.

Thus, the worlds collide.

Thus, the battle ensues.

The Chukchi believed that their dogs guarded the gates of heaven, and that the way you treated a dog in this life determined your place in heaven. If this is so then surely when time comes for us to pass we will be assured of a place of great honor.

It is said that your dogs wait for you, asleep until you come across, then they pull your sled through and into heaven.

— National Sanjankah Dog Association

CHAPTER ONE

The far-northeast Siberian coast ~ a Chukchi village ~ Winter 1908

The huskies lay still in their snowy circles, tied to their posts, eyes closed, with their noses tucked under the curve of their thick tails to help warm each breath against the frozen air. Somewhere between awake and asleep; silent yet aware, they waited as they had for centuries. Darkness blanketed the isolated, craggy coast, where land met the sea ice. The Pole Star twinkled overhead. The Creator god could see all below on Native Earth, where the humans live, while the Earth god watched from beneath the Deep. The dogs continued to lie still, unmoving but for the rustle of their fur against the arctic winds. Senses sharpened, muscles tensed, they waited. Summoned now by the Gatekeepers, they waited for their guardian.

Thirteen-year-old Anya had little time. Everyone would awaken soon. Chilled but determined, she slipped through the door flap of her home. She'd kept outside the warm, fur sleeping box in their tented yaranga the night before, leaving Nana-tasha and the rest of Grisha's family inside the polog. Anya had claimed illness, and no one paid her any mind except Nana-tasha. Anya shrugged her shoulders, used to the snub. But her grandmother had given her a second look, then a third. Anya had looked away, correctly reading disapproval on every wrinkle of her grandmother's face. Hers was the single face Anya cared to see each day. Nana-tasha cared about her, the only one in the village who did.

Vitya. What about Vitya?

Anya pushed his sudden image from her mind and swallowed hard against the upset she would cause her grandmother. Taking her knife from inside her seal-fur clothing, Anya held fast to it. She'd had the crudely fashioned blade for as long as she could remember. "A gift from the gods," her grandmother had said, telling her to always keep it close. Right now Anya wished she'd never been given the knife and wished she didn't have to use it on this day for such a purpose. She'd no choice. Calling silently to the Morning Dawn, she prayed for help from the Directions.

Quick as she could, she cleared the rest of the village yarangas. The dogs lay just beyond, between the village and open tundra. She was glad it was not the dead of winter — most of the dogs would be outside, not inside sleeping with the children. Only on the coldest of nights, during Days Grow Long, were dogs invited inside to warm the children — children of breeder families. Grisha was a breeder of sled dogs. Grisha was important, a leader in the village. She'd no idea what he or the other breeders would do to her on this day.

The winds howled around and through the village. Anya shivered despite her knee-length kerker and high booted leggings. The howling picked up. She dropped to her knees, then stretched out face down in the snow. She must pray to the Morning Dawn. The howling kept on. Intuitively, Anya lifted her head, pulled off her fox-trimmed hood, and put her ear flush to the snow. The moment she did, she knew the sound and where it came from.

It wasn't the howl of the wolf or the dog. It wasn't the mournful song of the whale or bark of the seal or great walrus. It wasn't the music of the wind from any earthly direction. The cries came from another world — the spirit world. Sick to her stom-

15

ach, she hated the familiar sensation she faced whenever the spirits, good or bad, neared. She was no shaman. She was *not*.

Anya pulled herself to a stand. Her heart beat in time with the drums of the ancestors, steadying her, helping her stay calm. She refused to be afraid. What did the spirits want with her anyway? Why did they come now? She didn't know. She never understood their whispers, once close in. She never saw them clearly, but just a blur of shapes, some dark and some light. Right now the spirits didn't scare her; they made her angry. Even if she knew what they said, she didn't have to listen.

"Go to the shamans and leave me alone!" She whispered hard into the darkness, taking equally hard, determined steps toward the dogs. The images and shapes surrounding her dissolved away beneath each icy step she took; their ghostly murmurs and undertones quickly melted into the spring snow. This was the first time she had actually spoken to the spirits. She supposed it wouldn't be the last. But still, she was not a shaman. She was *not*.

She'd reached the dogs. Grisha's huskies would be first. Resolute, Anya clasped the knife in her hand and gripped it hard. The entire team of twenty sled dogs stood at alert attention, quiet, waiting, their keen eyes filled with trust. Tears trickled down Anya's face. She remembered helping to select each one of them as pups. Doing her best not to think of that time, she approached the team. Zellie was the first to lick Anya's cold hands, then Xander.

Instinctively, Anya let the knife slip from her fingers and fell to her knees between the black and white pair, hugging them both tight. Even though they'd been born to separate litters two seasons ago, Xander followed Zellie around from the start. Anya's heart lurched, remembering. She'd done the same, following both pups, shepherding them as best she could. Zellie pushed her cold muzzle against Anya, nestled her husky mask into the curve of Anya's neck, then heaved a contented sigh. Xander broke from Anya's hold only to push against her back with both front paws, trying to knock her down as he'd done since his mischievous puppyhood. Xander won, and down they all went in a black and white furry pile, ties entangled, with Anya laughing as she always did during their play.

For the briefest of moments Anya forgot what she had to do before the village awakened — before Grisha awakened. Anya, a mere girl, remained amazed that Grisha had allowed her to work with the dogs and help train them.

When Anya was born — under the flashing sky of an arctic storm, a bare-skinned babe all shivers and alone on the frozen earth inside the spacious yaranga — the huskies came and lay with her, bringing with them a curtain of light from the skies overhead, shielding her from the cold and showering her with love. The bonds were immediate and fierce, as if she'd been born into their world instead of the other way around — as if she belonged with them and not humans.

It wasn't natural to have such careful recall of the day you were born, or to feel you belong in a world other than human. In truth, Anya had no memory of a mother's touch, only the soft down of the dogs, cuddling her and keeping her safe. As she grew up, she always felt more secure around dogs than humans; except for Nana-tasha. Her grandmother did not know how to be loud or cruel or unloving. Her grandmother told her that being different meant being special.

"Hah, different," Anya hissed. Angry with herself for wasting time, she mechanically broke free of Zellie and Xander and got up, already hating herself for what she had to do. She looked over her shoulder to make sure no one approached, then bent down to collect her knife, but hesitated.

Maybe there was another way.

She tossed her knife onto the nearby snow bank. The impulse to hitch Zellie, Xander, and the rest of the team to their sled, and then speed across the ice to the very edges of Native Earth, hit hard. Why couldn't she do that now? Why couldn't she harness the dogs and leave the village? No one could catch up to her. Her dogs — Grisha's dogs, that is — were the fastest in the village. Nearly lighthearted now, she turned around to fetch the needed hitch lines and sled. The moment she did, she stopped short, her purpose forgotten.

The night sky was on fire!

She should be afraid, but she wasn't.

Waves of bright light streaked across the heavens in rays of red, yellow, and green, fast-moving and changing shape in a whirlwind of color. The skies filled with curtained light, changing night to day in the time it takes for a heart to beat, giving life to all things. Anya felt a sharp pull, drawn in by the fiery storm overhead. Strangely, she wanted to go toward the light and not run from it. Even if she did run, which direction should she take?

The winds around her died down, as if all

four Directions had been overpowered. Without them, she could not find her way. She fought panic; Anya hated being lost. Used to surviving alone and relying on her keen sense of direction, she imagined she stood on an ice floe, broken off and drifting away into midnight, leaving her dogs on the other side, helpless, never to return. No thought struck more fear in her.

The colorful storm overhead showed no sign of letup. Anya studied the dancing lights, and wondered if the Creator god might have sent them. A memory stirred, at first a faint glow in the distant shadows of her mind. She'd seen these lights before. Straining to remember, she shut her eyes tight to better concentrate.

Zellie whimpered from behind her, and then Xander. Anya opened her eyes and turned to check them. The moment she did, the moment she matched looks with her dogs, she remembered when she'd seen the lights before — *when I was a babe* — when the huskies brought the shimmering curtain of light inside, surrounding her, protecting her, and keeping her warm. She didn't know how she knew this. She just did.

Without warning, her insides tossed so hard she dropped to her knees. The familiar sick feeling sparked her anger, helping her get right back up. From whichever direction the spirits tried to come, she'd face them all! Slowly, deliberately, Anya pivoted in place, and stared out over the frozen tundra, then the craggy shoreline, then out over the sea ice. Seabirds swooped low in the distance, their calls eerily silent. The village remained quiet. She saw no one about. Not even the shamans.

Were they so lost in trancelike sleep, they couldn't awaken on such a night? If only they would come outside and see, once and for all, that she never lied to them about the spirits. From the first time she'd gone to the shamans and told them about the whispers and shapes appearing before her, and asked the shamans to heal her, they accused her of being possessed by bad spirits and had refused to help her.

The main reason so many in the village had little to do with her was because of the shamans. Nana-tasha told her they were jealous of her, since Anya could see and hear spirits without ritual or ceremony. She didn't need any conjuring to connect with the spirit world. She didn't need the shamans to mediate for her. "This makes them angry," her grandmother would say. "You are born of the very world they fear. You are a medium, a child of the spirits."

Whenever Anya would question her grandmother about what she meant, Nana-tasha fell silent.

No matter now. No spirits came. *Good.* Anya didn't have to worry about them. The shamans, either.

The skies abruptly shifted into a featureless, blue shimmer; all other color disappeared except for a faint swirl of green at its center. The swirl took no form, no shape. Anya stared deep into the blue and thought of the watch eyes of the husky. Many held the same sky-blue color, like the Gatekeepers.

Anya had always believed the eyes of the Gatekeepers — the pair of huskies that guard the gates of heaven — must be the same, unmistakable blue. If anyone showed cruelty to a dog, the Gatekeepers kept them out of heaven. Gasp! In that moment, she knew. The dogs stirred. They knew. *The Gatekeepers had come.* They'd left their watch over all the other worlds to make contact with Native Earth! Anya couldn't believe it, but it *had* to be true. What else could this sign be? She felt their spirit wash over her in the same way she'd felt as a new babe. The Gatekeepers spoke to her, not in whispers but in silent understanding. She listened. She understood.

As suddenly as the heavens lit up, they darkened. The Pole Star twinkled. Glad for direction again, Anya could feel the winds whoosh by. Afraid Zellie and Xander and the rest of the husky pack would start to howl with the break of dawn, she hurried over to them and quickly scooped up the knife she'd pitched away. She cut Zellie's tie first, then Xander's, then went down the line of Grisha's dogs, not stopping until she'd freed each one. Instinctively the dogs knew to run, as far and as fast as they could.

Only Zellie and Xander hesitated. They watched Anya instead of leaving.

Time stood still for Anya.

The black and white pair didn't match in all things.

A female, Zellie wasn't as large as Xander. She was a leader dog, smart and pretty as could be, with her white legs and tail tip that curved up at her back. Her thick, soft, predominantly black body fur stood shorter than Xander's, with her black ears lined in white fur coming to more of a point than his more rounded ear tips. Her facial markings were typical of the husky mask, the area above her eyes circled in black with the rest all white. She had one watch-blue eye and one brown eye, not uncommon. Her intelligence and heart shone through her eyes.

Xander's thick layers of soft, black-mixed-with-white fur stood longer than Zellie's, his mask less distinct with his face mostly white. Both of his eyes were watch-blue. His white legs and tail tip matched Zellie's, but his eagerness and strength couldn't be matched among any of Grisha's dogs. To Anya, two more beautiful and loving dogs than Zellie and Xander had never been born on Native Earth.

The distant howling of wolves jarred Anya back to the moment.

"Go. You must go!" She whispered hard. Tears welled in her eyes. It took everything in her to shove Zellie and Xander from her. "Go!" Zellie let out a single bark in protest. Xander whined. "Go now," Anya pleaded. This time they did. Anya watched them disappear across the open tundra for a few precious seconds, before she rushed to the other tied huskies. Despite her shaky hands, she worked as fast as she could, afraid someone would stop her before she'd finished.

"Find the girl, old woman!" Grisha bared his teeth and roared so loud, the center pole of their home shook. He yanked off his sealskin hood and pulled hard on his steel-black hair. His bronze complexion steamed.

"*The girl* happens to be your daughter," his mother replied evenly, alone in the spacious, walrus-skin-covered yaranga. The years had taken their toll on Nana-tasha. Her eyes, once dark and luminous, shone a dull gray. Streaks of the same gray ran through her wiry, bound hair. She gathered up the folds of her beaded, loose dress and slowly rose from her spot on the fur-covered floor, then padded over to the door flap Grisha had left open. She smacked it closed. The thud sent the amulets overhead rattling and swinging. She'd been waiting for her son and expected his anger. Nana-tasha was angry, too, but she refrained from behaving in such a way as he. Chukchi men, when angered, acted like children! She fumed inside. Anya deserved better than this from Grisha.

"The girl is not my daughter. She is not of my blood," Grisha spat out, while he searched all three compartments of his dwelling.

"Anya is not here." Nana-tasha whispered softly. It was customary for Chukchi women to speak thus. More out of habit than submission, she sat back down next to her cook fire, checking the oil lamp, making sure the kettle hanging over it heated properly. She had to stay in her place, no matter if she were Grisha's mother. Women had to get up early, work hard, and do as they were told. A weak woman would not survive very long. Nana-tasha smiled inside. *Anya is a strong girl.* For Anya, she needed to be just as strong and stand up to her son.

"You do not ask me why I want to find Anya. Do you know what she did?" His words were more accusation than question. "Do you know what trouble she has made in our village?" Grisha seethed, pacing back and forth across the widest space in the yaranga. He still wore his outer clothing and hadn't stripped down to his inner fur shirt.

Nana-tasha knew the time grew close for the Markova Fair in Anadyr. She could guess what Anya might have done.

"Answer me, old woman."

Grisha's sour tone sent a chill down Nana-tasha's spine. She did not like this side of her son; it reminded her of bad spirits. She thought of the time, soon to come, when she could no longer do her daily chores. Would Grisha kill her, or would he give her time to announce her own death? He held the power.

"Grisha, my son, think of Tynga. Think of your wife."

He stopped hard in his tracks and stared

at his mother, his weathered face unreadable.

Nana-tasha knew the risk, bringing up his dead wife. How else could she protect Anya, if not to remind Grisha of his love for Tynga. Tynga died giving birth to Anya. That had to count for something to her son. Anya was a part of Tynga, if not him.

Groaning outwardly, Grisha stripped down to his kukashka, his inner fur shirt. He rubbed his face hard, then recaptured his mother's look.

"This is not right, my mother. You should not speak of Tynga, who is lost to me." Unexpectedly, he collapsed in a sit next to Nana-tasha, looking into the cook fire and not at her.

"Tynga cries in the heavens, upset at how angry you are with Anya. She worries for Anya. I worry for Anya," Nana-tasha began softly.

Grisha put his head in his hands and appeared to listen to his mother.

"Tynga's tears dry and she smiles down on you when she remembers what good care you have taken of Anya all these years. She smiles down on you for such care of her daughter."

Grisha shot up at her words and began to pace again.

Nana-tasha tried to stay calm. She was so worried for Anya.

"Thirteen unlucky years I have sheltered another man's child. I have done this for my Tynga, who I loved more than my own life." Grisha spoke with difficulty. "I do not know which whaler, which fisherman, which trader took my wife to his mat. I do not know and I do not care anymore. It is the way of the Chukchi to welcome any stranger. I cannot blame Tynga. It happened. It is our way."

"Yes, my son," was all Nana-tasha could manage.

Grisha threw his hands in the air. His mood changed. His roar returned. "I can no longer allow Anya to live in my yaranga. The shamans have warned against her. I will listen to them now. She has committed a crime against us. She has released our dogs, our livelihood. Without them our people cannot herd the reindeer or find the seal and bring food back from the hunt. The hunt is long and the miles are many. The shamans are right. Anya is possessed by bad spirits. I will take care of this bad business."

Nana-tasha sat frozen.

Grisha threw open the tent flap and stormed out. The amulets overhead swung back and forth; this time they fell to the ground.

Nana-tasha cringed at the ominous sign. Gripped in panic, she slapped her hands together, fastening and unfastening them in prayer to the Creator god for help. She prayed to the gods in all of the worlds, human and spirit, from wherever they must travel, to help her Anya.

"Everyone is mad at you, *gitengev.*" Vitya crouched down next to Anya where she hunkered behind the craggy embankment. He knew she'd be hiding in their secret place. No one ever ventured this far from the village to such an unforgiving point, with its sharp ridges and deadly cliffs. This was not a place to begin the hunt. No reindeer hunter traveled this way. No sea hunter set his baidarka in the water from here. Lone sea birds swooped past, their calls piercing the breaking dawn.

Anya shrugged and kept up her stare out over the ice; she did not look at her childhood friend. Stars still illuminated the fading darkness. She didn't argue with Vitya for teasing and calling her *gitengev,* the name in Chukchi for pretty girl. Always before, she'd deny her good looks. Her attention went to Zellie and Xander at the moment, not Vitya. Fighting tears, she wondered where they'd run and if they were all right, and imagined herself drifting away from them on an unfriendly ice floe. Deep in thought she pulled her hood off. As soon as she did her long hair escaped its bindings and blew in dusky, seal-brown waves across her face. She let it. She didn't care.

Vitya wanted to comfort her but he didn't know how. She looked so thin and fragile. Her heavy kerker couldn't hide her slight shape from him. She never ate enough. Things were really bad with Anya. She'd let him call her *gitengev*. Her light-skinned, rosy complexion appeared to glisten in the frosty gusts. The faint sparkle reminded him of the white blood in her. But she was Chukchi, like him. She had the heart of a Chukchi, the heart of a husky. He reached over to pull her hood back up.

"No, Vitya!" She pushed his hand away, suddenly aware of the brush of his warm fingers on her cheek. He'd never touched her like this before. Surprised and confused, she scooted away from him. A few lengths of her rich, wavy hair still blew across her face. She wiped them away.

"Anya," he said softly, feeling stupid, embarrassed. Since he'd reached fifteen this past midwinter, in the Extending Days,

Vitya had different feelings for Anya, but until this moment he hadn't realized what the feelings meant. Now he knew she was more than a friend to him. He couldn't call her *gitengev* anymore. He just couldn't. Snatching up his gloves, he slid his fingers inside the hide mitts then stood, his back to her.

Anya stared out over the frozen Bering Sea, her straight, soot-brown eyes fixed ahead. She tried to concentrate on the horizon and what might lie beyond on the other side of the great sea, instead of thinking about Vitya. She'd never thought of him as a tall hunter, so strong and handsome. That's how he seemed to her now. She'd never thought of him as anything at all except her friend. His dark attractiveness made her uneasy inside. She shifted her position, then dared a sideways look at him. His back was turned. *Good.* But for some reason this upset her instead of making her feel better.

Vitya turned around.

Their eyes met.

Anya looked away and got up in a hurry, more uncomfortable than she could ever remember.

"Grisha means to find you, Anya," Vitya warned, his voice breaking a little. "Tell me how I can help you."

Her awkwardness vanished into the cold. She didn't feel anything now but the harsh reality of the freezing day. Shivering, she tilted her head up to face Vitya. Tufts of his steel-black hair dusted up with the winds. She couldn't let him get involved or he would be punished, too.

"Anya, what do you want me to do?"

"Vitya, you must return to your family. They will miss you. They will worry." Instinctively, she put her bare hand against his chest because she wanted him to listen to her and to understand.

"Where are your mittens?" he grumbled. "You know better than to expose your skin to the temperatures. What if you lost your fingers? How could you drive a sled?" He pushed her hand from him.

Hurt that he scolded her, Anya gave him her back.

"Please look at me," he said gently, and pulled her around to face him.

She let him guide her. When he picked her sealskin mittens up from the ground, she let him push them over her stiff, icy fingers. It hurt now to think of how much she would miss him.

"I will leave our village with you. It is the only way," he insisted.

"No, Vitya. It is not the only way. I'm going back."

"You can't. You know what will happen."

"And where would I go, if not back to my grandmother?" She didn't cower at his roar.

"We can cross the tundra and find the reindeer hunters, Anya. I will go to the nearest village and get a sled and dogs. Twilight becomes daylight in two warm moons. I will be back by then and we can leave together." Although he hoped to change Anya's mind, he already knew her answer. He couldn't remember a time when she changed her mind on anything.

"Vitya, go home. I will follow soon," she said, pretending a smile. The corners of her mouth felt frozen. She shut her eyes against the pain of his leaving, but opened them instantly at the warm touch of his lips on hers!

"You will always be my *gitengev,*" he whispered, and gave her shoulders a last squeeze before he let go of her.

Anya shut her eyes again, this time against the confusion of his quick kiss. The feeling was new to her; she wasn't sure if she liked it. When she opened her eyes, he'd left. She put a hand to her stomach. Did Vitya leave or was he *taken*? She let her hand slide away. She didn't feel sick. Vitya hadn't been

33

spirited away — changed and unrecogniz-
able to her. Shaking her head to clear such
mystic beliefs, she carved her way down the
craggy embankment. Something made her
look up at the dimly lit sky. Was the Raven
flying overhead? She thought so.

A powerful god, the Raven could bring
good luck or bad. On edge, she wondered
which one the Raven carried within its
sharp claws for her.

The ghostly day was half gone. Anya
trudged into her Anqallyt village, exhausted
and downhearted. She walked past face
after familiar face, all busy at work. The
recent hunt brought in a great whale. There
was much to do. Few Chukchi dared look
at her. Those who did turned their backs
when she passed. Children, unmindful,
played along the path, giggling and squeal-
ing as they chased the new pups around.
Not long ago Anya was one of those children.

Just then a copper-red and white husky
pup toppled at her feet. She bent down and
scooped him up, easily becoming a child
again when he licked her cheeks and nuzzled
at her chin. Her arms suddenly ached. The
puppy almost fell from her grasp. Her fear
took over. She set the puppy back down and

kept on her way.

Grisha's yaranga loomed at the head of the village, the easternmost point. Anya very nearly expected the shamans to come out of their tented huts as she passed and taunt her with their drums and curses; she was sure they would try to conjure bad spirits to harm her. Hah, she thought. They don't have to; not with Grisha waiting.

"Stop there, Anya," Grisha thundered.

She had her answer. The Raven brought *bad* luck.

The harpoon in Grisha's hands gave Anya proof enough. She imagined the sharp point already pierced through her, killing her. Resolved to her fate, she stood tall, eyes wide open. Her grandmother did not come outside. Good. She did not wish for Nanatasha to witness her death. Steeling herself to the moment, Anya shut out all the noise around her and waited for Grisha's strike. Just then a great howl erupted from behind their yaranga, breaking through her silence. Panicked, she recognized the call.

Zellie howled again, and then Xander; both tied, both caught.

Anya's insides seized. If only her dogs were wolves. The Chukchi *cannot kill* wolves. Even though she didn't think Grisha would kill Zellie and Xander along with her, right

35

now she didn't feel sure. He was so mad! She made a dash for the back of the yaranga.

Grisha stuck out the harpoon to stop her, its point rested just at her chest.

She jerked away from the harpoon, but the quickly formed line of Chukchi men behind her caught her and held her. The fierce look across their warriorlike faces told her what she already knew. She was the enemy. Dangerous moments passed. Anya heard her dogs, and she twisted out of the warriors' hold, the element of surprise on her side.

But the shamans, there was no escaping them. She struggled to get free from their unnatural grasp. Zellie and Xander barked excitedly, still hidden from her view. Other huskies barked now. Anya stopped fighting the two shamans and cast her head downward. Her soul lay dead at her feet. She had failed. She was desperate to become a human sacrifice to the Gatekeepers; the killing strike of Grisha's harpoon couldn't come soon enough. Nothing else would appease.

"Let her go."

"Grisha, this one is possessed by bad spirits," one of the shamans leveled.

"You must kill her," the other pronounced.

"Let her go."

Neither shaman obeyed their village

leader, and they tightened their punishing grasp on the *possessed girl.* The amulets and tassels worn around their necks and adorning their reindeer pelt clothing rattled and clanged together, the sound sinister, foreboding.

All of the dogs brought back to the village barked at once. Their cries and howls fueled the already tense atmosphere.

Anya listened to the dogs, only the dogs. She'd worried that Zellie and Xander might return to the village to find her. But they knew to leave. *They knew.* The other dogs, too, or so she thought. Their instincts should have told them to run. Their keen sense of survival should have told them to run — to run from the danger of returning to the village before the next coming of winter. Anya couldn't imagine what had happened.

Had the dog owners in the village gone on the hunt for their dogs? Had the wolves chased them back? Had the shamans conjured a dark spirit, so evil it changed the wolves into something far worse — something from the darkest of spirit worlds, so beastly, so unearthly that the dogs fled? Anya never doubted the shamans had such powers, but until now, she didn't actually believe it.

She carefully raised her head and met Grisha's stern regard, suspicious, as if seeing him for the first time. Had he ever taken any form other than human? For that matter, had she?

"Grisha, use the harpoon on the girl."

"Rid our village of this evil now."

The shamans kept their hold on Anya, shoving her closer to Grisha's killing strike.

"Let her go," Grisha said again, his tone calm, severe. "I will deal with the girl."

"Then do it now," the shamans demanded. "Her blood must be a sacrifice. She is cursed. The gods will smile when she is dead. We will make sure all of her souls die with her, Grisha." Both shamans took their turn with their cold pronouncements.

Anya stood limp, her shoulders slumped, between the Chukchi holy men, her eyes on Grisha. She already felt dead. She hadn't protected the huskies. Now they would be scattered all over Native Earth, loyal dog teams broken up, never to run together again across the great tundra or the great seas of ice. Tears welled, not just for Zellie and Xander, but all of the huskies.

Which would be selected this season?

She felt a part of all of them, and she couldn't stand to watch the dogs be split up and herded to the Markova Fair. She couldn't stand one more season of feeling adrift on one side of an ice floe while she watched the dogs trapped on the other. The dogs should all run free, hard, and strong as they were born to in this life, and only stop when they could run no more. That's exactly how she felt now, like she would never again run with the Chukchi dogs *as I was born to.* Then an odd pull tugged at her insides, just enough to get her attention.

Anya straightened, still held fast by the shamans. The pulling inside her didn't make her sick to her stomach. In fact she didn't feel anything. The strange sensation puzzled her. It wasn't spirits coming to torment her — or else, shouldn't she feel sick? It didn't make much difference now anyway, if she felt anything or not.

She swallowed hard and focused on the tip of the killing harpoon, waiting for her life to end. She deserved to die.

She'd failed to help the dogs on this day, and she knew the Gatekeepers would be unforgiving. Embarrassed by her tears, she hoped no one saw. If only she could see Zellie and Xander one last time. How she longed for the coziness of the huskies, just like when she was a babe; their soft down the only comfort she needed. Her tears kept coming. Scared and embarrassed, she dared not wipe them away.

But then, all of a sudden Anya felt drawn into a mystic world of shadows and forms where nothing seemed clear. She immediately thought of the spirits and forgot about waiting to die. A surprising calm settled over her. Her tears dried. Her body relaxed. Soft flashes of red, green, yellow, then blue swirled around her, soothing her, reminding her of the Gatekeepers.

She was in her body, yet she was not.

She was changing, yet she was not changing.

She was moving, yet she stood still.

Was she being *spirited* to another world, taking on another form, no longer human? She glanced up. The skies had lightened, but Anya could see the Pole Star twinkle overhead as if it were the darkest time of night, when the star was most visible. She had the oddest notion she'd just traveled through one of the holes around the Pole Star, the connections to the worlds beyond. Only shamans could do that. An unearthly silence draped over her. Her senses stirred. Her heart pumped. No voices, human, animal, or spirit broke through the silence, yet she listened, and strained to hear.

Someone, something was there.

Grisha kept his eyes on Anya. He didn't

want to care about the child, but he did. He didn't want to believe the shamans were right about her, but he knew they were. Bad spirits haunted her. The way she stared at him, seeing him but not seeing him, gave him proof enough of her possession.

He never once believed she could become a shaman. Yes, girls could become shamans, but not Anya. He would never allow such an honor. Tynga might be her mother, but Anya was not his blood, his true daughter. He would accept what the village shamans said. Bad spirits and bad luck followed her. Anya put all of them in danger when she released the dogs.

Every dog in the village had great value. Every dog meant survival. To release even one before it was time endangered all in their village. Much depended on sled dog trades in Anadyr. The best dogs could bring a good price at the Markova Fair. Many tribes come to trade. Outsiders come to trade, outsiders from other parts of Siberia and from across the great seas.

An idea dawned. Grisha knew what Anya's fate must be.

"There, you have all you need for your journey," Nana-tasha said as matter-of-factly as she could and then stepped away

41

from her granddaughter. The old woman finished inspecting her handiwork, making sure of Anya's food store of boiled walrus and whale, and she added warm clothing; not wanting to forget anything — Anya's knife especially — and not wanting her granddaughter to notice her upset.

Anya stood mutely before her grandmother. Grisha and the rest of his family left them alone in the spacious yaranga. His wife, Gyrgyn, had never been kind to her; neither had his sons, Rahtyn and Uri. Though fierce warriors, the Chukchi always showed kindness and generosity to everybody, even strangers who came to their village.

Not Grisha's family. They ignored her. Anya never felt a part of them, except for her grandmother. Anya shrugged her thin shoulders. No, she would not miss Grisha's mean family. She would not miss Grisha. He'd given her food and shelter, but never love. No, she would not miss Grisha. Her chest tightened. He had given her one thing — permission to rear and help train sled dogs. He had given her that. She softened inside, but the feeling didn't last. Now he was taking it all back.

Grisha pulled open the door flap.

"It is time, Anya." He shut the flap and

stayed outside.

The dogs barked loudly, jarring Anya's nerves even more. The thick, hide walls of the yaranga offered little protection against their excited cries. Anya took a last glance at the only home she'd ever known, then dared a look at her grandmother. They would never see each other again. They both knew it.

Nana-tasha took Anya's young, tear-streaked face in her aged hands and touched Anya's nose with her own.

Anya wrapped her arms around her grandmother and sobbed against her.

"There, there, my child," Nana-tasha soothed. "Have no fear. I will always be with you. When you lie down, and when you rise up, I will be with you. You will know I am there. You will know."

Anya pulled away from her grandmother, enough to study her face and remember every detail of these last moments. After this day there would be no one to comfort her, to care for her, to love her. Not even the dogs. She loved her grandmother. She loved her dogs. But after this day, there would be no one.

Nana-tasha gently gripped Anya's arms.

"You are a child of the spirits." She whispered quickly yet quietly, not wanting

Grisha to overhear. "You are a child of the great storms begun when worlds collide in our heavens. You came to us on the arctic winds. The Gatekeepers watch over you. They have given you a great burden to carry, my little Anya. But they have also given you great powers. The shamans have always feared you because of this. You are the first of your kind, the first Native-born of the spirits. There are others created by the spirits, some for good, some for evil. You must become master, little Anya. This is all I can tell you. This is all I know," Nana-tasha finished, then eased her hold on Anya and finally let go.

"How do you know these things, Grand-mother?" Anya didn't understand what she was hearing. The prophecy scared her. She was scared enough already.

Nana-tasha tensed. She saw the fear on her granddaughter's face.

"The ancestors speak to me in dreams; only in dreams do I imagine these divinations. Do not worry over what I say, little Anya," she replied in a whisper, and hoped to reassure. The last thing she wanted to do was frighten her granddaughter. Too late; she knew she already had.

The dogs barked outdoors.

Anya jumped. Zellie and Xander were

among the ones chosen for Markova!

This awful day had no end. Anya reverently touched her grandmother's cheek in goodbye, then turned and quickly passed through the tent flap. Just when she thought the day couldn't be worse, she ran right into Vitya the moment she stepped outside.

He shoved something at her.

Anya grasped the object in her heavy mitten and kept on walking. She refused to look at Vitya. It hurt too much. Tears stung her eyes.

"Anya," Vitya called from behind.

Grisha stepped in between them to make sure Vitya couldn't follow.

In front of her, the selected dogs had been readied for travel, the teams hitched to lightweight whalebone sleds. Anya focused on the dogs and the journey ahead, and didn't look back at Vitya. Like her grandmother, she and Vitya would never meet again. She dared a quick glance at the object in her hand.

It was a Chukchi dog carved out of walrus tusk. The handsome husky howled at the heavens, calling to its pack. Anya removed her mitten and clasped the necklace to her chest. She would hear Vitya calling her *gitengev* when she held it so.

Gasp!

The carving turned hot in her hand. She pulled down her hood and quickly slid the necklace around her neck, risking any burn. It cooled right away against her skin. On her guard for spirits, she eased her mitten back over her hand, and wondered if this sign came from good spirits . . . or bad?

She didn't have any time to think on this — she hurried toward the noisy, excited group of dogs that waited. She needed to find Zellie and Xander. When she did she saw they'd already been separated, split up and hitched to different sleds!

Both dogs quieted and calmed to a sit when Anya neared. They'd forgiven her. She could see it in their eyes. She'd never forgive herself for failing them, for letting them be caught and sent to drift away from her on dangerous ice floes into the unknown. It was her fault. Her throat ached from wanting to cry, but she didn't want the dogs to see.

Zellie and Xander would be traded at the Markova Fair. Anya doubted she would make it that far.

CHAPTER TWO

*Markova settlement near the Anadyr River,
Gulf of Anadyr, Bering Sea ~ late May,
1908*

"Rune, go back to the *skepp*." Lars Johansson commanded his son to return to their
steamship, the *Storm,* and then climbed out
of the undersized boat — the "lighter" —
used now to navigate the Anadyr River.
Their Seattle-based steamer had made it
three-quarters of the way through the Gulf
of Anadyr before being stopped by ice. The
rivers already flowed in Siberia, but the
thick pack ice along the coast hadn't melted.

The *Storm* wasn't an icebreaker, a cutter
able to withstand the crushing power of ice
and push through it. Polar explorers used
the modern, steam-powered icebreakers.
Not Lars. His crewmen had helped slide
their small boat, used for lightering passengers and supplies ashore, on makeshift
runners over the ice to the mouth of the

Anadyr River. They had traveled the remaining short distance to Markova by way of the river.

At sixteen, Rune didn't think his father should order him around, especially in front of the crew. He was a man now, a full hand on deck.

"Far, I came to help like the rest of the crew," Rune shot back at his father.

Lars let the crewmen offload the trade goods and supplies, and kept his eyes on his son. Rune reminded him of their ancient Viking heritage with his blond good looks, strong, lean body, height that matched his own, and his sky-blue eyes. Smart, too. Lars couldn't forget that his son had a quick mind, and a stubborn streak that sometimes got him in trouble. Like their ancestors, his son loved the sea and anything to do with it. Everything about the sea seemed to come naturally to Rune, as if he had been born with the ancient sunstone of the Vikings in his hand. He could navigate the ice better than a schooled sea captain, yet Lars still worried over him.

"You will be needed back at the ship." Lars concentrated on using the English word for ship; his tendency was to revert to Swedish. Here in Siberia there were already too many languages spoken in trading. In

48

Markova, an old Cossack settlement, Russian and English could be understood among most. Lars scanned the crowded river embankment for the native translator he was accustomed to meeting on these stops. In all his years of trade along the Siberian coast, the native languages never came easily to him. Russian, either. He needed that translator if he expected to find Boris Ivanov.

Rune ignored his father and helped with the offloading. He always helped and couldn't imagine why he'd been told to return to the steamer. This trip brought everything from food staples to clothing to household goods to firearms and ammunition. No alcohol. His father never brought alcohol to these trade stops. Unlike others from America and Europe who traded along these shores, his father never thought selling alcohol was right. Since they were successful enough without bringing alcohol, Rune didn't question this decision.

"Rune, come here." Lars took hold of his son's fur parka and pulled him away from the supply boat.

Rune shook himself free. Angry now, he looked at everything around them and not at his father. He'd never been to the Markova Fair. The sights and sounds immediately drew him in: switching his focus to the reindeer-drawn carts rolling by, piled with furs. Rune picked out Siberian fox, polar bear, reindeer, arctic wolf, and seal fur. Native tribesmen, dressed in some of the same fur, shouted out to one another over the din. Funny; he only saw men. Evidently women and children didn't come to the fair. Only men traded, he guessed.

"I need you to go back to the *Storm.* This is our last stop before we head to Nome!" Lars had to shout to be heard over all the noise.

"Nome!"

"Yes, Nome," his father echoed.

"But we have to return to Seattle, Far, not Nome. That will take us weeks out of our way!"

"Rune, this trip is different. We'll have cargo to deliver to the Alaska District. This is why I need you to return to the ship. I need you to get the cargo hold cleared for our passage across the Bering Sea to Nome."

"Cleared?" Rune didn't understand. He wanted to see the Markova Fair.

"We'll have live cargo this time."

"What?" Rune didn't think he heard right.

Frustrated and short on time, Lars turned his son about and pointed him in the right direction.

"Expect us back at the ship late tomorrow. Clear enough space for at least a dozen dogs."

"Dogs?" Rune wheeled around, and glared in disbelief at his father.

"Chukchi dogs," Lars added, then turned his son back toward the Gulf of Anadyr. "Go now."

Rune fumed as he started out along the Anadyr River, his mukluks sinking in the slushy mud.

"Chukchi dogs," he grumbled. "I'm a seaman, not a dog keeper."

During this whole trip, his father never said a word about ferrying dogs across the Bering Sea to Nome. Rune didn't have anything against dogs; he just wasn't a gold miner or a freighter or a mail carrier or any kind of musher. A sled dog racer, either. He never stayed on land long enough to become a part of racing, like so many had in Nome and the surrounding villages.

Racing wasn't important to Rune. Fishing was important. Trading was important. Sea navigation was important.

Not dogs!

He picked up his angry pace and kept his eyes still cast down on the slushy embankment where he walked.

Ooooph!

"Hey, watch where you're going!" Rune yelled reflexively at whoever had just bumped him.

A fur-clad figure quickly sidestepped him then kept going.

"Hey, I said —" Rune turned and watched the slight figure continue walking. "I'll be. It's a girl." Although he didn't see her face, still, he knew she was female. He took off after her, wanting to apologize for the bump, but pulled up short.

Dogs!

Teams of dogs were everywhere, a sea of them, in every color — black and white, gray and white, copper-red and white, some pure white and even piebald spotted. Chukchi dogs, he bet. They came out of nowhere, just like the girl. Were they dogs or wolves? They sure looked like wolves that belonged in the wild, not hitched to sledges. They were smaller than huskies in the Alaska District, and Rune immediately questioned why his father wanted to bring any of these dogs to Nome. Too small for distance racing or pulling heavy loads — what good would they be?

Still mad at his father, yet resigned to his task, Rune didn't have a choice. The day turned warm, too warm. His cropped, straw-colored hair clung straight on his forehead and neck. He roughly brushed it away with his hands then undid the front of his parka and grudgingly set out for the *Storm.* By now he'd forgotten all about the girl he bumped.

"Hallo, I'm Lars Johansson."

"Privet," the big man responded in kind. "Boris Ivanov."

Lars studied Boris Ivanov's face to take his measure. Thanks to the native translator, who knew some Russian and English, he'd found the right fur trader. Much of the day was gone, but at least Lars and his crew had taken care of all their business. He'd made decent profit. The matter of finding Boris Ivanov had weighed on him — that, and transporting Ivanov's dogs to Nome. Lars already regretted the undertaking, but he'd promised an important business relation at the trading post in Vladivostok. Trade stops in the Russian port were vital to Lars and he didn't want anything to interfere, especially since Vladivostok never became trapped in ice. Waters stayed navigable the year round. Still, he regretted not telling Rune about Nome sooner. He should have.

"Engelska? Do you speak English?" Lars asked Boris Ivanov, needing to focus on the

task at hand.

"*Chu chu,* a little," Boris answered. "*Russkiy yazyk?*"

Lars shook his head, no. He'd picked up some Russian words over the years, but not enough to count.

Both men looked at the translator at the same time.

Boris spoke first.

"Ya . . . *koddah?*" he asked, his beefy hands upturned in question.

"*Gedh?*" the translator responded.

Apparently frustrated, Boris looked at Lars now.

"Kepten Johansson," he began, his hands outstretched to Lars. "Ya . . . eh, I pay you rubles take me and *Sibirskiy haskis,* Nome."

"Yes," Lars acknowledged, relieved they'd gotten this far in the conversation. He hadn't expected any payment for the trip, but he wasn't about to turn the offer down. This stop in Nome was unscheduled. Time is money. He'd never have agreed if it were winter and not summer. He'd never be out in such dangerous waters in the colder months, waiting for the ice to trap him, and run the risk of his ship being crushed and his crew lost. Summer was trading and traveling time. Not winter.

He thought of Rune. His son, if given the

chance, would venture into icy seas and face into the sudden squalls rather than turn away from them. As soon as the *Storm* returned to Seattle, he knew Rune would be impatient to set out again. This winter would be no different.

"*Dobry,* Kepten. Gud, Kepten," Boris smiled, then gestured for a handshake.

Lars shook his hand and gave a friendly nod, yet still thought about Rune.

"Where are your dogs?" Lars asked Boris, looking all around. He saw a lot of dogs hitched to sledges. Native Chukchi, Evens, Chuvans, and Yukaghir, along with local Russians walked the team lines, talking and bartering over the dogs.

The translator said something to Boris in Russian.

"*Da, kanyeshna.* Yes, of course." The big fur trader started out through the maze of people and animals.

Lars followed, and motioned for two of his crew to do the same. The excited dogs barked louder as they passed. Lars was reminded of the frenzied, noisy dog yards in Seattle. When the gold rush to the Klondike began in '98, every kind of breed could be found, all yipping and yapping and snapping excitedly, just like these dogs. Same kind of bartering went on, too. The dogs all

brought a stiff price. The miners needed
them to survive in the harsh wild. Trade had
always been good with the gold miners in
Nome, but Lars never thought of bringing
dogs from Russia to the miners until this
trip.

Dogs were still vital for freight and transportation on the Alaskan frontier. Couldn't
get anywhere in winter without them. Vital
to gamblers, too, since so many miners in
the Nome area, including local Eskimos,
liked to race their dogs for sport in the
winter months when nothing much else
happened. Serious sport meant serious
money. Ever the businessman, Lars always
assessed the value of goods bought and sold.
Already lucrative stops in Nome might
become more so.

In a hurry to set up camp for the night,
Lars noted the still-lit sky, then relaxed
about the time. Night had begun turning to
day in the Arctic where the sun wouldn't
set again until the end of summer. Still, he
and his crew needed to eat and bed down.

"Here, Kepten." Boris stopped short and
pointed to a field of tethered dogs up ahead.
"Chukchi *sobaka*, Chukchi *ezdovaya sobaka*," he said. "Kepten . . . eh, Chukchi
sled dogs. Here are my *sobaka*, my dogs."

"All of them?" Lars couldn't take so many

on his ship. He wouldn't. He counted two hundred if he counted one.

"*Nyet,* Kepten. I pick eight *sobaka.* I pick eight dogs," Boris explained then held up the same number of fingers to underscore the correct number.

Better, Lars thought; only eight. Rune could manage eight dogs in the hold. It wouldn't be easy keeping the peace with eight dogs barking and snapping at each other across the Bering Sea. It occurred to Lars that the hold wouldn't work. Tied on deck was the only place for any dogs on the *Storm.* Besides, these dogs belonged outside. He didn't know much about *Sibiriskiy haskis,* but he could see they belonged outdoors, not in.

"Ya . . . eh, I go now. I pick my dogs, Kepten." With that, Boris set out among the field of dogs and their masters, looking for his eight Chukchi *ezdovaya sobaka.*

Lars watched Boris walk through the maze of animals. Something about these dogs seemed peculiar, something beyond the notion they looked like wolves that belonged in the wild. The dogs lay in sleepy circles, all tied together, all quiet, all waiting, calm and easy. Even with the big fur trader stomping among them, along with native traders, who signaled for their dogs to stand

and be examined, the huskies didn't protest.

The contrast between these Chukchi dogs and the other dogs at Markova struck Lars as remarkable. A businessman, Lars immediately assessed their value. Still, he scratched his head. He'd never seen a breed like this. Maybe that's why Boris Ivanov wanted them. Nome hasn't seen a breed like this, either.

She was in Markova at last, but the trek had taken its toll on Anya. Daylight had burned through her all day long, the warmer temperature unnerving. She'd never rested on the journey, even when the sled drivers stopped to eat and sleep. She didn't eat and she didn't sleep. Dead inside, she couldn't. Dead inside, she'd cried her last tears, she thought. On each step taken, away from her village and away from the only home she'd ever known, she'd built a wall higher and higher around her, and made a vow that for whatever time she had left on Native Earth, she'd never care about anyone or anything again. Her souls, all of them, died with her back in the village. Downhearted, she believed there would be no afterlife for her in the spirit world or any world. She didn't deserve it.

She'd struggled to keep pace behind

Grisha's sled instead of running alongside as she'd been told to do. In a fan hitch, each dog had been harnessed to their own trace line which allowed them plenty of room to maneuver. Zellie and Xander ran on opposite sides of the fan. Right before leaving the village, Grisha untied Xander from a neighbor team then rehitched him with Zellie. Anya had held her breath, mistakenly thinking Grisha might leave Xander home after all. But he did not.

Other dog breeders from her village had driven their sleds on past. None of the drivers looked at her or spoke to her. Sometimes she felt the dogs try to turn to her, but then their driver would call out and press them forward. Trapped on separate ice floes, she and the dogs drifted far apart. It would just get worse. Her head ached. Her heart broke. She guessed she wasn't dead yet, or she wouldn't hurt so.

Anya hadn't really thought about what might happen to her in Markova. What did it matter anyway? She still didn't understand why Grisha hadn't killed her. When he ordered her to leave the village with all of the dogs set for trade, she believed he meant to leave her out in the open tundra, lost and alone to die. That she could understand.

But Grisha had not left her behind. He

had not left her alone. If she'd had the chance, she would have run off. The trek had been warm, too warm to stay covered. She'd pulled her fox-trimmed hood down and wished she could shed her fur kerker. Instead she slipped the sealskin bag of walrus and whale meat off her stiff shoulder, and let the food fall to the ground. None of the meat had been eaten. Not hungry, she didn't want it anyway. The foxes and wolves were welcome to it.

Her parched throat scratched every time she swallowed. Handfuls of slushy snow brought some ease. She'd had to squint most of the day, not yet used to summer's light. When dark specks formed into a darker line across the horizon, she'd grudgingly pulled her hood back up to help block the sun for a better look at Markova, innocent of the fateful stranger about to brush past.

"Adin, dva, tri," Boris counted — one, two, three — pointing to each of Grisha's dogs he'd selected.

Anya stood close by and watched, silent, unmoving. She didn't want to see. She didn't want to hear. What she wanted to do was bolt, to be anywhere but here. Zellie's searching eyes kept finding hers, forgiving her all over again.

Xander had already been traded. As if that wasn't bad enough, she had a *bad* feeling about the Yukaghir tribesman who took him. Something was wrong. She didn't know where Xander had been taken, and she was anxious about him.

And now Zellie would be lost to her. The big Russian had picked Zellie as one of three he wanted from Grisha, to take across the great Bering Sea to the very edges of Native Earth, taken from the only world Zellie knew! Anya had picked out most of the exchange used to bargain. She understood some of the Russian words. When whalers came to her Anqallyt village, she'd paid attention and learned. She understood a little English, too.

"Staamat?" Grisha barked out.

The translator shook his head, no. The fur trader wanted three dogs, not four — "not *staamat.*"

Grisha ignored the translator and gestured out over his entire team. *"Staamat? Talliman?"*

Vigorously shaking his head no, the translator indicated the fur trader didn't want four dogs, or five. He wanted three — *"pingayun."*

Grisha let his arm drop and finally nod-

61

ded the agreement.

Anya watched the big Russian give Grisha something. *Money,* she hissed to herself. She'd seen rubles before, in the pockets of whalers and fishermen when they came to her village. Money is evil. Money is greed. No Chukchi admired greed. A trade with other breeders, dog for dog, she might come to accept — never money, never greed.

Money for her Zellie!

Anger flared inside her. It wasn't right for her Zellie or for any of the Chukchi dogs!

A sharp pain cut through Anya's carefully built, frosty exterior, making her feel fractured into pieces of useless, broken ice. She'd failed them. Zellie, Xander, all of the dogs. She watched the big Russian take Zellie and the two selected, copper-red and white huskies from their ties then move out into the sea of other dogs for trade.

Stupid Russian!

Wiping her tears and her runny nose, Anya passed her fur sleeve across her face, unaware she'd done so. Doesn't the stupid Russian know that Grisha's dogs are the fastest, most sure-footed, hardest working, best at seal hunting, and most valuable of all the Chukchi dogs? A hundred miles out on the ice, Grisha's dogs would bring you safely home. The stupid Russian should have wanted all of Grisha's dogs.

"Anya!" Grisha suddenly roared.

Anya jumped, but stared across the field of dogs, straining to keep her eyes on the three just taken, especially Zellie.

"Anya!" he roared again, this time he grasped her arm hard. "It is time to go. I have traded you."

"Tr-traded me?" she stammered. Now she looked at him.

Grisha gave a curt nod, but said nothing else.

She jerked her arm away. Lifting up to her full height, all five feet, two inches, of her, she gave Grisha the same curt nod he'd just given her. If she had to go, she'd do it willingly, not dragged for all the dogs to see.

"Come," Grisha said, his voice uncharacteristically quiet. He began to walk in the same direction as Zellie and the copper-red and white huskies.

Anya quickly heeled.

Bedded down in the open, bundled under reindeer blankets, Lars and his crew slept peacefully alongside the Chukchi dogs selected by Boris Ivanov for transport to Nome. Accustomed to the midnight sun over the years, Lars had no trouble falling asleep. Their group had pitched camp away from all the noise and trade, on a far bank of the Anadyr River. The dogs had acted up a bit when first tied together, but soon quieted. Lars fell asleep on the thought that Rune would have little trouble managing this lot. If only Lars would have such luck with Rune.

Awakening first, before his crew, in the early morning, Lars looked over at the huskies. He climbed out from under his blankets and stood. All eight of the huskies looked back at him. He wondered if they'd fallen asleep at all, the way they stared at him, alert, sitting up, watching him as if they'd done so the night through. Never a dog owner, at sea most of his life, he guessed this was typical for the Chukchi husky. They must be good guard dogs. Why else would they all be doing the same thing now, unmoving but for their watch-blue eyes.

"Gud morning, Keptan." Boris woke next.

"Good morning," Lars said, forgetting about the watch eyes of the huskies and remembering their translator had left last night.

"Everyone up," he routed his crewmen. "We have a long day's travel ahead."

The huskies began to stir. They moaned a little, no doubt hungry.

Lars noticed.

"Got anything for these dogs to eat, Boris?" he asked, hoping the Russian understood.

The big man threw off his blankets.

"*Da,* sure," he mumbled, and got up.

Lars watched Boris uncover a bucket of fish, then give one to each of the dogs.

Even more astounding than the dogs being so well-behaved thus far was that the dogs didn't fight over the food! Lars expected them to. Stories from dog drivers in the Yukon had led him to believe the world of dog driving was naturally brutal, complete with competition over food. On his stops at trading posts, he never liked to hear the bloody details of how hard a dog could be driven. Yes, freight was important. On-time deliveries meant good profit. But was profit in the fur trade important enough to whip dogs into submission on hauls, bloodying them, cursing them, often maiming them, driving them hard, some to their deaths? He didn't think so, and he was glad he wasn't in such a heartless business as freighting.

Lars watched the gentle Chukchi dogs finish their breakfast. He didn't know what Boris intended exactly for these unique huskies in Nome, but he hoped it had nothing to do with freight hauling.

Xander!

Anya ran over to him and fell to her knees, then threw her arms around his neck. She hugged him with everything in her. Nothing ever felt as wonderful as his soft fur against her cheek. She breathed in deeply, his scent familiar, taking her home.

The young husky licked her face, whimpering low in apparent acknowledgment, then abruptly pushed against her with both front paws.

Anya giggled when he knocked her over in play.

"Up, Anya!" Grisha roared.

Brought back to the uncomfortable moment, Anya forced herself to stand. She put her hand out for Xander to nuzzle, needing his companionship to give her courage.

Grisha charged over to her and grabbed her away from the dog.

Xander growled.

Anya had never heard him growl. She'd never seen him scared. He didn't shake, but she felt his fear. It matched hers. They were afraid for each other.

Grisha eyed Xander hard. The dog had never crossed him like this. He raised his arm at Xander, ready to strike as if he held a sharp-knotted whip in his tight grasp, but then he mumbled something under his breath and dropped his arm, his hand open.

Anya had never seen Grisha raise his arm to a dog other than to give a command. No need to strike a dog! No need to use a whip to force a Chukchi dog into action, to punish them for not working hard, for not running straight and true; never resting until they were told, willing to give their lives to finish the hunt for their master. No need to ever be mean to a Chukchi dog, especially to Xander who didn't have a mean bone in his body. Anya's heart pumped in her chest, and she felt frightened all over again for Xander.

Grisha roared something at her, but strangely, she couldn't make out what he said. No words, *just noise,* as if he spoke a different language she couldn't understand. The noise faded. Grisha's shape muted into a blur.

Instinctively she found Xander's face, his husky mask was still crystal clear to her. She relaxed with Xander close, and her fears diminished. All stayed eerily quiet around her. Her stomach turned. Spirits — it must be spirits coming, she thought. She listened hard, needing to understand what the spirits wanted with her. But no voices spoke to her. No shapes hid in shadow. Still she listened and watched.

Someone, something was there.

Whatever it was that hid in the dark recesses of her awareness, it *wasn't* good.

"Anya, come here. Mooglo is your master now."

She didn't jump at Grisha's roar this time, his words clear again. He came into sharp focus, but she refused to show fear.

Xander, either. He didn't growl.

"Leave Mooglo's dog and come here," Grisha repeated.

Mooglo's dog? Anya rubbed behind Xander's downy ears, upset by Grisha's cold heart. She stayed in place, stubborn to the core, a trait not uncommon to Chukchi dogs. Forcing herself to, she glanced at the man who stood next to Grisha, knowing who it had to be. Her master in this slave trade was the ugly Yukaghir who took Xander away earlier, the one she mistrusted. Her intuition told her the Gatekeepers would *never* let him into heaven. Ugly on the inside and outside!

His yellow eyes bore through her, and made her uncomfortable. The broken teeth in his crooked smile were the same sickly color. An evil aura coated him, bringing darkness to the day. She easily read the signs.

How could Grisha do this to her and to Xander? He had to really hate them and not care at all what happened to them. Anya wished he'd left her to die on the tundra, preferring that fate to whatever lay ahead. Then she thought of Xander. At least she had him close.

"Goodbye, Anya," Grisha clipped out, then briskly turned and left.

Anya stood silently and watched his back disappear into the crowd of dogs and men still gathered for sale and trade. She hadn't expected a fond farewell from Grisha, but she'd expected more than a simple good-bye. Even with what she'd done in the village, she still expected more from the man who'd fed and sheltered her for thirteen years. He had let her help raise and train his dogs. She grabbed onto this thought, the only good one she had left for Grisha.

Mooglo's clawlike hand touched her face.

Repelled, Anya jerked away.

The Yukaghir laughed, low and mean.

Xander, at Anya's side now, growled.

Mooglo kicked him away, still laughing low and mean.

Taken by surprise, Xander fell from the swift blow. He didn't yowl in pain but got up and stood straight, his watch eyes on Mooglo.

Anya put herself squarely in between Xander and the Yukaghir. If he tried to hurt Xander again, he'd have to kill her first. The cold-blooded expression on Mooglo's ugly face told Anya all she needed to know. He would use the whip on Xander and all of the dogs he'd just bargained for. He would use it on her, too.

Mooglo smiled at her.

The otherworldly change on his face sent a cold shiver through her.

"Bed down now. We leave early in the morning," he snarled, then waved her away with his clawlike hand, still laughing low and mean.

Before she could react, Mooglo grabbed Xander's hide collar and had him tied securely to a post near the other trapped huskies. Anya stayed glued to the spot and watched the slave master's every move. She wouldn't make hers until he fell asleep.

Lars wondered how much Boris Ivanov actually knew about these Siberian dogs, as he saw him organize the huskies for their return to the *Storm*. Disorganize was more the appropriate word. Lucky for Boris, the dogs still wore their hide harnessing, bought as part of their trade. The dogs had obviously been gentled by the Chukchi and were accustomed to cooperating in teams, getting along and not fighting. Boris tied them all to one hide thong line, then must have thought better of it and gave each dog his own. No matter — the watchful dogs allowed Boris plenty of leeway to experiment. He had purchased a lightweight sledge — *umiaq* to the Eskimo — at the fair, and tried to get all the dogs' lines set up right before he started out.

The plan discussed was to trek the huskies along the Anadyr River while Lars and his crew floated their supply boat upriver until they met the Bering Sea ice. Maybe Lars didn't know anything about sled dog driving, but he believed that once the huskies broke into any kind of run, Boris might be in big trouble. You have to know how to drive a dog team as well as hitch them up right, Lars supposed. The trek over slush and snow could be tricky with Boris at the team's helm. The distance across the Bering Sea ice to the *Storm* would be an even bigger test for the Russian fur trader. More likely, the dogs would be at the helm all day, and tug Boris along.

Scanning the group of huskies under Boris's command, Lars sensed these intelligent animals, once started, would get their driver and the sledge to the ship, or die trying. He'd never owned a dog in his life, but he already had a grudging respect for these little *Sibiriskiy haskis.*

Lying on the cold, unforgiving ground, Anya had no reindeer blanket for protection. She didn't need one anyway; she was determined to stay awake and keep her eyes on Mooglo, waiting for him to fall asleep. She'd pretended sleep. The ugly Yukaghir hadn't let her bed down near Xander and the other dogs like she'd wanted. At least he hadn't tied her to any post.

Mooglo turned in his sleep, his back to her now. He slept too near. His smell, like something dead, nauseated her. She heard him snore. Unwittingly, she ran her hand inside the neck of her seal-fur kerker until her shaky fingers bumped against the necklace Vitya had given her. She clasped it tightly in her hand. The carved husky warmed her. She missed Vitya and would give anything to have him with her. She let go of the necklace.

Vitya wasn't here. He never would be again.

Anya refused to be upset. She didn't have time. Her eyes fixed on Mooglo's ugly, snoring back. Running her still-unsteady hand inside the pocket of her kerker, she found the crude blade she needed and pulled it out. Determined in her purpose, her hand steadied at the feel of her knife. Rolling onto her side, she faced Xander and the rest of the caught huskies.

The dogs slept in lazy circles, eyes closed, somewhere between awake and asleep, the only movement the rustle of their fur against the chill winds, waiting obediently for their guardian. Xander opened his eyes and sat up. He hadn't been asleep. The rest of the dogs did the same. Unmoving, they all watched Anya. The arctic winds picked up force when they brushed over each dog. The music of the winds echoed through the tense atmosphere. All the Directions took their turn speaking.

Anya carefully sat up and put a finger to her lips, motioning for the dogs to stay quiet. She made sure Mooglo still slept then got up off the cold ground. Other camps had been set up in the area, but none in close range. Wolves howled across the expanse. Anya swallowed hard. The wolf is a good sign, she told herself. She did have good luck in the fact that she hadn't been tied like the dogs. Mooglo thought her a mere girl, his willing slave, and didn't even bother to keep watch on her. Grateful for his mistake, she remembered Nana-tasha's prophecy.

You came to us on the arctic winds. The Gatekeepers watch over you. The shamans fear you because of this. You are the first of your kind, the first Native-born of the spirits. There are others created by the spirits, some for good; some for evil. You must become master.

If her grandmother spoke true, Anya suspected Mooglo was created by the spirits for evil, appearing in ugly human form on Native Earth. He could be. She'd find out soon enough if he awakened. She swallowed hard again, a little afraid to find out the whole truth of Nana-tasha's words. The shamans might be afraid of her because of some kind of mystical power her grandmother said she possessed, but she was afraid, too — afraid to find out if the shamans were right. What if she *was* possessed, and she had traveled to Native Earth through one of the holes around the Pole Star from a dark world?

Anya shook her head to clear it. This was no time to worry over prophecy and superstition. Spirits did come to her; they had her whole life. So what! Nothing ever came of it, and nothing ever would. Only whispers in the wind she couldn't understand and shapes in the shadows she couldn't make out. That's all they'd ever been or ever would be. Nothing to be afraid of from any dark world!

Mooglo stirred in his sleep then coughed.

Anya's heart jumped to her throat. She prayed hard to the Morning Dawn for help.

Mooglo coughed one more time then settled back to sleep, his loud snores proof he had.

Able to breathe easier with Mooglo's back to her again, Anya slipped over to Xander and the rest of the huskies. Using her knife she cut Xander's bindings then nineteen more, and freed all of them. Once she'd let each husky go, they readily slipped out of sight, disappearing into the mist of the open tundra. Anya didn't think they'd return.

No other dogs, amid the sea of sleeping huskies traded at the fair, barked. None stirred that Anya could see. She silently thanked the Morning Dawn, the Creator god, and the Earth god, and realized what a miracle it was that no other dogs howled in alert. No trader woke up shouting after the escaped huskies. Anya strained to listen. Only distant wolves called across the winds. Xander had stayed put, waiting obediently for her. She turned to him and motioned for him to follow.

"Run *now,* Xander, run!" she whispered out loud, the instant they'd cleared all the encampments. The belief that Mooglo might not be the only one sent to the Markova Fair by evil spirits who could awaken and come after them was foremost in her thoughts.

CHAPTER THREE

Anya stopped short, unsure of her direction. Her ragged breaths steamed in the air.

Xander ran ahead then must have sensed she didn't follow; he finally turned to pad back to her.

Anya pulled off a mitten and threaded her fingers across Xander's back. His thick fur gave her the comfort she sought. Ahead lay open tundra, *not* the Bering Sea. Too late, she realized she should have followed the river out of Markova. Time was wasting. The baidarka that would take Zellie and Grisha's other dogs across the Bering Sea might be gone by now! She'd understood some of the trading words and knew there was a big baidarka, a big boat, at the edge of the ice that would carry the dogs across the sea to — to whatever lay beyond. When whalers and fishermen came to her coastal village, they spoke of their big boats full of steam needed to hunt in the great sea. She knew the land. She knew the ice.

Why hadn't she taken the time to determine the right direction out of Markova!

Upset, she hadn't paid attention to the winds and let the Directions guide her. The night sky wouldn't reappear for many new moons. There were no stars overhead at this time of year, no constellations. Orion couldn't show her the way. Uneasy, she looked around for any sign of Mooglo. The very thought of him upset her stomach.

All at once she jerked her hand from Xander's back, as she felt something warm and sticky on her fingers. *Blood?* She hastily examined Xander, worried he'd somehow been cut along the way. Relieved to see no blood on him and not worried about herself, she started to put her mitten back on when she saw the blood on her hand, oozing down her fingers in painful, gluey trails. She shot a look up, expecting to see Mooglo. The ugly Yukaghir wasn't there, but she could see the bloody lash marks from his whip on her hand, and she knew the bad spirits had found her and drawn first blood!

This fact made Anya believe her grandmother's divination — *all of it.* Spirits from a powerful dark world had broken through into Anya's, and marked her. The blood on her hand gave her all the proof she needed that evil spirits were trying to prevent her escape, just like her village shamans had done. Shivers ran up and down her. Anya never thought the whispers and shadows from any world of the spirits would ever be anything but annoying. She'd never really been afraid of them, until this moment. Her bloodied hand fell to her side, limp — hurting, useless.

Xander whimpered softly, then nudged his snout into her hand and began licking her fingers clean.

Anya felt the life return to her hand and was immediately comforted. She bent down and hugged Xander protectively; not needing to look at her fingers to know he'd cleaned the blood from her. She felt healed, her pain gone. She'd never sensed a stronger connection to the Gatekeepers, to their healing spirit, than she did now from Xander's touch. Reluctantly, she let go of Xander and stood tall.

He looked at her expectantly, his tail wagging, and waited for her guide.

"Find Zellie," Anya at last thought to say.

She'd no more finished her command before Xander sped off across the snow-covered open, his way seemingly clear.

Anya shoved her mitten back on and followed him — both of them running as if they knew their lives depended on it.

"Might not be so easy, getting your dogs onto shore at Nome," Lars warned Boris after all eight huskies scrambled up the gangplank and had boarded the big iron steamer.

"*Da,*" Boris agreed.

Although he was exhausted after the day's travel, Lars could see the dogs were not. In fact, they appeared more energized than when they all set out in the early morn. These dogs had remarkable stamina. Well, they'll need it, Lars thought, to make the two miles necessary to reach Nome's unfriendly beaches. Ice bound in winter; no problem. The dogs could walk to Nome from the ship. Summer was a different story. The shallow waters and rocky reefs around Nome created a problem for large vessels to offload. It might work better to go to Saint Michael's port, across the Norton Sound, and then run the dogs overland along the edges of the Seward Peninsula.

On second thought, rough waves or not, Lars would have Rune get the dogs to Nome in the supply boat. Anything else would take too much time. Besides, he didn't think Boris could manage the dogs any easier across the wilds of the Alaska territory then he'd managed them across the ice. Lars had to laugh. Managed wasn't the right description. Hitched to their sledge, spread out in separate lines, the dogs tugged the big Russian the whole way from the Siberian coast over the ice to the open waters of the Bering Sea. Boris should have sat in the sledge instead of trying to drive it, trying to keep balance on the runners and keep his mitts on the handles. It would have been a lot easier on him.

"Hallo, Far," Rune called, appearing from below deck, where he'd been helping shovel coal to fuel the steam engine and start up the propellers. He itched to get under way as soon as possible. Wiping his grimy hands with a rag, he put out a hand to welcome the newcomer.

"Rune Johansson," he introduced. His pushed-up shirtsleeves were covered in the same coal dust as his hands.

"*Privet.* Boris Ivanov," the Russian greeted him, and exchanged handshakes.

"Wh—" Before Rune could ask his question, it was answered. The Chukchi dogs came up behind him, friendly, their tails wagging, curious, nudging him gently. "Hey, guys." Rune shoved the dirty rag in a corduroy pants pocket and put both dusty hands out to the dogs. They sniffed his fingers, and licked away the grime, their curled tails still wagging.

I'll be, Lars thought. He hadn't seen the dogs take to anyone like this since Markova. The dogs acted familiar, like they knew Rune. There was a *jente*, a girl, Lars remembered, an older girl with one of the dog traders. Probably the Chukchi's daughter, Lars assumed at the time. The dogs acted just like this around the girl.

As if he'd done so a million times over, Rune dropped to a squat among the frisky pack, letting them paw and play like old friends. The crossing to Nome would be all the shorter if they got on well enough. A seaman and not a dog driver, he hadn't thought much about these furry passengers that took them out of their way, except that they would be a nuisance on the *Storm*. Maybe it wouldn't be so bad after all. Abruptly pushed over by friendly paws, Rune found himself flat on his back on the planked deck. "Hey, I'm not dinner, guys," he laughed, and then pulled himself up and out of the mix of huskies.

"You're a natural," Lars said.

"Nej, no," Rune quickly protested, then quickly brushed his hands back and forth across each other to underscore his point. "Nuisance dogs," he mumbled, and shooed them away.

The pack backed off but their tails still wagged.

"Keptan," Boris spoke up. "Where do dogs stay on ship?"

"Rune will show you," Lars said. "He'll find a place on deck for them."

"But, Far, I thought you wanted them in the hold?" Rune ran his hand across his forehead to clear his sweaty hair away. The streaks of coal dust didn't go anywhere.

"These dogs belong outside, Rune. They'll cook in the boiler-heat below."

One look at the thick fur on the dogs made Rune agree. They'd probably be miserable below deck. He didn't care one way or the other, he told himself, but his father was right.

"Mister Ivanov."

"Boris. *Pozhalujsta,* Boris," the big Russian insisted.

Rune nodded in the starboard direction.

"This way, Boris," he said, then took off along the right side of the ship. He didn't look back at the dogs. There was a space near the front of the ship that should work fine for them. The dogs were Boris's problem, not his. Rune had a steamship to help get under way. He'd no time to worry over any Chukchi dogs. Besides, he could hear the warning sounds at the ship's sides. Jagged edges of sea ice nipped at the *Storm*'s hull, threatening to trap them and crush them in their powerful icy jowls. No matter that it was summer; the seas ahead would provide rough going. Rune could feel it in his bones.

Crewmen busied past, hoisting ropes, securing sails and hatches, calling out checks to each other, and made ready to pull up anchor. Shouts between crewmen from the engine room vibrated through the deck.

"Let me know if you need anything," Rune told Boris.

"*Da,* gud. I will. Looks gud," Boris said as he surveyed the assigned area. Without notice he bent down and collected each dog, nervously tying them separately to the ship's rail.

The dogs didn't protest. They'd never been shipboard before, much less taken from the only home they'd ever known; still, they didn't protest. Their guardian neared.

Rune headed back down to the engine room. The gleam of the midnight sun followed him. There was much to do. He didn't look behind him at the dogs. He was a seaman without any ties, not a dog driver. He didn't want to like the fur trader's dogs,

84

and never expected them to like him. Why the dogs didn't yip and snap, like most did around him, seemed odd. He fought the urge to look over his shoulder to make sure. Hah, what did he care?

He was a seaman without any ties to land, and that suited him just fine.

Caw! Caw! A raven flew overhead, its eyes trained on the two specks that traversed the ice below. Storm clouds gathered. Other ravens gathered and darkened the sky with their numbers. They cawed out to each other, all watching the tiny figures below on Native Earth. Caw! Caw! Caw! The ravens flew in swift circles, closer and closer to each other until they formed into a maze of thick, icy fog. Then the storm clouds burst open.

Xander slid to a sudden halt. His watch-blue eyes fixed straight ahead over the ice. He didn't move a muscle.

"What's wrong, boy?" Anya stopped, too. "What is it?" She looked in the same direction as Xander. She saw nothing. They had to keep going. Time was running out. The baidarka could be gone by the time they reached open water. Zellie would be lost to them forever!

85

"Xander, come on, boy," she urged.

He barked sharply — once, then again. His cry echoed across the ice.

Anya recognized the bark. It was the same one she heard him use when he found his prey on the hunt.

Xander's body stood alert.

Anya knelt next to him and removed a mitten. She stroked his back to reassure him there was nothing up ahead but the ice and the sea. No danger.

Xander whimpered and gave her a quick lick on her cheek, then faced ahead again.

Could be an arctic wolf up ahead or a polar bear, Anya reasoned. The arctic wolf would avoid them, and they would do their best to avoid the polar bear. Two alone in any fight, the polar bear would win. They'd avoided such encounters before and would now.

"Come on, boy. We'll be all right. Come on, now," she urged, still kneeling down.

Xander barked again, more forcefully than before.

Anya didn't recognize his bark this time. A razor-sharp chill cut through her, causing her to look away from Xander and stare ahead at the silent horizon.

An ice storm blew.

She could see it now and hear it coming.

But this was the season, in the New Summer Growing, when storms quieted. What could bring such an outburst? She listened hard for the Directions to answer, anxiously waiting for them to brush past. Her hand began to throb, the same hand on which Mooglo had left his ugly mark. She looked at her hand expecting to see fresh blood. She saw nothing, but in that instant she knew the icy curtain ahead meant to stop their escape.

Anya straightened to a determined stand and ran steady fingers over Xander's back, then abruptly let go. Time was running out.

"We've weathered storms worse than this. Go on boy, find Zellie!"

She watched Xander head into the ice storm and followed him, fully trusting in his keenness and strength to take them through the fearsome blindness.

Rune met his father in the wheelhouse, summoned there by the alert bell and the sudden squall outside. The *Storm* listed to one side, then the other, the big ship knocking hard against the edges of the Bering Sea ice. Waves thrashed against the hull, enough to throw the ship and its crew off balance. Shards of ice rained down — at least that's what the sleet and snow felt like to Rune.

He couldn't believe the gale all around! When he'd gone below deck the evening was calm and the water smooth.

"Away anchor now!" Lars yelled to his crewmen while he held onto the steerage with both hands.

Rune knew his father had no choice but to get away from the ice. To stay would mean the ship's hull could be pierced. They'd sink. Rune grabbed the nearest rail for support. No time for questions, only action.

"Far, let me take the wheel."

His father shook his head, no.

"See to the dogs and Boris Ivanov," Lars ordered.

Rune didn't think he understood right. The noise from the storm all around deafened him.

"Far —"

"Rune, see to the dogs. *Now!*"

Hurt by his father's command, Rune believed his father didn't trust him at the helm. He let go of the ship's rail. The moment he did, the big vessel listed, sending him hard against the deck floor. Angry and embarrassed, he scrambled back up then made his way starboard, not looking back at his father and not bothering to hold onto anything. His father shouldn't treat him like a boy when he was a man, a full crew member.

Two heavy cargo crates slid in front of his path. He shoved them hard to the inside wall, then lashed them down and kept going. As he'd come above deck without any protective gear, his shirt had soaked through. He brushed the cold aside, just like he did the wicked turn of the weather. *Damned dogs.* They were the reason for all this trouble, and now his father wanted him to help save them instead of the ship. *Damned dogs.*

Zellie watched Rune come near. The rolling deck didn't knock her off her feet. Senses sharpened, ears pricked, she waited. The other seven waited, too, all eerily quiet and steady despite the fearsome weather. Their guardian was here.

"Where's Keptan?" Boris yelled the moment he spotted Rune.

"At the wheel," Rune snapped, counting all eight dogs. None had fallen overboard yet. Boris, either.

"*Vy pozhalujsta* help me get *sobaka* below deck!" Boris had all the ties in his hands before he finished his sentence, his feet set wide for balance. The Russian trader seemed accustomed to such rough conditions but nervous about the dogs.

Just then a big wave sprayed them all, the gulf waters roaring.

Rune nodded yes to Boris, wiping his arm across his face to clear the wet. The dogs needed a safer hold. The ship started to move — this time propeller movement. Rune could feel the *Storm*'s power rage against the sea. He wished he were in the wheelhouse to help steer the ship to safety instead of helping guide *these damned dogs* down below. Grumbling to himself, he jerked some of the dogs' leashes from Boris and pulled the huskies along the unsteady deck.

Zellie went willingly. The others followed her lead.

Rune managed to tug the dogs along the main deck, then down ridged planks meant for supply loading, to the level below. Immediately warmed, he shook the cold and wet from his head and pulled his frozen, long underwear shirt away from his bare skin.

The dogs followed his example and shook the cold and wet from their fur.

Boris flopped down in an exhausted heap along the inside hull of the *Storm,* and still held onto his dogs. He was already fast asleep.

Less angry now, Rune took the leashes

from the older man. He looked like a big old bear settling in for hibernation, covered in fur gear head to toe. With his bushy eyebrows, mustache, and beard, he could easily pass for a grizzly.

The ship still rocked and swayed, but Rune felt the power of the *Storm* taking them out of danger. The burlap bags piled nearby should do fine for the dogs to bed down. He wanted to get back up on deck to his father and the wheelhouse, but he would report to the engine room instead. He didn't need to be told no a second time.

"One, two, three," he began his count of the dogs to ensure they all made it below deck. "Four, five, six, seven, eight, nine —" He counted again. *Nine?* The big ship lurched. Rune didn't have time to stand there and count any more dogs. He spread out the burlap and did his best to settle all nine dogs down, hitching their leashes over the nearby rail. As he hurried to the engine room, he thought he must have been wrong to think there were only eight dogs brought on board when he counted nine now.

Xander settled down next to Zellie, home at last.

"Kapvik!" Anya could use the same roar as Grisha on this wolverine who'd found her

91

hiding place!

As soon as the *Storm* had cleared the Gulf of Anadyr, in smooth waters for the present, Rune left the engine room and thought to check on Boris and the dogs before he went above deck. Along the way, he reached blindly into the same locker where he always stowed his navy seaman's jacket. The early morning was still cold despite the calm seas. Instead of his heavy wool jacket he felt fur — wet fur? It wasn't his reindeer parka. This was soft like seal. He tugged the parka out for a look.

"What the —"

"Kapvik!" Wolverine! How could she have been so stupid, being found out so fast? She should have searched for a better hiding place. Upset with herself; Anya refused to look at her captor or worry over her fate.

Rune couldn't believe what he was seeing, what he was holding. *A girl! A stowaway!* He'd found stowaways on shipboard before, but never a girl and never in his locker — and especially never one coming from Russia.

Anya tried to squirm out of her captor's strong grasp, and she still didn't look at him, busy planning her escape. His fingers suddenly let go. *This* made her look at him. The moment she did, she froze.

The eyes of the Gatekeepers met hers.

She'd never seen such a glacial blue, bluer than the heavens, gentle as the warmest day, yet powerful as the coldest night. She was instantly drawn to him; his watch eyes held her. She was feeling funny; her vision began to blur. Then her knees gave way. It wasn't spirits coming. Exhausted, she fainted from hunger and thirst.

Rune caught the unconscious, frail girl and eased her to the deck floor. Under all her thick, damp clothes, she'd no weight at all. The light in the narrow passage let him get a pretty good look at her. Strangest thing, he wished her eyes were open. He saw them briefly before she passed out, long enough to know he'd never seen any eye color or eye shape like hers before. They were brown, he thought, dusted with black lashes, like an ice seal's coloring. Her eyes struck him as large and straight, not small in thin slits like the natives of Siberia and the Alaska territory, the Eskimos.

He had the oddest notion she'd appeared from under the ice, finding a seal hole then climbing onto the *Storm.* He didn't know what world she was from, white or native, but she wasn't from anyplace he'd ever been. He thought again of the sea and looked at her legs, foolishly checking for a

93

tail fin. Some seamen *had* reported sighting mermaids. They didn't exist, of course, but still, he took a second look to make sure she was human. Her high mukluks proved she was.

Anya began to stir.

Startled, Rune moved back.

Her eyes stayed closed.

Rune kept his gaze on her. She reminded him of an animal in the wild. He thought of the ice seal, then the ribbon seal. The rare ribbon seal had the same white trim to its neck as she did around the edges of her white fox hood. Strands of deep brown hair splayed across her face. He crouched down and gently pulled the wet strands away. Her face was pale, too pale. On impulse, he touched her cheek to make sure she hadn't died or something.

His fingers seemed to pass through her like she was a ghost, before he knew he actually touched cool skin. Heck, if she wasn't a mermaid, she might as well be a ghost. He didn't believe in mermaids or ghosts. This girl was just that — only a girl, a stowaway.

Dog barks sounded through the narrow passage. Rune stood. He wondered what had the animals stirring so?

Anya opened her eyes at the barking. She

heard Zellie and Xander. Before she tried to move she mentally thanked the Chukchi gods for helping her and Xander come this far — for helping them find Zellie and the rest of the huskies that had been taken.

Anya realized she wasn't alone. Quickly, she picked herself up off the floor, before the good-looking boy with the bluest of watch eyes could stop her. Once she had a better look she wasn't at all afraid of him. *Hah,* he wasn't much older than she was. He was taller than her by a head or more; but his muscled frame didn't scare her, either.

Rune looked at the strange girl again, without a clue what to do. First the dogs, and now this girl . . . who else wanted to go to Nome? Maybe he should check the whole steamer for more animals and children!

Anya took off running in the direction of the dogs.

Rune ran his fingers through his thick, cropped hair then rubbed his jaws hard in exasperation. His beard stubble hinted of coming in, the layer of fuzz palpable. If he hadn't been so frustrated with finding the girl, on top of the whole issue with the dogs, he might have realized it, since he wanted to prove to his father he was a man, a full crew member, beard and all. He grudgingly started down the passage after the girl. No need to run. What would she do now, jump ship? He picked up his step as he realized she just might.

He found the girl, smack in the center of the Siberian wolf pack. Boris still slept. Amazing that he could sleep through all this! A bit relieved the girl had decided to dive into the pack of dogs and not the sea, Rune let them tumble and play like old friends meeting up. The gentle dogs were just that with her. Friends. Fine, let them play. What else was he supposed to do?

Anya looked up. She'd already undone all the dogs' ties. She stared holes through the Viking boy, daring him to interfere.

Zellie broke from the group and darted over to Rune, and immediately licked his hand in greeting. Xander broke, too, and ran to Zellie and Rune.

Anya couldn't believe it! Shouldn't they be growling at the Viking, their captor? She remembered the tales in her village of fierce, golden-haired Vikings invading in the old times, beating back the murderous Cossacks just like the Chukchi had always done. Humph. She was Chukchi. She had nothing in common with this boy! Still, she couldn't take her eyes off him. She'd never seen Zellie and Xander behave so with anyone but her.

Suddenly jealous, she brushed her fingers over the ears of the huskies still gathered round her. The copper-red and white pair she knew as Grisha's dogs; the rest she would get to know. They were Chukchi-bred, she could tell, and most likely from the Chawchu, the reindeer-hunters.

Rune fought the urge to pet the pretty little wolf dog. The bigger black and white who'd approached begged for a pet, too.

Zellie nudged harder, and wanted notice, while Xander reared up on his back legs and put his paws against Rune's chest in play.

"Easy, guys," Rune admonished. He tried to sound gruff but couldn't. He wanted to keep from petting the nuisance animals but couldn't, and abruptly put a friendly hand to each of their luxuriant, furry backs. For the second time in as many days, these dogs surprised him. They seemed to like him well enough. This had him stumped.

He was a seaman, not a sled dog driver. He didn't know the first thing about these Siberian wolves. The girl obviously did, the way they all took to her. At the thought, Rune suddenly looked up and right into the pretty eyes of the strange girl who'd been hiding in his locker. He thought she smiled.

Caught off guard, Anya bit her lower lip and tried to hide her expression from the outsider. She didn't want to give away anything to him and let him know what Zellie and Xander meant to her. She was still afraid for them; she didn't know why the sleeping Russian bear wanted to take them beyond the edges of their Native Earth. She didn't know their fate. At least she was going with them. *No one* would stop her. Not Grisha, not Mooglo, not the black-hearted Raven, not this Viking boy, not anyone, human or spirit.

They all had to be hungry and thirsty, Rune decided. The girl looked like she would pass out again, and he doubted Boris had awakened long enough during the night to feed and water his charges.

By now Zellie and Xander had wandered back over to Anya.

"You hungry?" Rune asked the girl, not thinking she might speak a language other than English.

She frowned back.

"Eat?" His brain kicked back in. He put his hand to his mouth as if he held a spoon.

Her quizzical frown turned to an understanding nod. She was hungry, but so must the dogs be. They had to eat and drink, too.

Without another thought she charged over to Rune then turned and pointed to the huskies.

"*Imiq? Meck? Tiblit?*"

It was Rune's turn to frown. He didn't understand her words, but her melodic tone took him by surprise. He was reminded of the sea again, thinking she sang like the animals of the deep. Darned if she didn't sound like what he'd imagined a mermaid would!

"*Vada? Miaso?*" Frustrated the boy didn't understand her native language, Anya tried again to ask for fresh water and food for the dogs, this time louder and this time in Russian. She hoped he could speak some Russian.

"Oh. Oh, yeah," Rune finally got it. She wanted the dogs seen to first.

Relieved the boy understood, Anya followed at his heels just to make sure.

Rune turned around and the girl bumped right into him. He put his hands up and gently pushed her back a step. Then he put his hands to his chest.

"*I* will do this. You go back," he said, and tried to pivot her around.

She shook her head no, and stood firm.

Rune nodded his head yes, and succeeded this time in turning her around and sending her on her way like she was a disobedient child. He heard her curse at him. He didn't have to know what language she spoke. Smiling despite his annoyance with this whole situation, Rune grabbed up a water bucket and headed for the fresh tap barrels. Boris should have some food stowed for the dogs. He meant to wake the trader up and find it. Passing the galley, Rune reached for the sourdough loaf atop a nearby shelf. The girl had to eat something, too. He snatched up the sack of jerked beef next to the bread. Boris might come up empty-handed.

"An-ya," Anya carefully pronounced the moment Rune returned. She looked at him, pointed to herself and said again, "An-ya."

Rune set down the pail of water. He splayed his fingers across his chest.

"Rune."

Anya watched his firm mouth and his white teeth, trying to understand.

"Run," she at last pronounced, half-smiling, proud of herself. "Run."

"No. Not Run. Rune," he corrected, emphasizing the *oo* sound.

"Roo," she parroted.

"Close enough, Anna."

"Roon," she repeated, this time with all the right sounds, she thought.

He set the bucket of water in the middle

of the waiting dogs. Boris slept on. Amazing! Rune handed her the loaf of sourdough bread.

She absentmindedly took the loaf then tapped him on the chest.

"Not Anna. An-*ya*." She shook her finger in front of him in a no. "Anya, *Russkiy yazk.*"

"Right, right," Rune understood. "Anya is Russian." Evidently, in the middle of all this craziness, getting her name exactly right was important to her — important to her, but trouble to him. The girl was turning out to be as much of a nuisance as the huskies.

"*Da, Russkiy yazk,*" she repeated and smiled up at him.

Her fluent Russian pronunciation was lost on him. Annoyed with her, Rune still fought his urge to give her a playful pat on the head, just like he'd given the huskies. Wherever she'd come from, she was one of the pack. A blind man could see their mutual attachment.

Anya bit into the loaf he handed her, forgetting she had no idea what she was eating. She coughed her mouthful right at Rune, and spit bits of bread all over.

"It's going to be a long trip to Nome," Rune prophesied, and wiped his shirt front. "Eat. It's good." He guided her hand that

101

held the bread back to her mouth.

She pulled her hand away and pointed to his arm, the one holding the sack of food. She gestured for him to show her what was in the sack.

"For the dogs," he said right away. "This food is for the dogs." He dumped the jerky in a pile on the floor, letting the dogs choose their own.

Anya dropped down and pulled a strip of beef out for herself, then quickly shoved the delicious bites in her mouth. She let the sourdough fall to the floor.

Rune picked up the bread. He'd put it back. Food wasn't to be wasted, especially not on any ungrateful stowaway. If she wanted to eat dog food, let her. In a huff over everything, Rune didn't think about how much he loved jerked beef, and jerked salmon as well.

"Here." He shoved the dipper he'd brought from the galley at the nuisance girl.

Anya took it, immediately filling it and taking a welcome drink of water.

Rune watched her fill the dipper to the brim three times, drinking each one to the bottom.

He picked up the bucket. The dogs and the girl would need more. He shook his head — nothing but trouble, all of them.

■ ■ ■ ■

"Rune, go back —"

"I know, Far. You want me to go back to the dogs." Rune pulled Anya into the wheelhouse with him before his father could finish.

"I was going to say the engine room," Lars said, his stunned focus entirely on the girl. He recognized her right away as the girl with the Chukchi dog trader. What in the world was she doing shipboard?

"Girl, did Boris Ivanov bring you with him?"

Anya stared at the man who guided the baidarka. Rune looked like him, only much younger.

"Girl —"

"It's no use, Far. She doesn't speak any English," Rune interrupted.

"*Da* . . . yes, yes English," Anya said, defending herself. "Hello . . . goodbye . . . fish . . . whale . . . ship . . . home . . . dog . . . thank you . . . snow . . . ocean. See, I can say English," she finished, her mutinous eyes on Rune. She remembered most of the words from Russian whalers and the English, but she was surprised, herself, at her memory.

Rune let go of her arm, shaking his head over her surprises. Nothing but trouble, Anya!

"You're a smart one." Lars smiled down at her; her pronunciation was pretty spot-on.

"Anya," she offered, and pointed to her chest. She thought she'd be afraid of wherever Rune was taking her, but the fair-haired baidarka driver, the *ship* driver, meant her no harm. His eyes were kind. His manner gentle, more gentle than Rune's!

"Rune, take the wheel."

Startled out of his annoyance, Rune slipped his hands onto the well-worn steerage. Only after he had the helm did he realize his father actually gave it to him. Maybe he wasn't so annoyed with Anya after all, seeing as how she caused his father to ask him to take over. It felt like "home" with his hands on the wheel, the only home he ever wanted.

"Anya, did Boris Ivanov bring you with him?" Lars repeated his same question, in an appeal to the slip of a girl. He saw something in her large brown eyes, as if she were older than her young years. She couldn't be more than thirteen or fourteen *ar-gammel,* a kid just like his son. She looked part-native, part-white — probably

104

orphaned by some whaler who left her with the Chukchi.

Lars thought of his daughter, Inga. If he'd left her in some native village, she'd never have survived. Soft and spoiled at fourteen, his daughter would have refused to live anywhere but their expansive home in Seattle's finest neighborhood. Inga wasn't made of tough stuff, but the girl who stood before him certainly was. She stood up to him, apparently not afraid and apparently running away from home. He studied her sad eyes, and wondered why she'd left.

The Chukchi dog trader came to mind, then Boris Ivanov.

"Child, did the Russian force you to come with him?"

Anya struggled to understand. She could pick out some of the words, but not all. "Boris" must be the big bear of a man sleeping with the dogs. She knew the word "Russian." She heard the name mentioned twice, "Boris." The ship driver might think she'd come with the Russian.

She shook her head firmly no.

More puzzled than before, Lars turned to his son.

"Where did you find Anya?" he asked, his tone suddenly gruff.

Rune got his back up a little at the question, but he kept his hands on the wheel and his eyes full ahead. One day he'd prove himself to his father; then his father wouldn't have to be so hard on him.

"In my locker," Rune said, agitated over the conversation already.

"Be serious with me, son. This is important."

"In my locker, Far. She was hiding there and must have boarded ship during the ice storm in the gulf." Rune thought about it for the first time. How the heck could anybody board ship during that squall? But Anya must have and with the ninth dog. Maybe he hadn't been wrong about his count. At that moment, with his father pressing him — eight dogs, nine dogs — it didn't seem to matter. Anya's sudden appearance did.

This barn boarded our skepp during the isen storm? Not possible, Lars thought. He still suspected the Russian somehow got her on board before the storm. Maybe he wanted a young wife to warm him on cold Nome nights, kidnapping or buying a child bride.

"I don't think she came with Boris." Rune had sensed where his father's thinking might be going. "Boris has been asleep since we left Siberia, and I don't think he even knows she's here. She came for the dogs,

106

Far. I think she came to be with the huskies and didn't want to be left behind. That's what I think," Rune said, explaining his theory on why the strange girl stowed away on the *Storm.*

"Huh," Lars grunted.

Rune tightened his grip on the steerage. His father obviously didn't think much of his theory.

"Girl . . . Anya," Lars said quietly to her. "Come." He motioned for her to follow him out of the wheelhouse.

Anya shot Rune a nervous look before she obediently trailed behind.

Rune didn't miss the appeal in her watering eyes for him to come, too. He hugged the wheel tightly and was almost willing to let go of it.

CHAPTER FOUR

Anya didn't understand kindness. She'd never known it from anybody but her grandmother and Vitya. The ship driver, Keptan Lars, was kind and didn't roar at her. When the Russian bear roared at her, Keptan Lars defended her. Although she didn't understand all the words exchanged, she thought the keptan explained that she came with the dogs, then saw the bear shake his head in a no, at the same time he pointed her way. He also pointed his finger at Xander, possessively Anya thought. It struck her that the bear would keep Xander as if *he'd* traded for him. So be it. There was no going back. The bear kept on roaring. The dogs barked again. They'd been retied. Feeling just as tied, she fisted her fingers around the rail and kept her watch eyes on the bear.

Lars agreed with Boris. Boris couldn't take on the care of this girl and the sled dogs. Lars didn't think it was a good idea anyway, for this stranger to be entrusted with the child. Lars had already gone over this in his mind before he went below deck. He believed that Boris had no idea the spindly girl had stowed away and that Boris didn't remember seeing her at Markova.

Boris the bear still pointed at her.

Anya watched him shake his head at her and gesture like he wanted to shoo her away. She dropped down to the dogs, kneeling next to Zellie and Xander, and wished she could disappear in the pack. She wished they all were running free across the open tundra instead of being trapped here. Sobs welled in her throat. How she longed for one more hug from Nana-tasha. She needed to feel her grandmother's protective arms hold her.

The oddest sensation hit. Anya didn't think it came from her grandmother. She got up off her knees and put her hands out in front of her, examining them — surprised not to see blood, and surprised to see her hands at all, she felt so funny.

She pressed her palms together, entwining her fingers, to make sure of them. It almost felt like they weren't attached to her. The pulling inside her strengthened. She gripped her hands together more tightly, her sixth sense telling her that if she let go, she would lose hold of her physical being and disappear. The spirits followed her, she believed. But were they good spirits or bad?

Forcing them apart, she let her hands fall to her sides. She couldn't help but wonder what just happened.

"Nej," Rune answered flatly, trying to hide his agitation.

"Ja, you will," his father argued.

"Far," Rune's tone turned more rebellious. "I made a place for the dogs, but I'll be darned if I'm going to worry over Anya."

Lars's big shoulders heaved. He didn't have a choice but to put Rune in charge of the child on the passage to Nome. There was no one else — the job was not going to go to any crewman, and certainly not to Boris Ivanov.

"Look, son, all you have to do is make sure Anya has food, water, a place to sleep, and doesn't fall into the Bering Sea. That's it until Nome."

"That's it?" Rune repeated, wanting to hold his father to his word. "All I have to do is make sure she eats and sleeps until we get to Nome, then that's it?"

"Ja," Lars answered stiffly.

"She gets off in Nome, then I can be done with her?" Rune pressed.

"Ja. She gets off in Nome," Lars answered truthfully.

"I'll find her after I finish my work on deck," Rune said curtly, then gave his father the wheel of the *Storm*.

Lars took over steerage. The collar of his heavy sweater irritated his skin enough for him to reach up and tug it away. Out of the corner of his eye, he watched Rune see to his duties on deck and realized he had a lot to think about, a lot to decide.

With her coastal village far behind, Anya became somewhat accustomed to routine aboard ship and learned her place. It certainly wasn't with the dogs — thanks to Boris Ivanov, she believed. Every time she'd come close to Zellie and Xander, he'd shoo her away. No matter; she kept coming back to check on them.

The big Russian bear might forget to feed and water them. He certainly didn't exercise them, even after he'd switched all the dogs to the open. At least they were outside and away from the heat of the engine room below deck. Left free to explore the ship, she'd done exactly that, more curious than ever to see for herself what kind of ships had brought whalers and fishermen to Siberia's fierce coast. She'd listened to tales

111

around the yaranga fires in the evening back in her village, but she still found it hard to believe she was actually on one of the big ships. This wasn't a whaling vessel, but it could be, she imagined.

As she leaned over the deck rail at the bow of the *Storm,* Anya peered into the noisy deep of the Bering Sea, listening as each wave crashed against the ship's sides. She pulled back inside the rail and glanced around her, eyeing the horizon in every direction. No land in sight, only water. She kept waiting to see the edges of Native Earth; half expecting the ship would drop off into some abyss that would send them all to their deaths or to another world below the Deep.

If they died, she knew Zellie and Xander would be rescued by the Gatekeepers, their sled pulled across into heaven. If they fell into the world below the Deep, she believed the Earth god would keep them safely hidden from the dark spirits that dwelled there. Thinking hard on her own fate, she leaned far out over the rail again, imagining what it would feel like to drown. The Earth god might welcome her, but then she had helped hunt the seal, the walrus, and the whale on Native Earth — only for survival, but still, maybe she wouldn't be so protected in the Deep.

"Aaaahhh!"

Anya shrieked at the powerful arms suddenly clamped around her, cutting off her air, and pulling her from the rail. She wasn't some wounded gull or puffin to be plucked out of the water! When she'd been let go, she spun around and expected to see Boris the bear, but it was Rune. She hadn't seen him for days, it seemed, and he took her by surprise.

"Are you crazy? You can't go jumping off this ship until we get to Nome!"

"Nome?" she repeated, worried more about the sound of *Nome* than his obvious upset with her. She should be mad at him, but she wasn't.

Upset, Rune started to walk away but then came back. He realized he should have been keeping a closer watch on Anya, who was still clad in her heavy fur parka. What if he hadn't come this way? She might have fallen overboard. The weight of her wet parka alone would have sunk her! No one would know. It would be too late to save her. Even if they managed to find her body and pull her from rough seas, she'd already be dead from the cold. A few minutes in arctic waters were all it took to kill.

"Nome?" Anya repeated impatiently.

Rune caved at her simple question. Her innocent look made him soften, reminding him she was only a child. She had every right to know where they were going, even though she'd stowed away. The *Storm* had just cleared the passage between the Chukotka Peninsula and Saint Lawrence Island, and headed straight for Nome's waters. In two days' time they should arrive. Rune wished the ship could travel farther north into the Arctic Ocean instead of stopping. He couldn't wait for the adventure of it — for the challenge of steering out of harm's way, out of the way of ice floes farther up the Alaska coast. The *Storm* would steam north right after the quick stop in Nome. The planned stops in Kotzebue, Port Hope, and finally Barrow would be lucrative fur-trading points. His father had already radioed ahead to find out about the ice pack, before he'd decided that rather than having to return to Seattle, they'd be able to venture north after all.

The ice might keep them from Barrow. If it was too dangerous, his father would turn the ship back. The *Storm* was no icebreaker. The change in schedule wasn't easy, but it would be better to return to Seattle with a profitable load of Klondike fur goods than an empty hold. Only one thing stood in the way: depositing Anya and the dogs and Boris Ivanov onto Nome's crowded, gold-claimed beaches. Rune would be glad to say goodbye to all of them. The way Anya stared up at him now, her innocent face full of questions, struck a nerve in him, a guilty one.

"Nome is the place you're going," he tried to explain.

"*Da,* Nome," she said after him.

Rune pointed across the Bering Sea in the direction of Nome.

"Nome."

Anya copied him, pointing and nodding her head, yes.

"Nome is your new home, Anya."

"*Da.* Nome. Home," she pronounced. She knew home.

Rune couldn't believe how calm she appeared. Although she was a mere child, a female at that, she didn't seem scared at all. The only thing she seemed scared about was the dogs. That's it, he reasoned. She ran away from her home in Siberia to be with the dogs. Rune thought there must be more to her story. There had to be. Suspicious, he wondered who or what she ran from. Catching himself worrying over some nuisance stowaway, he quickly looked away and glanced out to sea or anywhere, away from her trusting, sad eyes.

"*Sobaka?* Nome? D-dogs, Nome?" Anya struggled with the right words, still pointing in the same direction.

Rune heaved a sigh, understanding her. He believed she wanted to make sure the dogs were going to the same place she was. He softened more toward her.

"Yes," he reassured.

She smiled at him, a full, genuine, beautiful smile, seemingly happy for the first time since they'd left Siberia. Seeing Anya's bright smile, he suddenly thought of his sister, Inga. He'd never seen such happiness on Inga's pouty face. Hah, his mother's, either. His mother carried the same pout. His sister had never known unhappiness, he realized; she got everything she wanted from his father whenever she wanted it.

Shoot, he felt more of a tie to this strange girl than he did to his own sister, to his own family. Squirming under the thought, Rune knew he'd part company with Anya soon . . . and good riddance. The North waited for him. The Arctic Ocean waited for him. Not Nome. He didn't want anything to do with any females, family or otherwise, and especially not with this ghost of a girl.

Abruptly, Rune turned to leave, but Anya

116

caught his arm. She motioned in the direction of the dogs then tugged at his arm, dragging him along. He didn't have to guess. He knew where she was going to take him. Grudgingly, he let her.

"Nyet, nyet!" Boris bellowed his no to Rune and Anya. "My haskis *kharasho*. Haskis fine. Goodbye. *Do svidanya!"*

Anya started undoing Zellie's tie to the rail and ignored Boris the bear. The dogs needed exercise. They'd never been tied so long, kept to a post, unable to run. She'd tried to free them before, but Boris the bear never slept anymore, it seemed.

"Do svidanya. Goodbye," Boris huffed, then snatched Zellie's tie from Anya, which sent Anya off balance.

Zellie bristled. Xander, too, both huskies alert to the moment, their watch eyes on Boris.

"Hey, no need for that, Boris." Rune protectively stepped in front of Anya. "I think she just wants you to let the dogs run around deck a while. Can't do any harm," Rune said.

Boris eyed Rune suspiciously.

Anya peered around Rune, eyeing Boris just as suspiciously. The big bear didn't know about dogs, especially Chukchi dogs.

Zellie and Xander had been traded to a bear of a man who didn't know anything about them. Fear coursed through her. She was afraid for Zellie, Xander, and all the Chukchi dogs going to a home called "Nome."

What waited for them in Nome? What would happen to them in the hands of Boris the bear? Her hand throbbed. She had to look. No blood. She eyed Boris again, wondering if he owned a whip. If he did, did he crack the whip to guide dogs or beat them? Chukchi dogs didn't know the whip. She did. The scars on her hand were proof enough.

Light-headed all of a sudden, Anya grabbed Rune for support and managed to catch the back of his sleeve. Someone whispered to her. It wasn't Rune. Looking around him, she saw it wasn't Boris the bear. Clutching Rune's sleeve tighter, she closed her eyes, and strained to better hear the whispers. Her thoughts spun, and she tried to understand the voices on the winds.

It is time. It begins.

Anya threw Rune's arm from her as if it burned. She'd never understood any whispers from the spirit world until this moment! It is time? It begins? In her native Chukchi, she'd heard the words clearly. The whispers seemed familiar. She'd heard the

118

voice before. Anya calmed at once, thinking of her grandmother, letting Nana-tasha's soft whispers cuddle her close as if she were a babe. Then, in that split second, in the time it takes for a heart to beat and give life or take it, Anya knew her grandmother's heart beat no more; her life had ended.

The dogs howled; their mournful cries pierced the eerie silence.

Boris tried to settle them.

Rune tried to comfort Anya, although he had no idea why she just collapsed in a sobbing heap behind him.

Relieved that radio ship-to-shore reports of icefree water off the beaches of Nome were correct, Lars dropped the *Storm*'s anchor a mile and a half out at sea to avoid the hull-smashing sand bar hidden in front of them. Mid-June, with the waters fairly smooth, he hoped the trip up the coast to Barrow would be as welcoming. He hadn't slept well last night — nightmares again. The collar of his sweater irritated. He pulled it from his damp; itchy skin, then left the bridge, hopeful his talk with Rune would go as smoothly as open water, not head-on into pack ice.

Anya slept restlessly for two days, some-where between awake and asleep — between her grandmother's dying words and the fog of nightmarish ice storms colliding.

It is time. It begins.

What could her grandmother mean by such words . . . time for what to begin?

You are the first of your kind.

What kind am I? What burden do I carry? What must I master? I have no weapon but my simple knife! Anya thrashed in her sleep, feeling Mooglo's ugly whip cut across her back, each lash deeper, each drawing more blood. Dreams of her loving grandmother turned to misshapen nightmares of evil spirits coming after her and Zellie and Xander, spirits with their whips raised high, laughing at her simple knife.

Rune had taken Anya to his room after she collapsed. He'd given her his small quarters at the start of their passage, preferring the open deck anyway. He had no trouble finding a spot on deck to bed down. The more he checked on Anya, the more he felt sorry for her; for her and for the dogs on board that didn't belong to her anymore. Now that they were in Nome waters, he had to wake Anya up. He hated doing it. She had no place to go in the gold-digging city and would be dropped off cold, like so much cargo. Maybe his father would take her back

120

to Siberia, back where she came from.

Father and son collided in the narrow passage outside Rune's quarters.

"Get your gear, son," Lars ordered, and tried to turn Rune around toward his cabin. He'd decided not to have a talk with Rune. Talking wouldn't get this mission under way. Orders would. Rune understood orders, having lived aboard ship most of his life. Nothing got done unless every crewman followed orders. Survival at sea, especially the unpredictable Bering Sea, meant every man had to do his job and toe the line.

Rune shook off his father's hold. He refused to be pushed around anymore. He faced his father squarely and stood his ground.

"Rune, get your gear," Lars repeated evenly.

Rune said nothing; he watched his father's lips move but wouldn't listen and obey. He was so mad he forgot all about Anya and his purpose . . . Every single time he charted a course, his father put him off course! He watched the muscles tighten in his father's jaw and knew his father was just as angry as he. Rune crossed his arms in front of him, locking them at his elbows.

The *Storm*'s foghorn sounded, causing

both father and son to hurry above deck.

Anya awakened to the unearthly sound. *Someone was there. Something was coming.* She climbed out of her sleeping box and head straight for Zellie and Xander and the rest of the dogs. Her stomach turned to fire.

Spirits from the darkest of storms past, in the darkest of worlds present, had found them and were coming!

The misshapen evil had no form, no shape, but whispered only the promise of death. Running as fast as her shaky legs would take her, Anya unwittingly felt for her crude knife tucked deep inside the pocket of her kerker, reliving her nightmares each step of the way.

"Can't figure this." Lars rubbed his jaw hard as he stared into the dark curtain of sea smoke and fog lowered around them. It came out of nowhere, like his nightmares. When he went below, he could see Nome, but now the frontier boom town had vanished from sight. The seas stayed calm. He couldn't figure that, either. There had been no storm warnings, no reason to doubt their course.

Rune stood at his father's side, just as puzzled over the unpredictable weather. The whole ship seemed to stand still, all silent, with no crew that hurried to their tasks. The alert sounded again, jarring Rune into action.

"Where are you going?" Lars tried to catch his son's arm.

"To the huskies," Rune called over his shoulder, on his way to the starboard deck where he knew Anya would be by this time. He needed to keep her from going with Boris and the dogs. Whatever it took, he had to stop her. In the short time he'd known her, she'd become more like a little sister to him than Inga ever had. Like it or not, he needed to protect Anya and get her back to Siberia.

He knew it. There she was, climbing down into the lighter-boat already lowered to the water, the boat with Boris and the nine huskies ready to go.

"Nyet! Nyet!" Boris yelled at her, all the while trying to loosen her hold on the ropes she trailed down. "Go bek! Go bek!"

The frantic barks of the dogs didn't stop Boris. Xander nipping at him didn't stop him. Zellie's attempts at the same thing, didn't stop him. Two of the three crewman already on board finally pulled him away from Anya.

She scrambled into the undersized boat and dared Boris the bear to touch her again after she put her hand inside her pocket to make sure of her knife. Rebelliously, she took a position in between Zellie and Xander and sat hard on the floor of the boat.

"Here." Lars shoved his son's duffle gear at him before Rune had a chance to slip over the rail to fetch Anya.

"Wh—?" Rune pulled back onto deck. "Nej, Far! I'm not going with this boat to Nome. I need to get the girl and we need to get her back to Siberia where she belongs."

The seas started to act up. The boat began to toss.

Rune realized the danger. The crew had to get the boat, cargo, and passengers to Nome soon or not at all, the way the wind kicked up. They needed to beat the weather.

"No time now to argue with me, Rune. You're needed on the oars," Lars yelled, and strong-armed his son back over the rail. "I'll find another lighter-boat in Kotzebue. You stay in Nome with the crew and this one. I'll see you on my return," he promised. With that, Lars pitched Rune's duffle over the side.

"But —" Rune didn't have a chance to reply, to counter his father, before rough waves slapped against the sides of their boat, knocking it against the *Storm*. They had to go now before the weather got worse. Rune didn't want to think about that happening. He knew the crew could use his help. He glared up at his father, then looked at Anya.

Since the moment he'd met up with her, she'd brought nothing but trouble for him, one storm after another. Anya and her dogs! He'd much prefer dodging dangerous ice floes to this. But he had no choice. Rune kicked his duffle aside to secure it, then took to the oars with the rest of the crew, leaving the *Storm* behind him.

Thankful Rune was with them, Anya threaded her fingers across Zellie and Xander's downy backs. She needed them close. She'd spotted the Raven flying overhead. The sign could not be a good one, the way the winds blew dark. All she could do was watch as one raven became two, then three, then more, darkening the skies in frenzied circles as their anger grew. She felt their icy spirits cut in the air. What weapon did she have against such evil? Her simple knife? She didn't think it would be enough to defend against the Raven.

Her eyes went to Rune. The Raven feared him. She could smell the Raven's fear, even in the twisting air. She looked at Rune as if for the first time, and couldn't imagine what powers he must hold to frighten dark spirits so.

Anya took one look back at Keptan Lars. He had been kind. She would not forget. His ship had carried her all the way across the great sea and helped her escape with the dogs to the edges of their known world, plunged soon into the unknown. Praying hard to the Morning Dawn she appealed to the Directions to help Rune battle the evil that tried to stop them, that tried to keep them from reaching the village called Nome.

Her necklace burned like fire. She quickly pulled the carved ivory from her skin, and waited for it to cool, then let it fall back to her neck. Vitya's gift, she thought, before an even odder feeling hit. She darted a glance at each face onboard the boat, expecting to see Vitya among them. He wasn't. She tilted her head up and saw the dark clouds over-head, reminded of the blackest of ravens. The ominous sign frightened her.

Afraid something might have happened to Vitya back in their village, she prayed to the Creator gods in all the heavens, and to the Earth gods beneath all the waters, to protect her forever friend. The boat rocked hard. Sinking her fingers deeper into Zellie and Xander's thick fur, Anya held the dogs close and did her best to keep them all from be-ing tossed into the sea.

Rune had his hands full, trying to help the

crew keep the boat from overturning in the sudden squall. He knew the boat was sturdy enough; he just hoped he and the crew would be strong enough to keep on course for Nome and not head back out to sea. In the thick fog, he didn't want to make any mistakes. Pieces of icebergs floated all too near. Not a good sign. The waters evidently had churned up enough to bring some of the broken ice pack. Fighting four- and five-foot waves, Rune's arms ached from working the oars. The little boat could handle the waves for the moment, but he worried about capsizing if they got much worse. The seas always stayed rough around Nome, but not this rough this time of year. Late summer usually brought the rainstorms; they didn't generally come this early.

A big wave splashed across the boat, soaking them all again.

"Boris," Rune yelled. "Take the oar!"

Rune waited for the big man to climb over to him and take his position next to the crewman. He could see fear written all over Boris's face. The Russian had the grit to help, though. The weight of the boat shifted with Boris. Rune quickly moved to keep an even keel. He shoved a cargo crate to the opposite side of the boat before he made sure Anya and the dogs could hold fast in the rough water.

Rune wasn't certain what he saw on Anya's face, but he didn't think it was fear. She looked like a ghost; the blood had drained from her wet face, as if she'd already fallen into the sea and then returned to life through a breathing hole in the ice. Seals did it. Mermaids did it. The way she clutched the huskies for dear life made him forget his superstitions and think of her safety. She shouldn't be here. Neither should the dogs. They belonged back in Siberia, not in this storm-ridden boat headed for Nome.

While he fought for balance, Rune bent down to get the ropes coiled on the floor of the boat. He needed to lash Anya and the dogs down, and secure them to the boat before something bad happened. Just then another wave hit. This time it knocked Xander's tie loose and sent him into the water, dragging him down.

Zellie howled, excited and biting feverishly at her tie.

Anya tried to hoist her leg over the side of the boat, going after Xander.

Rune yanked Anya back and shoved her to the floor of the craft, then he leaned over the edge and caught Xander's hide collar, thankful the big husky had one on. The dog

128

fought hard, but his head disappeared below the water. Rune pulled with all his might, grateful the collar held; finally he managed to pull Xander's head above water. The dog was close to death, his fight gone. Rune leaned farther over the edge in a struggle to get an arm around the heavy animal caught in a merciless undertow. Rune didn't have time to think about the unnatural situation, the out-of-place undertow. The dog was dying.

The crew couldn't help; they were all busy at the oars trying to keep afloat. Boris didn't turn around, unaware of anything but holding onto his oar for dear life.

Desperate to hold on to Xander and Rune, Anya wrapped her arms around Rune's lower legs and mustered every ounce of her strength for the fight.

Even with the toss of the boat, Zellie stayed at alert attention with the rest of the dogs; their eyes were all on Xander.

The Gatekeepers watched.

So did dark spirits.

And now another peered up from the Deep, looming in the depths, having patiently waited to seize this opportunity.

Rune was about to let go of the half-dead husky. He couldn't risk the lives of everyone on board any more than he already had, by leaving the oars to save one dog. He'd make a last attempt to get the dog out of the water, and then it would be over. His muscles ached to a burn. He hated to watch this dog die. With strength he never knew he had, Rune held fast to the dog's collar with one hand and managed to hook his other hand beneath the dog's immersed body; then he lifted the animal up and into the boat.

It happened so fast, Rune couldn't believe it. He still didn't, despite watching Anya hover over the rescued animal. The dog's head twitched. Good; he still lived. Rune wiped his hair from his eyes then quickly retook his position at the oars; he didn't notice the bloody marks left on his hands from the struggle.

Anya watched Rune take up his oars, then leaned back down to Xander. She didn't know how Xander had survived, but he had. More than once while they were out hunting back home, she'd feared one of the dogs might fall through the ice and drown in the cold dark of the sea. That Xander hadn't drowned just now was a miracle.

Rune had saved him. Rune had pulled him from the Deep. Rune was master of the dark spirits on this day, she believed. No hunter was stronger than he. No shaman wiser. The ancestors smiled at Rune. Anya could feel their ceremonial drums beat softly in her heart, echoing their trust in him.

The winds died down; the waters calmed. Xander opened his eyes and tried to stand. Anya helped him get up.

Zellie touched noses and licked his face.

Coming back to life, Xander shook off the wet, knocking Anya away almost in play.

Zellie barked. The other dogs stayed quiet.

Anya wiped away her tears, able to breathe again. She'd never been happier. Xander was alive. The danger had passed. Anya felt her body relax as she watched Xander settle next to Zellie. She curled up with them needing to be close and reflexively shut her eyes. That's all it took for her to fall fast asleep.

When Anya awoke, the dogs were gone! So was the boat and Rune and Boris the bear! Waves rolled in from the sea, lapping at her feet. She scrambled up from the unfamiliar ground. In her exhausted nightmares, had she fallen through a hole around the Pole Star and landed in another world? Alarmed and confused, she quickly circled round. This place didn't look like any home, any village, she'd ever known, but it had to be Native Earth. *Nome,* she remembered, as she saw so many humans in front of her. Dogs, too — lots of them, tied in teams pulling odd sleds without runners.

None were Chukchi dogs.

Frantic, she forgot all about Rune and the boat as she bumped her way through the sea of men and dogs and mounds of strange objects, determined to find Zellie and Xander and the rest of the dog team from the *Storm*. No breezes blew to give her any sense of direction. Trapped, caught up in a whirlwind of unfamiliar sights and sounds, Anya appealed to the Morning Dawn for guidance.

She'd never seen so many people in one place in her life! Some were dressed like her, but most had on funny-looking clothes. She'd never seen so many different kinds of yarangas, different kinds of homes; some were so tall they towered over her. Poles shot up in front of the tall structures — and not inside the homes, where they should be to support them and hold up the walls. Out-of-place hitch lines ran from the top of one tall pole to the next and then to the next one after that. Funny, she thought, poles hitched together but not dogs.

Each dog team she passed along the crowded path looked nothing like her beloved Chukchi dogs. The big dry-land sleds that drove past were being pulled by larger, heavier dogs than hers. The loads they pulled outweighed anything she'd ever seen. Most of the dogs looked like Zellie and Xander with similar fur, but the resemblance stopped there. Other breeds were mixed in, she could tell, but that's all she could tell. The different breeds puzzled her, and made her wonder what unknown village they came from.

People shouted and called out over the constant hum of noise, drawing Anya's attention each time. She looked for Rune. She looked for Boris the bear. Her scarred hand throbbed. She looked for Mooglo, too, suddenly worried that the ugly Yukaghir might drive past on the next heavy sledge. Mooglo would use his whip on Zellie and Xander if he found them first! Setting one foot down hard in front of the other, she determined to find them before he did.

The tall towers had marks on them Anya didn't understand. The structures definitely were not built of walrus or sealskin. The steamship had the same floor as the walls of these towers. *Wood,* Rune had told her. She'd asked him a lot of English words on the journey from Markova, and remembered some of them; she remembered wood.

The people who came in and out of the

towers spoke in words she didn't understand. The way they talked was different,
making it hard for her to pick out any words
in Russian or English she might recognize.
In her Chukchi village women spoke in soft
whispers and men spoke loud and harsh.
Here in Nome men and women sounded
alike, making it difficult for her to pick out
separate words in all the chatter. Natives
passed her.

Inupiaq, she thought. Tales of the Eskimos
were part of her history — tales of their
battles with the Chukchi. That was another
time. Now she felt comforted seeing native
Inupiat and Inuit among the strange faces.
She was hungry and tired, and she knew
the dogs would be, too. She didn't trust
Boris the bear to feed and shelter the dogs.
She didn't trust him, period. Why did he
want to bring Zellie and Xander and the
other Chukchi dogs to this place? How
could Grisha trade the dogs to such a bear?
How could Grisha trade her to the ugly
Yukaghir?

She groped her way through the mix of
people and summer sleds and animals,
unwittingly landing inside one of the tall
wood buildings, beaten down by her pain.
It hurt so badly, being alone and feeling useless, with her grandmother gone and the

dogs lost to her. She'd failed them all.

A man bumped her. Another shoved her out of his way. She slid behind a wall of casks for cover from the unfriendly crowd in this lost world. She'd traveled all the way across the great sea to the edges of Native Earth, and for what? So she could die here? Ashamed that she wanted to die, Anya couldn't see any purpose to her life. She'd failed her grandmother and the dogs.

The smoke-filled room made Anya gag. The noise deafened her. Strange faces peered her way. The sea of men and noise came at her in nauseating waves. She crouched down as far as she could behind her cover, wanting to run from this place, yet held to the spot. Reminded of the shamans with their smoke and drums pounding at her, she thought this could be a gathering place for ceremony. Why, the whole village of Nome could be stuffed in here, except she saw only a few women and no children. In her village, everyone gathered for such ceremony. Nothing in this place spoke of tradition and ceremony, but then why did she feel its purpose was just that?

Something told her this was an important place, even a holy place. Something would happen here. Anya hunkered down farther behind the casks, and tried to imagine what that something might be.

Something is coming. Someone is there.

For the second time in her life she understood the voices from the spirit world, warning her of dark times ahead. Instinctively she felt for her knife. So it is not finished, she thought. The Gatekeepers are watching. She was not meant to die yet, not until she found Zellie and Xander and the rest.

"Out you go, dearie."

Someone grabbed Anya's ear, pinching it hard and pulling her to stand up.

"Git," a woman barked at her. "No kids, white or Eskimo, are allowed in this saloon."

Anya jerked her head enough to break the hold on her.

"I said git." The woman waved her arm in the direction of the front door of the saloon.

Frozen to the spot by the odd-looking woman in odd-looking clothes with odd-looking marks on her face, Anya stayed put. The woman's springy brown hair was wound on top of her head, jutting out like a twisted reindeer antler. Round, reddish splotches tinted her puffy cheeks. She reminded Anya of a puffin bird, all decorated and strutting. The sleeves of her top puffed up just like her nearly bare chest. To Anya she looked almost naked. She wasn't

136

shocked by the woman's exposure; many in her village undressed for ceremonies. Anya never thought anything of it.

A *dress* — she suddenly remembered the word for what the woman wore. One of the whalers brought something like this to her village, "a present for Grisha's mother." Nana-tasha had laughed as she watched the other women in the village pull and poke at the thin, close-fitting coverall. She finally gave it to them. Indicative of her importance as Grisha's mother, Nana-tasha already had a loose, beaded dress made of the softest of hides and the rarest of fox, worn for special occasions. She'd no need for something so thin it would not keep out the cold.

Before Anya could think another thought, the bold woman had shoved her through the crowd of blustering men and out the door of the Board of Trade Saloon onto Front Street. Anya turned around and saw the sign over the door but didn't know what it read. The Chukchi didn't have writing like this. They didn't have writing at all, making Anya feel even more a stranger in Nome. She might know some words in the white man's language, but not enough to sharpen her knife for the fight ahead.

CHAPTER FIVE

"Dammit," Rune cursed. Anya had disappeared. He'd only been gone a few minutes. The beach landing had been good, the surf pretty calm. Anya was passed out from exhaustion, and he'd decided she would be all right if he left her on the flat, harborless beach to sleep. He'd carried her from the boat and she'd not awakened.

He could kick himself. The surf crashed at his feet. Who was he kidding? He'd dreaded waking her up to watch Boris Ivanov take the dogs away, especially given the way they fought him. Better to leave her alone and asleep, he'd thought. Well, I thought wrong, Rune realized too late. Figures, he told himself. First thing I try to do on land, I mess up. He kicked at the wet sand, one foot, then the other. *Dammit.*

Taking a quick look out over the Bering Sea, Rune spotted a number of large vessels anchored in the distance. In the fog and kicked-up squall, he hadn't seen the ships until now, alongside his father's own steamer. Tugs and gasoline schooners pulled barges loaded with freight, for isolated Nome residents, to shore. Piles of freighted supplies dotted the beaches. The roadstead in front of Nome was much busier than he'd expected.

Some years ago the summer scene was always busy and the beaches always covered with mounds of freight. White tents, miners' tents, could be seen along the shore for miles. Rune remembered seeing some of the miners sitting atop their piles of equipment in tears. He'd never seen grown men cry until then. His father told him some of the men didn't have the money to get their equipment past the unsafe, lawless beaches and into warehouse storage on Front Street. Their life savings would be stolen or washed away on the tides, and they'd never make it to any sought-after gold claim. Some of the ill-prepared miners would give up and die right on that spot, his father had said.

Rune scanned the beaches again. No men cried. No men died. But he could hear them. He could hear the clamor and buzz of hammers and saws cut across Nome's sharp breezes. No more tents coated the landscape; just scattered, broke-down sluice boxes and other mine remnants. The gold on the beaches had played out, but men still cried, men still died, over gold fever — maybe not here at Nome's roadstead, but in the hills beyond the frontier city. Rune slung his duffle over his shoulder, carrying a heavy respect for all who'd landed on these rough shores, for all who cried, for all who died.

He caught himself lost in thought, then remembered where he was. The crew had helped him stow their lighter-boat ashore for safe keeping then took off for the nearest saloon. The men would find work at the gold mines, either for the Minocene Ditch Company or the Wild Goose Mining Company, until the *Storm* returned for them.

Rune had thought to do the same after he took care of Anya. Yeah, he'd taken care of her all right. He'd lost her.

"Nothing but trouble, Anya and her dogs," he muttered, then stomped through the mud to Front Street. Like it or not, he had to find her. Loud, angry waves crashed at the shore behind him. He hoped to God Anya hadn't been pulled back into the sea. The realization that she might have been taken by the same undertow as the husky had been scared Rune into a run. He had a lot of ground to cover if he expected to find the lost girl before something bad happened to her. He might be too late and he knew it. He counted on the midnight sun to help him; it was all he had in his favor.

Anya eyed every dog, every man's face she passed. She'd wandered for hours along the crowded pathways in Nome, studying stranger after stranger, but turned up nothing. No sign of Boris the bear. No sign of Zellie and Xander and the Chukchi team. Was she going in circles? She thought she'd been down this path before. Sweating, too hot, Anya wanted to strip away her kerker but didn't have anything on underneath her fur coverall.

Only then did she stop and realize she brought nothing from her coastal village for such a journey. She believed she'd die on the tundra, so what did it matter? She'd even thrown her food away. What did it matter then? It mattered now, since she had no food and no summer clothing, no thin hide or cloth to wear in this tangled village. How could her dogs survive in such a place? In summer they needed to run free and hunt, not be trapped by Boris the bear on these never-ending paths!

Her scarred hand throbbed. Her head ached. She thought of the dogs. Like them, she was caught in the same maze, the same jumble of unfamiliar faces and unknown places. Just as she imagined the dogs might, she longed to find the edges of the tundra and run as far and as fast as she could, away from Nome. They all needed to escape this river of mud — Zellie, Xander, the copper-red and white pair, and the remaining huskies. Nine all together, she counted: nine left unguarded, nine left alone.

If only it were in the Lengthening of winter days when the snows came. Right now snow and ice sounded heaven-sent. Chukchi dogs loved snow, not rain, not mud. They loved to run across the ice, not dodge little rivers at every turn. To Anya, Nome looked like a part of the sea with so much water all around. Waves crashed on the shore. She couldn't see them, but she could hear the sea roar. *It is time. It begins.* The words of her grandmother came in with the evening tide.

"Nana-tasha, what do I do?" she whispered, missing her grandmother, missing her home. If only she could thread her fingers into Zellie and Xander's fur and hold them close. If she found them, she'd be home; the only home she had. An odd tightening in her chest made her think of Rune. Rune had left her, dumping her out of the boat as soon as he had the chance.

Her chest hurt worse. Maybe Rune intended for her to die on the unfriendly beach, just as she'd thought Grisha meant to leave her to die on the open tundra.

She'd trusted Rune, especially when he'd saved Xander, especially knowing the Raven feared him.

Vitya's necklace heated at her throat. She wiped away the hot moisture and wished again for a thin coverall. She wished, too, that Vitya was here with her. Vitya called her *gitengev,* pretty girl.

Rune had said no such thing. This thought passed through her mind so fast it didn't register.

She put her scarred hand to her lips and remembered Vitya's quick kiss. When she did, the pain in her hand disappeared. The sign made her swivel around once, then again, and look for Vitya.

She expected to see his face in the lively crowd. Then she caught herself. He couldn't be here. It must be hunger and thirst that put such a notion in her head. But of one thing she was certain. If Vitya were here, he would never have left her to die like Rune had.

Still upset with Rune, Anya didn't look up and see the ravens circle overhead . . . one, then two, then three.

A sudden cloudburst sent Anya out of the rain and inside an unmarked structure, some kind of stable yard she supposed. She'd never seen horses before, although she'd heard of them from the traders and fisherman around village campfires. Reindeer and caribou weren't stabled and sheltered like this. The animals wandered in herds, outdoor always. To find the herd meant finding food to eat, to survive.

Anya wondered if the villagers in Nome ate horses. One of the big animals nudged against her outstretched hand, seeming friendly enough. She rubbed the big gray's nose, reminded of her dogs, their noses just as friendly and their manner just as easy. Wet dripped through the top of the stable causing the horses to stir. A yaranga wouldn't leak like this, she knew. Built of strong walrus hide, hitched and drawn tight around the center pole, the Chukchi yaranga would not leak like this poor excuse of a shelter, Anya decided.

She spotted sleeping blankets, a kind she'd never seen before. These appeared to be made of thick thread and not animal hide. The blankets hung from the shelter walls on large hooks. She grabbed one of them down then did her best to dry the backs of the seven horses. The horses were enclosed in separate areas, with a big wood stick used to hold each of them in. Anya fought the urge to free the horses, wondering where they'd go to better escape the weather. In turn, she patted each of their necks, and didn't want to think of any hunter aiming their gun at these beautiful animals.

She spotted whips looming overhead. Other gear was suspended, too, but she only cared about the mean whips; she yanked each one down, then threw them in a useless heap. The horses whinnied, reminding her of her dogs; both intelligent. The horses sensed the danger from the crack of the whip. They smelled it. They tasted it, just like she did. Quickly now, she scooped up the heavy pile of leather whips and dumped it out back of the stable, right into the nearest mud hole.

"Go, go to the shamans," she hissed, unaware of what she'd said.

The whips disappeared into the ground! Vanished in a heartbeat! Oozing mud and heavy slush covered them over and left no trace.

Anya dropped to her knees and stared into what she thought had been an ordinary mud hole. She didn't believe what she'd just witnessed. Impulsively, she reached her arm in. She felt no pull, nothing but thick mud.

No whips. They'd vanished! She felt queasy. Up to her armpit in mud, fur sleeve and all, she jerked her arm free, surprised it was so easy. In natural response, she hugged her arms to her but only felt *one.*

With the greatest of care she got off her knees and stood, before she dared look at her hands. She saw only one! Her fur sleeve was empty! Her ghostly shoulder tingled. She put her remaining hand to that shoulder and slowly felt downward to where her other hand should be. As she did this she could see and feel the life come back into her arm and hand. Able to hold both hands in front of her, she worked her fingers, out and in, in and out, and counted all ten of them each time.

Rain pounded, and made it harder for Anya to hold her ground. She had to, despite her doubts. What just happened — happened.

It couldn't have, but it did.

She rushed back inside the stable, out of the downpour. There had to be something for her to wear here. Her soaked kerker dragged her down. Never more uncomfortable, she slipped out of the burdensome clothes until she was naked as could be except for her knee-high leggings and her carved necklace.

No people passed by or came into the stable. The rain likely kept them away. Only the horses witnessed her discomfort. She grabbed another blanket from off its hook and wrapped it around herself, shivers and all. Hunkering low in a corner of the stable, trying to get warm, hidden behind the horses, she didn't want whatever was in that mud hole to see her, to find her. She didn't know if the spirits within were good spirits or bad, sent by the Earth god or the circling Raven.

Rain, *too,* Rune muttered to himself while he ducked inside the nearest shelter. Bad luck, being on land. At sea he could get his bearings easier than in this gold-fevered, wet, treeless, building-infested, people-infested, dog-infested frontier city. No matter which way he looked, he saw more buildings and more people and more unfamiliar dogs.

Anya wasn't in any of the buildings or among any of the faces he'd seen. He'd let her down. He'd let his father down by not keeping her safe. No matter how many times Rune tried to figure out why his father put him in charge of the stowaway girl in the first place, Rune had no answer. He set his duffle down hard on the entryway floor of the Nugget Inn. He felt as though he'd let himself down worst of all, leaving Anya alone on the beach where anything might have happened to her.

"Got one room left if you need it, son," the wiry clerk called from behind the hotel desk. The man peered through the small group gathered in front of him, at Rune.

Rune shook off some of the wet and looked the clerk's way.

"No thanks," he said, and gave a stiff nod in acknowledgment. He looked around the modest-sized lobby, past the men and women at reception to the velvety, stuffed couch and chairs, to the hanging paintings, to the fancy-striped wall paper, to the polished wood of the stair-rail, to the clear glass windows, to the coal-black heat stove in the corner, to the electric lights. This place looked modern enough. With all the gold in Nome, why wouldn't it be? His sister, Inga, would fit right in. She always demanded fineries wherever she went. Hah, spoiled through and through, Inga wouldn't last long in Nome outside of this fancy hotel.

But will Anya?

Rune opened his duffle and felt inside, searching through the gear his father had packed, not really knowing what he'd find.

His fingers bumped into a familiar pouch, his money pouch. Quickly, he pulled it out, then counted five hundred dollars cash and ten in silver; a fortune to most. He'd had that same five hundred dollars for a long time, since he never spent much money. Thankful his father thought to put his money pouch in his gear, Rune went over to the waiting clerk. The little group had cleared.

"I'll take that room." Rune tried to sound older than his years.

"Yes, sir," the watchful clerk responded as he turned the register around for Rune to sign. "That will be three dollars a night, payment in advance," he said, his manner all business.

It was Rune's turn to eye the clerk, suspicious of the extremely high price. Still, he needed the room and he had the money. Removing the needed coin from his pouch, he determined he'd leave the cash intact. He set down three dollars on the desk and signed the hotel register.

"Rune *Johansson*?" the clerk questioned. He immediately straightened his posture and adjusted the collar of his boiled shirt.

"Yes." What? Had he spelled his name wrong?

"I'm Elmer Henry, Mr. Johansson. Your

father is *Lars* Johansson?"

"Yes," Rune answered, on edge.

The suddenly animated clerk came around the front of the reception desk and tried to grab Rune's duffle from him.

"Hold on there," Rune cautioned. He wasn't about to give up his gear to this bean pole. In this gold-fever town, the clerk could easily be a claim-jumper, the way he was acting. Rune hadn't worked the mines before or panned for gold along Anvil Creek or any other, but he'd heard all he wanted to about claim-jumpers and crime in Nome. The only law was three miles away at Fort Davis. Rune wondered if there was any other law in Nome by now, besides the army outpost. He didn't feel like sticking around long enough to find out. He only needed to help Anya and then board his father's vessel on its return home. Right now even Seattle looked good to him.

The clerk appeared flustered, his bald head pinkening into an overripe tomato.

"Sorry, Mr. Johansson, I just meant to help get your things to your room for you. It's number nine. Just follow me."

"Do you know my father?" Rune asked, having made up his mind to follow the odd-behaving man up the steps.

"No, but I know *of* him," Elmer Henry

said the moment he'd reached the landing. He kept on to room number nine at the end of the hall, then took the skeleton key he held and unlocked the door.

"Everybody around here pretty much knows about Johansson and Son Shipping. You're as famous as the Pacific Steamship Company, even Hudson's Bay," the clerk went on. "You are the 'Son' in Johansson and Son, I take it?"

Rune gave a curt nod yes, then snatched the key from the clerk's hand.

"Well, yes, thank you. I mean, let me know if you need anything more, Mr. Johansson," Elmer Henry enthused, then shut the door.

Rune tossed his duffle onto the neat brass bed and went over to the room's only window. It gave him a view of Front Street. Rune stared into the rain. Yeah, he was that all right, the "Son" in Johansson and Son Shipping.

He didn't need anybody reminding him. His father owned six vessels, shipping and trading out of Seattle's huge port, and he didn't trust Rune to captain any of them. The sign would better read Johansson Shipping Without Son. Rune loved the sea. His father knew it. He worked hard. His father knew it. He didn't worship money as did his mother and his sister. His father knew

151

that, too.

Rune would never be old enough or good enough to do anything right for his father. He took off his wet sailor's jacket and dumped it on the bed, on top of his gear. Rain or no rain, he'd set out after an hour's rest to search for Anya.

So far, he hadn't done that right, either.

"Listen, Ivanov I ain't keeping these drowned rats for you. Take 'em somewheres else. Better yet, give 'em to the Eskimos for dog food." The swarthy miner shook his head at the Russian trader and the pathetic excuse for huskies that just arrived at his claim off Canyon Creek, above the Bonanza Hills outside Nome. The Snake River ran close by.

"I pay gud," Boris defended.

The rains poured down.

No matter how often the enduring Chukchi dogs tried to shake off the water soaking them, they could not. Being left to stand in all the wet was new for them. Their instincts were trained for snow and ice. Standing still, one of the copper-red and white huskies tried to circle down for protection and rest. Too agitated, the dog appeared to not find a comfortable place. Zellie and Xander watched. Nonstop rain pelted their fur. The other dogs moved in closer, all nudging each other, all trying to give each other some comfort. They all whined, but Xander most of all. He tilted his head back and howled. His sharp call cracked the dismal, dank atmosphere then faded.

"Shut yer yap," Frank Lundgren yelled at him. The miner's pock-marked face was set in a scowl.

Boris shot Xander a sour look.

"Get going, all of ya," the irritated miner spat out, then turned his back on Boris and the dogs and headed inside his cabin.

"*Pozhalujsta,* Frank. Please," Boris pressed. "Let me come in. We talk. I pay."

Frank Lundgren turned around at the mention of money.

"Yeah, well, leave the rats," the wily miner said, and then motioned for Boris to come in.

Boris nodded gruffly. Frank Lundgren acted funny. It made Boris nervous. Boris did a quick survey of his dogs and their harnessing to make sure they stayed tied. The separate hitch lines in his hand had coiled into a gummy, knotted clump. All Boris could think of was his upset over the bargain he thought he had. Boris needed the miner's help, bad. With no time to untangle the lines, Boris left the dogs tied

153

together in the deluge and went inside the dry, warm cabin behind Frank Lundgren.

The door slammed shut.

Xander howled the moment it did, and then folded to the ground in a soaked, wet heap.

Zellie whined and curled next to him.

The rest of the dogs tried to settle down themselves. All were tied in a mangle with little room to spread out.

Xander's already weakened body suddenly seized, fell still, then quaked again. This repeated over the next few minutes.

Zellie edged closer to Xander when he quieted and had stopped moving. She licked his face through her own whimpers, then settled next to him.

The rain wouldn't let up.

The circling Raven smiled; the gods were temporarily appeased.

Upset with herself for falling asleep in the stable, Anya opened her eyes. Into what world had she awakened — the world of spirits or the world of humans? More cautious since she'd crossed the great sea to Nome, she realized they might be the same. She realized something else: she might be more spirit, more ghost, than human.

Such an experience had happened twice

154

now, when she'd felt a part of her disappear then return. Goosebumps rose all over her shivering body, naked but for the square of horse blanket she'd taken. The spirits walked this place, good spirits and bad. The pulling inside her that she'd experienced time and again, the pulling that made her sick in her stomach, had to be someone or something trying to *pull* her from one world to the other, from human to spirit then back again. Hadn't Nana-tasha told her she was a medium between worlds, a medium the shamans feared?

Anya swallowed hard past her own fears; she knew her grandmother had to be wrong. The shamans had nothing to fear from her.

A heavy dread settled over her, forcing her to hunker down farther into the damp, musty stable corner. The awful feeling of not belonging anywhere in this world or any other hit hard. Accustomed to being snubbed most of her life, Anya didn't think she could hurt any more than she already had growing up in her village. She refused to cry. She refused to care, since she didn't need friends or family in this world or any other! She didn't need anybody!

Who would want her anyway, split in half like an ugly, broken ice floe, always drifting from the edges of one world and colliding with the next? No one will. Not human. Not spirit. Not white. Not native. Not Rune. Not Vitya.

Why their names came to mind, Anya had no idea; she was upset with herself for even thinking them. She didn't need either one!

A mournful howl pierced the dense stable air. Anya scrambled to her feet. She recognized Xander's call, unmistakable to her since he was a pup. He called to her; the whispers in her head told her as much. The whispers turned to shouts from the spirit world.

Something is coming! Someone is there!

Whatever was coming, she didn't doubt it was an evil meant to harm Xander first, before the others. The spirits were warning her. She had to find Xander!

Anya's discarded kerker lay toppled on the floor. Scooping it up, she pulled the weighty fur parka over herself and shook off as much wet as she could, then stilled. Another howl came across the wind, this one weaker, quieter.

Something had hurt Xander! Anya raced out into the rain. She must trust the Directions to guide her through the maze of Nome's crowded streets, through the tricky network of rivers, creeks, ditches, claims, dredge camps, Eskimo villages, windy gaps, hills, glacial lakes and mountains that lay beyond — to find him.

"Sekston ar gammel," Rune answered in his home tongue. He'd been stopped by a fellow Norseman the moment he entered the busy Board of Trade Saloon.

"I'm sixteen and so what?" Rune glared at the stouter man, wondering what this was all about. He'd come in to look around for Anya, that's all.

"You off an *angare?*" the grim-looking doorkeeper asked.

"Yeah, I'm off a steamship." Rune switched to English, annoyed with this sourpuss of a man. He didn't look like any fellow countryman Rune wanted to talk to.

"Where's your Far and your Mor?" the doorkeeper asked mockingly. "Did your papa and your mama lose you when they came off the *skepp?*" He laughed out loud at Rune. "If you all came to Nome for the gold, it's near gone." The man's laugh changed. He sounded resentful now, as if he knew from personal experience that what he'd said was true.

Rune didn't have time for this. He broke away from the hold on his arm only to run right into another roadblock of a man.

"Toss this young'un out, Neils, unless he's

157

got money in his pocket or a claim to put on the bettors' table."

Both men laughed and both men had hold of him, one at each arm.

"What are you two old sourdoughs doing to this young sailor?" A curvy, fancy-dressed woman approached.

Rune had never seen any gal so pretty. He forgot about the men holding him back; going all weak inside, he stared mutely at the red-haired beauty in front of him.

"Listen, Reba, we mean to boot this one outta here," Neils barked. "The boss don't want any young'uns bothering paying customers."

Reba smiled at Rune but spoke to the saloon's gatekeepers.

"I'll handle the boss," she said.

Both men exchanged a knowing look.

"How do you know this fine-looking sailor isn't a paying customer?" Reba asked. The words rolled off her tongue in syrupy notes. "You got no call to keep this deserving young man out of here, boys. No call at all," she said, taking Rune's arm from Neils and glaring at his counterpart until he'd let go, too.

Still tongue-tied, Rune let the fancy gal guide him inside the smoky saloon, past tables of men playing cards, past shouts of hurrah and curses, to an empty spot at the bar. He looked in the huge mirror behind the brass-railed bar, while he tried to think of something to say to the pretty Reba.

She was nearly naked!

His manhood stirred; his boyhood left at the door.

"You are a handsome one," Reba said, at the same time motioning for the barkeep to pour a drink for the boy. "Here's just what you need on a nasty day like this." She shoved the whiskey in front of him.

Rune stared at the glass but didn't pick it up. He'd didn't want any spirits, even from the pretty Reba.

"Aw, honey, take a little drink. Don't you have the money to pay for it?" she asked coyly.

Feeling every bit a man now, Rune didn't hesitate. He reached inside his jacket for his money pouch.

"Course I do," he answered, and made sure to keep his voice low and deep. He set his money pouch on the bar next to his glass of whiskey, one hand on each. With money in one hand and a drink in the other, he did feel all grown up, as good as the rest in this saloon anyway. He downed the whiskey in one swallow then set the empty glass hard on the bar. In a quick move he wiped his mouth with his sleeve, reflexively trying to hide his sputtering coughs from pretty Reba. His stomach soured. His face flushed.

"What's your name, handsome?"

"Rune Johansson," he answered right away, still trying to cover his embarrassment over the fact he wasn't used to whiskey.

"What ship are you from?"

Not a bit suspicious of the pretty gal, Rune was relieved to answer questions instead of trying to drink more whiskey to prove his manhood.

"The *Storm,* my father's steamer," he said readily.

"Well how about that," she lightly intoned. "Some of your mates were here yesterday, sailors from the *Storm.*"

"Yeah," Rune acknowledged blankly, unable to take his eyes off Reba's rouged lips. He ran his tongue over his own lips, imagining her touch.

"Where are you staying, Rune Johansson?" she purred her question.

"The Nugget Inn," he said right away.

"How long will you be in Nome, handsome?"

"Reba, get back to work," a gruff voice burst into their conversation.

Rune pulled his gaze from Reba's soft mouth and looked at the intruder.

"I *am* at work, Sam," she defended, her light tone gone.

"You know the rules. Tell this boy to be on his way. Now," he ordered.

Reba put a hand to her boss's shoulder.

"Aw, Sam, I was just playing. You know I like to play," she cooed.

"Yeah, well, not now, Reba," he muttered, slipping her hand from his faro-dealing arm.

Rune tightened his fingers around his money pouch and returned it to the inside pocket of his jacket, suddenly remembering where he was. *Dammit.* The pretty gal in front of him didn't look so pretty after all. Suspicious of "Sam," too, Rune soured to the whole place. He shouldn't have bothered to look for Anya here. An innocent like her would never come inside the Board of Trade Saloon.

"You heard Sam, boy. Now git," a changed Reba barked at him.

Mad at himself, Rune turned from the saloonkeeper and the fancy lady, and charged out the swinging doors onto Front Street. At least the rain had stopped. The muddy streets slowed him down, but he kept to his search. He needed to check each and every street in Nome all over again for any sign of Anya.

The Raven circled wildly overhead, unsmiling, angry at Rune.

The sun beat down. Anya crouched behind the rocks and low brush, her eyes on the white man's camp, hungry for their food. She'd found the river snaking out of Nome, and followed it here. The rain had let up miles ago, making her way a little easier. Until now, so shaky from hunger she could pass out, she hadn't thought of needing to eat and stay strong enough herself, to find Xander. The merciless heat beat down. Suffering under its burdensome weight, she pulled off her kerker.

The men broke camp, but left their tents behind. Anya watched the group walk together up over the next hill. She stealthily followed. Voices rose from behind the mounds of dirt. Noises clanked. Anya peeked over the rise. The men busied around and picked at the dirt like hungry gulls. Reminded suddenly of the sea and her purpose, she took a last look at the workmen to make sure no one followed, then hurried back to their camp. No other camps were set up close to this one. She hadn't seen any activity nearby.

Without knowing or caring what food was left on the white men's meal boards, Anya scooped the remains in her mouth. She didn't taste anything but bitter and salt and fat. No fresh blood here to give her the sustenance she needed for the fight. Opening the flaps of the biggest tent, she went inside and rummaged through the yaranga's contents. She grabbed up the pile of clothes thrown in a corner and rushed outside to put them on.

A scratchy, dirty top now covered her from her neck to her knees. A pair of bottom coveralls, fitting over her female parts, bagged on her, clumping at her feet in shackling folds. After a quick survey of the area, she spotted hide ties, snatched them up, and fastened them tightly at her waist to hold up the clothes she'd just put on. Easily enough she tucked the cuffs of the bottom coverall up over her ankles. At least she should be able to move without stumbling.

The men were coming back!

Anya ran out of the camp, hiding behind the same rocks and brush as before. The men sounded angry. She pulled her kerker in closer; she didn't want the men to see it on the ground where she'd left it, and come looking for her. She was glad these men had no dogs; dogs would follow her scent. She didn't want to waste any more time hiding here, and she wished all the men would go back to their dirt yard. What did they look for, pecking in all the dirt holes?

The whole time from Nome village, she'd passed the same kinds of dirt mounds and holes, some with funny wood tents built over them. Water gushed down the sides of the funny tents, funneled through channels and then flooding the ground below; Anya didn't know the reason. She saw only a muddy mess! Men worked in this camp just as in others she'd passed, picking and pecking at the ground and at any water flowing past. It made no sense to her. Little in the white man's world so far did.

She hadn't heard Xander howl again, not since last night. He *couldn't* be dead. She'd know, wouldn't she? She thought of Zellie and the other dogs. All of them were in danger, not just Xander. But something, someone, wanted him first. Why? None of this made any sense, just like everything else these days. It occurred to her that the one thing in life she disliked the most — whispers from the spirit world — was the only thing she wanted to hear.

She needed the ancestors to help her. She needed the Gatekeepers to guide her. This place, this Nome, was no decent place for Chukchi dogs. Chukchi dogs needed to run and hunt in the great Open, not bog down

164

in mud, running from one dirt pile to the next. She saw nothing to hunt here. No place to call home.

She couldn't fail Xander.

Maybe if she followed the river, as she'd been doing, she'd find a sign. Boris the bear didn't know dogs. Maybe she could count on him leaving some kind of trail. In all the weather, he couldn't have gotten very far without stopping. The dogs would need shelter. She cringed inside, and realized all over again that Boris might not care how damaging the rain could be. He might not care about the dogs' need for any kind of shelter from the storm.

Why did he want Chukchi dogs in the first place?

The same questions refused to go away. Why did dark spirits want to harm them?

She had to find the answers, and quick.

Anya heard nothing but the river rushing past. The ancestors said nothing. The Gate-keepers fell silent. Feeling completely alone, she waited a few more moments, wishing with everything in her Xander would call out. Just once and she'd hear it; just one more time. Anxious but determined, she came from behind the cover of rocks and brush; she would head upriver, her best bet, she decided. Tears blurred her vision. Fear set hard in her bones — fear that when she found Xander and the rest of the dogs it would be too late.

CHAPTER SIX

"But you good racer," Boris insisted. "You race my dogs and win big for us."

Frank Lundgren jerked away from the sawbuck table and got up to throw another stick of wood on the fire.

"It's cuz I'm a damn good racer that I'm not running with yer Siberian rats. I'd be the laughingstock of Nome. Scotty Allan and Percy Blatchford would beat me again. I ain't letting that happen, no sir. I'd lose big and there ain't no money worth it. Besides, yer rats are half dead anyways," the surly miner said with a sneer.

Boris left the table but didn't go outside to see for himself if what Frank said were true.

"I trade gud in Russia for *haskis*. These dogs special. They run fast. They run far. We win big money in Nome sweepstakes," Boris defended.

The mention of money grabbed Frank's

undivided attention.

"I said no, and I ain't saying it again," he snapped, his look malevolent. "Not that it's any of yer damn business, but I'm running a top team from over Port Clearance Mining District way. Best mix of malamutes I ever come across. What's left of yer rats wouldn't even make a decent supper for 'em. The sweepstakes are already mine. I'll have enough winnings to get the hell out of this played-out claim and find pay dirt again. So you and yer damn rats get off my place," Frank snarled. "Good luck on finding anybody stupid enough to race yer rats."

"We make agreement last year, you and me," Boris said quietly.

Frank kept up his sneer.

"Give money back I gave you."

"Hah," Frank laughed.

"You give —" Boris began.

Frank pulled his whip down from over the hearth, and in the next second, wielded a cutting lash to the tabletop that sent the half-filled tin cups of coffee flying.

"You wanna be next, Boris?"

"Nyet." The big Russian opened the cabin door and gently pulled it closed behind him. He didn't want to give Frank Lundgren any reason to follow, or feel that whip across his back. Boris noticed the rain had stopped.

His dogs were all lying in a quiet, muddy heap. They did look half dead, like the snake, Frank Lundgren, said. Maybe just as well, Boris grumbled to himself.

His idea to come to Nome and win big in the Big Race in spring with this pile of "half dead rats" didn't sound so good at the moment. He should stick to the fur trade, where he still made decent money. But the fur trade wasn't as profitable as it once was, because it was harder to find the sought-after pelts these days, what with the hunting grounds less and less in the Yukon.

The last time he passed through Nome, he got the idea to race Siberian dogs against the American mixed malamutes. Money, more each season, was put down in betting on the American races in the cold months when mining shut down. The Chukchi dogs *could* outrun the American dogs. They'd outrun the Cossacks, hadn't they? Boris was sure the *Sibirskiy haskis* could win enough money for him in America to make up for what he lost in the fur trade. Easy money, he'd thought. Looking at the pathetic dog heap in front of him, he feared he'd thought wrong.

Awake, Zellie pricked her ears and raised her head when Boris showed up again. She left Xander and got up. The rest of the pack, all weaker than before the rain, stirred and then got up to try to shake off the wet and mud. Xander didn't move; not a twitch.

He lay flat on his side, lifeless.

Zellie nudged him, first at his head, then his middle. She repeated this several times over, her low whine barely audible.

Xander had turned cold.

Zellie's desperate howl reached out over the tundra and icy sea to the Gatekeepers, asking them to watch over Xander and pull his sled across to heaven if he should die. Centuries-old breeding and animistic instinct forced Zellie's mournful call to the Gatekeepers, not training or words or reason understood from anything a part of Native Earth. Ancestral forces no human could define bred this understanding into her canine makeup.

She gave out a last whine, then nudged Xander once more before she flopped to the ground and curled next to him.

Boris had watched but his mind wasn't on the dogs.

The cabin door flew open.

"Shut yer yap," Frank spat at Zellie, not caring that he saw a dead dog next to her.

"*Da, da,* we go," Boris tried to reassure the upset miner. Boris stooped to Xander and put his big arms under the lifeless dog, picking him up, along with the clump of dog ties still knotted together. He didn't even stop to see if the dog were dead or alive.

"We go," he mumbled this time and started down the hill, wanting to get as far away as possible from Frank Lundgren's sharp lash.

His money was gone. Rune searched his room again, and turned everything upside down, looking for the pouch. He dumped out the contents of his duffle and rifled through any pocket, any crevice he could find. Nothing! Shoving his gear aside, he flopped down on the rumpled bed and put his arm over his brow, trying to figure this out. Hah, not much to figure out. He'd been robbed, plain and simple.

The back of his neck hurt like crazy. He saw nothing but nines . . . *nine* days at sea with *nine* dogs . . . room number *nine* . . . *nine* hours gone looking for Anya . . . *nine* feet of beach where he'd left her . . . *nine* times over his father warned him to keep watch. His new unlucky number, number nine. Why the heck was it showing up so many times? Lately he'd thought thirteen his unluckiest number, blaming his woes on thirteen-year-old Anya. Damn, he couldn't blame her for this. He couldn't blame her for his stupidity in leaving his money pouch in his hotel room for all of Nome to come steal! He couldn't blame Anya for his running his mouth at the Board of Trade Saloon, where he evidently signaled to Reba and Sam the saloonkeeper that he was the son of Lars Johansson and had a fat money pouch with him!

No, he couldn't blame Anya for any of this.

Put out at how stupid he'd been, Rune cursed the pain at the back of his neck and got up off the bed, surveying the mess he'd created. He didn't think Elmer Henry had done this, since he ran the Nugget Inn. It wouldn't do any good to go downstairs and browbeat the guy. Nome was a breeding ground for crime and corruption. That he'd just been a victim was his own damned fault!

He never needed much money before, living and working on shipboard much of his life. His family provided for him, and he never thought about money one way or the other until this moment. He needed money now where he hadn't before. Stranded in Nome until the *Storm* returned from the North, he had seven silver dollars left to his name, and he had to find Anya and take care of her with that many dollars.

His room cost three dollars a night. He'd passed the Bath House on Front Street, the sign reading twenty-five cents for a fresh, hot bath and five cents for used water. Food would cost a lot. Had to, Nome being so isolated. Seattle was two months away by dogsled and weeks away by steamer. Most everything had to be brought by dogsled or ship to Nome, foodstuffs included. His seven dollars had to stretch.

He was certain of something else besides his thin pockets: Anya was gone just like his money. Three things could have happened. Either she washed back into the Bering Sea, left the beach on her own, or was taken. None of the possibilities were good ones. She wasn't in Nome, that was for sure. He'd covered the frontier city, beach to tundra, and had found no sign of her, her dogs, or Boris Ivanov.

Could the Russian have taken her?

He didn't think so, since he'd seen Boris grab up the dog lines and drag the huskies off. As he thought about it, he realized the dogs weren't too keen to go along, and had fought Boris when he took them from the beaches — *from Anya.*

Rune wondered why he cared so much about her? She wasn't his sister or any kind of friend. She wasn't anything to him. Like it or not, he felt a connection to her. Rune remembered her teary look when he'd stayed in the wheelhouse of the *Storm* and not left with her, when she'd asked him to with her eyes. She'd been afraid to go with his father without him coming, too. Upset at the memory, Rune imagined that same look when she woke up on Nome's beach, left alone and scared. He'd give anything to have that moment back and be there with her when she opened her eyes.

If she was alive, only one thing could have happened to Anya. She'd taken off herself, out of Nome, to find her dogs. That had to be it. The alternatives were unthinkable. For his part, he'd never ventured too far outside Nome, never having needed to worry much about navigating on land, never heading to any of the outlying trading posts or Eskimo villages. He'd hunted at sea but not on land, and he wasn't any kind of tracker, either.

Well he had to learn and learn fast, didn't he? The Fates might be against him, taking him from the sea, from his father's ship, and leaving him alone on Nome's beaches, but he had to find the lost girl from Siberia or die trying. She needed him. His father didn't. His mother and sister certainly didn't.

Anya had depended on him, had trusted him. He couldn't let her down. He wouldn't. They'd both been left on Nome's beaches, and that linked them together in the wilds of the Alaska District. They did have that in common, Rune thought, and he hoped this fact might in some way help guide him to her.

In one quick move he grabbed up his gear and shoved it all in his duffle. He made sure he had his seven dollars then left room nine at the Nugget Inn, slamming the door hard behind him.

The brass number nine jarred loose from the door and jangled to the wood floor, nine times over. Already gone, Rune didn't notice.

Anya had arrived at the outskirts of an Eskimo village after hours of travel. She crouched behind tundra brush to hide. Trees surrounded her. She'd never seen trees, but that's what these green giants had to be. She didn't see anybody. Good. No one would see her pass through their land. Maybe the Eskimos would help her, maybe not. She couldn't be sure the Chukchi's age-old enemies were *all* friendly now, and she couldn't risk being stopped.

No village dogs roamed close, since they

were usually released during warmer months for hunting and breeding. During colder months, dogs were tied. Maybe there was a trading fair and the dogs had been taken there. This grim possibility upset her. She looked to the skies, halfway expecting to see ravens circle overhead. She only saw lines along tall poles again, just like in Nome, making her wonder what the strange harness lines were for, hitched in the air and not to a dog team.

Funny, she didn't see any dogs or hear any barking. There was usually more commotion in a village. Summertime shouldn't be so quiet. Then she heard something, at first distant but then . . . distinct.

Zellie!

Anya froze, listening hard to the familiar howl that cut across the wind. There was no mistaking Zellie's exact pitch. It was her. Not Xander. Anya didn't hear his cry. If he could, he would have called with Zellie! Anya fell to her knees. Something had found Xander!

She prostrated herself on the reverent earth, face down, her shaman cries sent to the Earth god below to hold Xander close. Xander never liked being alone. Please don't leave him alone. She sent more prayers to the Creator god and to the Gatekeepers, to pull his sled across to heaven. The drums of the ancestors pounded in her head, in her heart, and sounded her grief.

She could feel something lift out of her, as if one of her souls had just escaped her body. At least this was her first thought at the never-before-experienced sensation. This must be a good sign, she thought. This must mean the ancestors were allowing one of her souls to find Xander and comfort him. The new sensation struck her easy. She believed in it. These were mystic times. Maybe the ancestors allowed this because she was shaman. Maybe they wanted this for Xander. He'd depended on her. He'd trusted her. She'd failed him.

"I am with you, Xander. When you lie down and when you rise up, I am with you," she mouthed to him.

Weighed down by grief and doubt, Anya realized she had to find Zellie and the others before the evil that had sought Xander and found him found them, too. She didn't have time to worry about why this was all happening — about why the spirit within her felt so threatened — about why the lives of her dogs were so threatened. Like everything else, time was against her. She strained to hear any guide the Directions might give her. No wind blew past. All was eerily still.

Anya closed her eyes and lowered her head in respect, calling on the shamans of her ancestors to help again, as she believed they just had. But no sound, no sensation, nothing.

Then she remembered Zellie's echoed howl, every sound within it broken down and put back together; the picture was as clear in Anya's mind as if it were a roadmap imprinted there. She knew which Direction to take.

Wasting no time, she headed back the way she had come.

Only eight *haskis* now, Boris counted, letting the unresponsive dog slip from his arms onto the uneven ground. He should have bought more, and brought more *Sibirskiy haskis* to Nome for the Big Race. Down one dog already. "*Nyet* gud," he muttered, then wedged the clump of dog ties he still held into a convenient rock crevice. After he made sure the remaining eight dogs couldn't run off, he looked in the direction of the Snake River. He thought to dump Xander into the river. It would be easier than trying to dig any kind of grave.

The dog wasn't dead yet, or else he wouldn't have carried the burdensome load all day as he headed back toward Nome.

He might as well be dead, Boris grumbled to himself as he looked down at the still-breathing animal. There wasn't any point in trying to save the dog. All Boris could see was how much money he'd wasted in Markova and how much money he wasn't going to make in Nome. Boris had long ago lost sight of the fact he never traded for Xander but took possession of him from the Siberian girl. Frank Lundgren wasn't going to help him win big. Boris had a worse problem now than the untrustworthy miner going back on his word. Boris needed to find somebody else, and fast, to race the rest of his *Sibirskiy haskis* in the Nome sweepstakes.

The dogs had been watching Boris; in fact, they hadn't taken their eyes off him or Xander. All of them were restless and all of them started to bark. Zellie's barks turned to growls. She bit at the leather straps holding her and tried to chew them off.

His concentration bent on Xander, Boris didn't notice. He heard the dogs but didn't bother to look their way. Nudging Xander with his heavy boot, Boris contemplated digging a shallow hole in the dirt underfoot. The dog was all but dead, so it wouldn't matter if he buried him early. *Nyet.* It would be better to toss the dog's body in the river, he decided, and crouched down to lift Xander back in his arms. Xander was heavier than the other *haskis,* and Boris could see why this one would have been a so-called wheel dog on the team, meant to pull the heaviest load.

Zellie barked wildly at Boris; she hadn't broken through the hide straps that held her. Not yet. She kept trying.

Boris started for the river's edge, Xander's motionless body in hand. The sooner he dumped the now-worthless *haski,* the sooner he'd get back to Nome and find another dog driver — in spite of being short a dog. If I'm lucky enough, Boris thought bitterly. Other drivers might think the same as Frank Lundgren, and not want anything to do with *"Sibirskiy* rats!" Angry every step of the way, Boris didn't notice the dog he carried begin to move.

Xander was coming to.

Boris didn't see or care at this point. Frank Lundgren was a son of a bitch!

Xander's watch eyes opened. He immediately tried to twist out of Boris's hold.

Taken by surprise and unable to keep hold of the thrashing animal, Boris dropped Xander right at the surging river's edge.

Half in the water and half on the slippery bank, Xander fought to stay out of the swift current.

Boris did nothing but stand still and gape. How could the dog come back to life like that?

Zellie at last reached them.

So did Anya. She'd come upon the scene in time to grab Xander's muscular front shoulders and worn harness, then somehow find the strength to pull him to safety. The moment she did, Xander's harness snapped in two.

The Raven cawed wildly from its distant perch.

The Gatekeepers stayed silent.

Xander stood on wobbly legs, but he stood. He shook off the wet and tried to bark.

Anya put her hands to Xander's face; it was a miracle he was alive. She rubbed his ears, then ran her hands down his neck and across his back, to make sure of him, that he was real.

But something had happened to him, something besides almost drowning. Something else happened that had weakened him, *marked* him. She thought of Xander's mark and then her own. Her hand throbbed, the same hand marked by Mooglo's whip. Their wounds, both hers and Xander's, had left scars. The danger wasn't over. The battle her grandmother foretold was far from over. A battle to the death, Anya mentally repeated, recognition coming from a place inside her, a place beyond fear.

"Nyet. Nyet!" Boris bellowed, pulling Anya away from Xander. Or so he tried. When he took the slight girl by her shoulders, he couldn't get a hold on her. He hadn't had a drop of vodka for days, so he couldn't be drunk. He wasn't sick with gold fever or any other kind of fever. At least he didn't think so. Shaking his head to clear his confusion, he tried again to take hold of the little Siberian girl, this time more gently; this time he succeeded.

When Anya jerked out of his hold, he let her bend back down to her dog.

Her dog?

No, the dogs were his.

He'd traded for them in Markova, and paid good rubles, still losing sight of the fact he'd traded for eight dogs, not nine. For the life of him, Boris couldn't figure why or how this little Chukchi half-blood nuisance of a girl had followed him and the dogs from Siberia to Nome. There had to be more to it than met the eye.

Though freed from her tie, Zellie hadn't run off. Her instincts held her to the spot. Born to run, not to fight, still she stood by

Xander and Anya, her guard up against Boris. The rest of the dogs, all still tied, had quieted, their eyes trained on Boris. They waited side by side, their ties untangled enough to allow it. They were ready to run as a team just as generations of breeding taught them.

But nothing in their breeding had prepared them for this new challenge, for the ordeal of trying to survive in a world where they were the prey. All the dogs sensed this new world and this new danger. Gentle by nature, their best defense was to follow the team's lead dog, to watch her, to run, to hunt, and to fight as a pack, their howls joining the cry of the wolf.

To stray from the pack meant death.

The copper-red and white pair, the gray and white, the all gray, the black, the piebald spotted, and the white husky — all instinctively knew the danger ahead. Their canine nature told them what to do — that in order to survive, they reflexively had to band together. The ancestors howled across the winds. The dogs understood. They were not alone. Their guardian stood fast. The Gatekeepers had sent her. She was one of them. Her human shape could be trusted.

Trust in Anya wasn't something either Zellie or Xander needed to learn. Her world was theirs and theirs hers. *She was one of them. Her human shape could be trusted.* Until recently they had never been parted, never met with the challenge of life without her, or of surviving in a world where humans treated them as prey. Until now, humans hadn't mistreated them. Born to run, to work, to hunt, to watch over their humans, to endure at all costs, they did so willingly, instinctively.

The unmistakable smell of danger came across the winds, filling their nostrils, clouding their inherent reflexes, and tried to stop them, to silence them. *Something is coming. Someone is here.* The ancestors spoke; the Directions swirled loud and clear. The dogs listened to the winds howl. They understood. The cry of the husky joined the cry of the wolf — a battle cry. Zellie put her muzzle in the air, howling first. Xander followed, then the rest, their pack mentality set.

Anya reacted instantly, the shaman in her most of all. Her heart sounded the beat of ancestral drums. The dogs sensed their danger. The spirits must have reached them, and this fact made them call out. Anya looked around her trying to spot shapes and forms that might be visible on Native Earth, but saw nothing. She closed her eyes to better hear what the spirits must be saying, but heard nothing. Then she opened her eyes to the reality of the moment, one with the dogs, their instincts matched. They must stay together to survive, to defend against whatever evil lay ahead. To stray from the pack meant death, not just for one but for all.

Anya stood and faced Boris the bear.

The big Russian shook his head at all of them, and tried to figure his next move. The girl had saved a valuable race dog for him. He still couldn't believe the animal had come back to life, with or without the girl's help. He had nine racing dogs again. He just didn't have anyone to race the dogs to a win in the big sweepstakes. Taking care of the dogs wasn't as easy as he'd thought. The girl could help.

She had value to him, for a while at least. He'd get rid of her once he'd found a driver. Boris smiled to himself. The girl could help him with the dogs, and it wouldn't cost him a thing. Frank Lundgren had cost him a lot of money already, the son of a bitch. The bastard will be sorry when I win big, Boris ruminated.

"Russkiy yazk?" Boris hoped she spoke Russian.

Anya shook her head no. She knew some

Russian words, but she wouldn't give Boris the bear the satisfaction of knowing it.

Boris didn't understand any native words, whether in Siberia or the Alaska territory. He motioned for her and the dogs to come with him.

Anya nodded yes. Checking Xander one more time, satisfied he was all right, she collected the lines of all the dogs together; at the same time she removed any remaining worn harnessing. All the animals alerted to Anya immediately, their tails wagging, their excitement obvious. Still, weakened and weary, they needed food. At the next river's edge she would fish and find food for the huskies. Boris the bear would have to stop. He would have to listen to her. He was a stupid Russian who knew nothing about Chukchi dogs. She hoped he wouldn't be so stupid about the care they needed.

The dogs belonged to Boris the bear and not to her. At least they didn't belong to Grisha anymore, she thought to herself, all the while almost wishing they did. If they were Grisha's, they would at least be in their homeland. She knew the enemy in Siberia. In this place, she wasn't so sure. Shapes could change. Shapes could fool. No, she wasn't sure of the enemy here in this wilderness.

■ ■ ■ ■

Rune set out from Nome without a clue about which way to go. Just not to the sea. That was the only direction of which he was sure. Yet the sea drew him. The back of his neck hurt from its pull. Anya hadn't gone that way, so he wouldn't. Not now. When this was done and Anya had been safely returned to Siberia, then he could return to the sea. Rune still didn't know what was wrong with him, why he worried so much over a lost girl. He'd never cared this much about his own sister, much less a stranger. Rubbing the back of his neck hard, trying to clear his thoughts for the journey ahead, he took the first trail out of Nome. It led from Anvil Creek up the Snake River into the Bonanza Hills.

The sign read Bessie #5 Dredge Camp. An arrow pointed right. Rune didn't take that trail but kept on his way. He came to signs marked Boulder Creek, Canyon Creek, and Windy Creek. Claim numbers had been posted along the way, with trails leading to each designated camp. He continued up the Snake River and passed miners busy working their claims, or working for companies running hydraulic mine operations. Hoses could wash larger quantities of rock using hydraulic pressure than men could wash on their own. Some mine operations used dredges, working gulches and streams for gold. This ongoing, large-scale mining was often financed by absentee investors.

Northwest and arctic Alaska, coastal and inland, had been charted and mapped out by US surveyors from the US Coast and Geodetic Survey and the US Geological Survey soon after gold was first discovered in Nome. The entire Seward Peninsula was claimed and mapped out in mining districts, but certainly not played out.

Gold was still there to be found, but the means to find it had become more difficult. This separated the determined miner from the lazy miner. Mining in creek beds and sandy beaches was one thing, but heading into the vast goldfields, into the hard dirt and rock outside of Nome, was another.

The day was half gone, and Rune wanted to turn back. His neck hurt. He stopped more than once to shake off the queer pain. Angry at himself for not keeping better track of Anya, he doubted he could track her here in these wilds. The unfriendly hills, carved into ditches and creeks and canyons, gave away no secret as to where she might be.

Trails snaked everywhere.

He'd come upon an Eskimo village and thought to stop, but what could he ask? Through sign or broken language, he might make himself understood, that he was looking for a lost Siberian girl and nine small huskies. How could he make the natives here understand about a small husky breed they'd never seen before and about a girl from a place they'd probably never heard of?

No matter if he passed miners or Eskimos, few looked his way. He needed to get into the open. He needed to feel like he was at sea. That thought made him head off the proven trails and head straight for what he thought would be open tundra. The light would stay with him. There was no night, and wouldn't be for the next month.

There were no edges to anything, it seemed to Rune. How could you get your bearings with so many rivers connecting to streams connecting to gold-mined hills connecting to gold-mined claims connecting to foothills connecting to glacial mountains? *Open* — he needed to find the open. At last he came to a crop of evergreens. The tall pines showed him the way to fields of arctic grass and wildflowers; as far as he could tell, the fields were still untouched by gold-hungry miners.

Rune breathed in the sweet air. He settled a little, and felt the best he had all day. A large herd of reindeer, not caribou as he'd expect, grazed across the field. Eskimo herders shepherded alongside. The reindeer had been brought to the District of Alaska to help the Eskimo prosper in trade when their whaling grounds became depleted. Rune studied the lay of the land more carefully, and spotted moose in the distance, a mother and her calf. Animals could breathe easier in this place, just as he could. There were animals he couldn't see. He kept his guard up. He wasn't worried about wolves as much as bears. Birds suddenly squawked overhead.

He looked up and tried to shield his eyes against the sun; he thought he saw two hawks — or maybe they were eagles. On second glance, he recognized ravens. Ravens lived year round in the Arctic. He didn't think anything of seeing the pair of birds. He just wanted to head into the open to get his bearings. No sooner had he taken a step than one of the ravens swooped low in front of him. He still didn't think anything of it; his mind was on finding Anya.

The big black bird took another pass in front of him. Rune reflexively swatted at the raven. The bird flew back to the tree top then charged again, this time with the second raven. At sea he watched for signs from seabirds, sometimes getting his bearings from them. But these were not gulls or albatross or any waterfowl like the puffin or the fulmar. The way these ravens swooped low, they reminded him of birds at sea diving for food. He kept his eyes on the birds, waiting to see what they'd do next, ready if they took another dive at him.

Both birds perched in the same tall pine.

Rune took off across the field of tundra. He was a fool for wasting time on birdwatching. He also felt the fool because he didn't know which way to go. Wolves howled in the distance, causing him to stop and listen. He didn't want to be prey for wolves or bear; he hadn't seen either so far. At sea he'd never had to worry about such predators. If he were smart, he'd start worrying now. The squawking ravens pursued him again; this time they circled overhead. Rune stood still and kept his head tilted to them. If he didn't know better, he thought the birds wanted his attention.

His neck still hurt. The annoying birds made him mad. If only he had a couple of good rocks to throw, he'd take care of the nuisance. The two birds suddenly stopped their caws and flew in calmer circles, then flew west toward Nome and the sea.

Why Rune knew that, he'd no idea, but he knew their direction, and they gave him his bearing.

It hit him then, the important sign of the raven to the Vikings. He started back down the trail to Nome. Never one to admit trusting in sign or superstition, he couldn't believe he was following a pair of birds. More than that, he couldn't believe he was going back to a place where he knew he wouldn't find Anya.

But then, maybe he would . . . *dead.*

Gloom set hard in his bones at the thought he just might find Anya in Nome, but she'd be dead. Wasn't the ancient sign of the raven taking him there, to Nome, to the sea? Anya's body could have washed up on shore, the same shore where he'd left her. He couldn't shake the idea. The pain at the back of his neck stabbed.

This was his fault, all of it.

Anya would be alive if he hadn't left her at the edge of the Bering Sea. If only she'd really been an ice seal or a mermaid, as he'd imagined when he first met her, she might be alive.

But he killed her, the same as if he'd struck a harpoon right through her heart.

What about her dogs?

Rune got more upset. He should have helped, done something to get her dogs back to her. In Siberia, then all the way across the Bering Sea to Nome, he did nothing to help her keep her dogs. His chest hurt the same as his neck. He'd never experienced these emotions before.

Wolves howled again. Rune slowed down, not over any concern for prowling wolves, but over the fact that Anya could be a ghost now, dead. When he'd first touched her, he'd thought her a ghost. Now he'd made certain she *was*. If she haunted him until his last days, he deserved it. He'd never hated himself more. He didn't need his father telling him he couldn't take the wheel of the *Storm*. He didn't deserve the honor.

Rune had energy left for only one thing: to find Anya's body and bury her properly. Then he would find her dogs. He didn't think about what he might do when he tracked down the Siberian huskies, just about finding them. He couldn't think much past Anya being dead. Taking slow, unsteady steps, he imagined Anya's pretty face in front of him and felt her near. Their friendship was over before it had even started. He forgot about the pain at his

193

neck, filled with regret over what might have been.

The snap of Boris the bear's rifle stopped Anya and all the dogs in their tracks. His move had been quick — impressive to Anya. The big Russian was good for something: hunting, evidently. She watched as he charged over to his kill, an arctic hare. Food enough for one, maybe two, she calculated.

The animal was a gray color and not white, as it would be in wintertime. Anya thought there could be others, staying together for protection while they grazed on nearby grasses. In the tundra and ice she knew, there was little for them to eat but roots and plant stubs. Arctic hares were always busy hiding from foxes, wolves, owls, and other predators.

Anya's stomach growled. She could taste the succulent meat. She had no weapon to hunt with but her crude knife. She'd never shot a gun. Maybe Boris the bear would hunt more hares for them all to eat.

She tapped the big Russian on the back.

He turned about fast with his rifle pointed at her, then immediately lowered it.

Anya gestured toward the dead hare and then his gun, and did this repeatedly before she also pointed to the dogs. To indicate "eating" she put her hand to her mouth.

"*Nyet, nyet,*" Boris said.

She tried to take the hare from Boris but he pulled the dead animal away from her.

She tried to take his rifle but he wouldn't let her have it.

"*Nyet, nyet.*"

Stupid Russian, she thought — stupid, selfish Russian. The dogs were hungry. She was hungry. A river ran close by. She could catch fish if she made a spear with her knife.

Boris used his knife to skin the hare.

Anya turned her back on him and headed toward the river, determined to catch dinner for the dogs and for herself. Zellie and Xander went with her.

By now Anya had set all the dogs free. Boris the bear didn't seem to mind since none of them ran off. She wasn't even sure if he'd noticed. If he had, he might have protested. The Chukchi dog could take off and be miles away in the time it would take him to skin his hare. Boris trusted her. *Stupid Russian.*

It didn't take Anya long to catch enough fish for all of them, even for Boris. This world in Alaz-kah might be strange and unfriendly, but it had plentiful waters. She tossed a fish to each of the dogs, the rest having joined her at the riverbank. She gave

195

Xander one more salmon, because she knew he needed extra nourishment. Then she watched all the dogs eat their fill and quench their thirst at the river's edge.

When they'd rested, she would examine each one, paw pads and webbing especially, for any injuries from their ordeal. Contented when they'd curled up in sleepy circles, she picked up a still-squirming salmon and took a big bite. The meat was fresh, delicious. The blood of the seal or the reindeer might give more nourishment, but the fish satisfied her hunger. Anya ate her fill, all the while wishing she knew a place to take the dogs and hide them. If she had a hiding place, she'd steal them away from Boris the bear. Tired herself, she sat down next to Zellie and Xander, determined to keep her eyes and ears open for any place they could hide out from the predators that stalked them — the predators in this world or any other.

The Creator god and the Earth god, and all the Chukchi spirits — already awakened from prayerful trance to whisper among them about the breach — talked again of the unnatural rupture between their worlds and that of the humans, and talked of the beginning of time and the end sure to come.

Good spirits aligned against bad.

The breach could never be wholly mended.

A fanatic evil had been born on Native Earth, its power growing stronger with each year of life, bringing the ice storm.

Thirty times over the evil is born.
Thirty years coming and all will mourn.

The Gatekeepers listened. The Gatekeepers understood. With what time was left, they would be vigilant, and guard the gates of heaven, more precious now with the darkness coming. A guardian had also been born on Native Earth, and given the spiritual power of the ancients.

She is a shape-shifter, a medium, a shamanistic sprite, able to pass between the spirit world and the human world. She must hold back the great ice storm long enough for some to survive. The prophecies created her for this task. If she fails, their worlds end in the time it takes for a heart to beat, in the time it takes for life to begin, or end. Worlds ever brush past, both human and spirit. The hand of the guardian has brushed the hand of the runes. In a split second this chance connection between Anya and Rune, two humans born out of two ancient prophecies, has sent a powerful signal. Other gods have awakened from worlds far removed in time and space, existing eternally in their own realms, brought now to Native Earth by the breach.

Some have come to help, some have not.

The timeless layering of worlds and beliefs, and the fragile lines between them, have been upset enough to cause this rebirth of good and evil.

The only thread strong enough to slow the fatal breach must be sewn by human hands. The Gatekeepers can guard the heavens, but they are not master on Native Earth. The gods can destroy, but they cannot mend. The human spirit must prevail over the darkness coming.

The challenge is set.

The battle started.

CHAPTER SEVEN

Albert Fink pulled out a chair and sat down to call the meeting of the Nome Kennel Club to order. The members quieted. The Board of Trade Saloon worked nicely for the year-old club to conduct its business. A lawyer by trade, Albert Fink took the helm as the club's first president.

The idea behind the need to form the club, comprising mainly miners, came about, in part, due to Nome having become a bettor's paradise. Dog races were numerous. Purses into the thousands were being put on the betting table, the money often coming from friends living on the Outside. Dog races broke up the monotony of the long winter months for miners, from the end of October to the beginning of June. Miners couldn't work as much in the winter, but they could enjoy the sport of dog racing.

There was little else for folks to do, being

cut off from the rest of the world by a thousand miles of ice and snow. The only communication from the Outside came through the new telegraph system and the weekly government mail deliveries by dog team. Before the telegraph lines were installed, Nome had to rely on ship-to-shore as its sole means of radio communication.

To believe reports, up to twenty thousand people lived in Nome during the first decade of the twentieth century, with many dependent upon dog teams for work and transportation. The fact was everything that moved during the frozen months of winter moved by dogsled, including prospectors, trappers, doctors, the mail, freight supplies, and all trade and commerce. With dogs becoming the primary focus in winter for racing and for betting, the Nome Kennel Club wanted to make sure the dog owners and dog drivers — dog punchers to some — took great care with their animals, in breeding and in racing them. Until now, until racing became so important, not everyone had worried over scrupulous breeding of sled dogs, primarily needed for freight hauling. A standard of care for the sled dog hadn't been clearly set, but the era of dog racing brought focus on the need for such a standard to be put in place.

"Let's have this meeting come to order." Albert Fink pounded the table with his gavel.

"Shoot, Albert, this isn't any courtroom," one of the members shouted out.

"Oh, yes it is, Bartholomew. The rules we set down for our sweepstakes will stand as if made by a judge and agreed to by a jury. There won't be any room for discussion on the rules we set down. Today we need to amend the constitution for our club, and make any necessary amendments governing our big race at the end of the season. There are too many dogs and dog drivers involved, and too many bettors waiting to put their money down, to leave any question about how the race should be run and won."

"Hear, hear," others members called out, agreeing with their president.

"Mr. Fink!" Hester Bloom shouted.

"No need to shout, Hester. I hear you fine." Albert Fink shot the sole female member of the club a smile.

"Yes, well, I would like us to start with the rules against cruelty and abandonment during the race. We must not allow any whips to be used, and we must make sure each dog driver returns with *all* of his dogs," Hester declared.

"Some of the rules are already set, Hester,

as you know. The race last April was a slow one and an experimental one, but nonetheless, we made good rules, which we will add to if necessary," Albert Fink informed her.

Hester cleared her throat loudly.

"We have *no* rule about whips, and I think we should add that now."

"Hear, hear." The membership agreed.

"But how will this be enforced?" Hester asked. "How will you protect the dogs?"

Albert Fink gave her his full attention.

"The same way we protected the dogs and mushers last year. We'll post judges at each stop along the trail to Candle and back to oversee the progress of the four-hundred-and-eight-mile race and report any infractions. No ill treatment or unsportsmanlike conduct will be tolerated. The penalty for cruelty by any driver will be losing the race and forfeiture of the owner's team. Your comment earlier, Hester, is a good one. We will vote today on the rule that each dog driver must cross the finish line with all of his starting dogs. Need I add that the dogs must be the *same* dogs, start to finish."

"Albert," another member spoke up.

"Yes, Horace."

"There needs to be a ruling on the number of dogs that make up a team. Most mushers use sixteen dogs, and I think that number should be the one set, no more, no less."

"Hold on there, Horace," Hester butt in. "We've let drivers determine the number before, and I think we should again this year, with one additional stipulation. Drivers should only have the number of dogs they can take good care of and the number they need to power to Candle and back in a timely, humane manner. I say this, Horace, because we all know sometimes drivers can't take good care of every dog they hitch to their sled. While one dog driver might be able to handle sixteen dogs, another might not. We shouldn't force drivers to have a set number. It might be too much for them to handle. I don't want to have any injury and death on my hands."

"Hester is right," Albert admitted "I don't want dead dogs on the race trail, period, but certainly don't want any to suffer and die because of anything we or the drivers did. Let's leave the number up to the mushers. Do we all agree with Hester?" he asked, and looked around the room for confirmation. No one disagreed.

"If a death occurs, I don't want any dogs left on the trail, either," Albert had more to say on the subject. "They must be brought back to Nome and remain covered across the finish line. A driver *must* return with every single dog he started out with in the sweepstakes."

"Albert, do we need to make changes to passing rules?"

Albert pulled out a sheet of paper and read it.

"We've stated that 'if one team in a race meets another, the right of way belongs to the homebound team. It shall be the duty of the outgoing team to get out of the way and to assist the homebound team in passing.'

"We've further stated that 'when one team overtakes another going in the same direction, the team behind shall have the right of way. The driver in front must pull out of the trail and assist the team behind in passing.' " Albert looked up at the membership.

"Shall this stand?"

"Hear, hear," the group echoed.

"As for the route," Albert said, "it roughly follows the telegraph lines, the same survey trail going from one mine to the next. The checkpoints for the nineteen-oh-nine race and their distance from Nome are as follows: Fort Davis, three point five miles. Hastings, nine point one miles. Cape Nome, thirteen miles. Safety, twenty-two miles. Solomon, thirty-three miles. Topkok, forty-seven point two miles. Timber, sixty-seven miles. Council, eighty-five miles. Telephone, one hundred and twenty-five miles. Haven, one hundred and forty-three miles. First Chance, one hundred and sixty-five miles. And Candle, two hundred and four miles, which is the halfway point."

Albert put down the paper he'd been reading from and addressed the club. "This route crosses all kinds of terrain, as you know. It tests the mental and physical abilities of all drivers and their teams. It's challenging. You all know it. It runs over ice, across tundra, through timber, up high elevations and down into stormy valleys. It's meant to test the iron will in every dog and every dog driver.

"The first team to arrive at any road house or public stop will have first choice of stable room. Teams will start at fifteen-minute intervals."

"Will John Hegness, last year's winner, race again?" Sam, one of the members asked.

Others chuckled at the question to Albert Fink about John Hegness, since Albert owned the winning team.

"He's in Kotzebue now, Sam, so I don't know. Our mixed malamute team ran in one hundred nineteen hours and fifteen minutes. If John drives my team again, I don't think

205

he'll use that heavy freight sled of his. Fact is, I'll make sure of it. Drivers around here are starting to build lighter-weight racing sleds. Should be interesting, folks," Albert said.

"You can bet that's what Scotty Allan is doing." Sam wasn't finished. "He's about the best musher in these parts. Odds are in his favor already, according to the Bank of Nome."

Albert rubbed his jaw hard.

"There's a lot riding on this race, and not just the money. It's our job to make sure the race is run fair and square and that the dogs are protected. It's also our job to keep standards high and our focus on improving the breed. In the meanwhile there are plenty of shorter races being run around here to places like Fort Davis and Cape Nome. Folks will bet on just about anything that has to do with dogs, as we know." He winked at this.

"With all the press in the *Nome Nugget*, the *Nome News*, and the *Nome Gold Digger*, folks from the Outside have gotten the word on the running of our sweepstakes. With this attention on Nome, we need to make sure the Nome Kennel Club represents the highest standard possible for our unique breed of sled dogs. Their care, their well-being, and the improvement of their bloodlines are first and foremost."

"Hear, hear," the members echoed again. All stood and applauded.

"The next meeting will be at the beginning of the race season," Albert announced when the room quieted. With no objection, he adjourned the official summer meeting of the Nome Kennel Club.

Anya took more notice of the "Alaz-kah" — she sounded out the word — native dogs she passed than she did the people. She'd retied all nine of her Chukchi native dogs in a straight-line collar hitch when Boris got upset with them being free. She didn't know why he got so angry so fast, but he did. She wasn't really afraid of Boris the bear, but still, she needed to mind him so he wouldn't make her leave.

The dogs were her family, her only family. She was mother and father and brother and sister to them, as they were to her. She didn't need anybody, not Grisha or Vitya or Rune. Grisha had never been any kind of father, at least not the kind who might love you. Vitya had been her friend, but he was across the great sea in Siberia.

Almost fourteen, she would be considered a "woman" in her Anqallyt village. If she'd never released the dogs and if nothing had changed in her life, would she and Vitya have married? She remembered his brief kiss, and wondered if that was any kind of love. Remembering Vitya hurt, but thinking of Rune hurt worse.

His wound cut deeper. He certainly didn't care about her, deserting her, leaving her for dead. He'd hurt her and she'd let him. She'd never be so stupid again.

Rune's unwanted, handsome image loomed in her mind's eye.

"Go to the shamans," she hissed out loud. Now she saw Rune's face and not Vitya's, kissing her! She wiped her mouth with a hard swipe of her hand, needing to brush away any kind of connection to the Viking warrior. She hated him! How could she have thought the powerful Raven feared him?

Hah, Rune had no powers to be feared. He was no warrior. She was glad to be rid of him; he couldn't help her fight the ice storm coming anyway. Conveniently forgetting that he had helped her get the dogs safely across the Bering Sea to Nome, she wished she'd never met him, feeling more like an ordinary girl than any kind of shaman.

Zellie whined, enough to take Anya's attention off Rune. Anya watched more big

Alaz-kah dogs pass, pulling dry-land sledges. Men in clothes like the ones she'd found at the miner's camp drove the sledges. Some native Eskimos walked by on foot, their village dogs beside them. She saw only brown-eyed dogs, never blue. Some of the white men who drove sleds had whips in their hands while some did not.

She fumed inside, eyeing every driver and every hitched dog as they went by, and she fought the urge to grab each mean-braided and knotted hide whip she spied. Good dog drivers don't need whips. Bad dog drivers use whips. Not now, over dirt and rocks and tundra grass, but in winter over ice and snow. That's when bad drivers unleash their whips and force their teams to run for their lives.

Boris the bear signaled for Anya to stop.

She led her dogs off the heavily trod roadway to the side, and waited with them. She stayed alert with the dogs, watching Boris's every move.

He'd slowed down one of the drivers and dog teams and was talking to the man.

The driver held a whip.

Anya recoiled inside.

The dog team driver looked her way, then at her dogs, and then back at Boris. The driver laughed in Boris's face and shook his

209

head no. Boris the bear kept talking to him, but the driver just laughed harder and pointed again to Anya and the Chukchi team around her.

Although unsure what was going on, Anya didn't like the stranger laughing at her and the dogs. The roadway was too noisy. Frustrated, she couldn't pick up any of the words exchanged between the two men. Why did the stranger laugh at them? Maybe he laughed at her and not the dogs. Maybe it was her funny clothes. She looked a mess and she knew it. So what? She couldn't care less about what she had on, but evidently the dog driver found her a pathetic sight. What she wouldn't give to grab up the dog driver's whip and threaten him with his own weapon. He deserved it.

The stranger shot her another look. He didn't laugh now.

She felt uneasy inside at the curve of his smile. What if Boris the bear tried to trade her to the stranger? For the first time since she stopped, she looked away, uncomfortable under the stranger's sneer. Her heart jumped into her throat. She couldn't swallow, so afraid was she of what might happen next, of what might happen to her.

Xander whined then licked her fingers. Zellie bumped her, she stood so close. The dogs brought her out of her fears. She felt better.

Whatever happened, she would not leave her brave nine. She would *not.* Grisha's harpoon hadn't stopped her. Ugly Mooglo hadn't stopped her. The great sea hadn't stopped her. So far, the Raven hadn't stopped her. This stranger's glare wouldn't stop her, either. Determined, her mind set, Anya looked at the dog driver again.

He'd gone?

Boris the bear gestured for her to follow him again. She quickly led the dogs back onto the roadway, relieved the sneering dog driver was nowhere to be seen. Other teams brushed past, other sets of drivers and their dogs created dust clouds in their path. The dry day chafed.

Boris sputtered and sounded angry.

He cursed, Anya thought. The dog driver must have made him mad.

She was relieved the man with the un-friendly smile and a whip in his hand had disappeared. Boris wouldn't stop any more drivers, she hoped. Walking with the dogs, behind the big Russian, Anya didn't know what was going to happen next, to her or the dogs. She didn't know what Boris the bear had in mind for any of them. So far she hadn't found a good hiding place from

Boris the bear *or* the ice storm coming. She didn't know what was coming from either, but she doubted Boris wanted her or the dogs dead.

The ice storm did.

Zellie and Xander paced companionably side by side, hitched in a way so they could. Anya petted both their backs in turn, her fingers soothed by the touch of their protective fur. The remainder stepped jauntily in front, and appeared recovered from their ordeal so far. By now Anya had given them all names. They were her family. They should have names.

The mystic, copper-red and white pair she named "Magic" and "Mushroom," since their coloring reminded her of the red mushrooms with white spots the shamans ate before going into their trances. Magic was female, and Mushroom male.

The sweet-natured, multicolored dog became "Flowers." In the short summer on the tundra near her village, when the sun shines all of the time, the ground is covered in fragrant flowers like forget-me-nots and daisies, with rivulets of water running around and through it. The piebald female brought this image to mind.

The all-black, staid male became "Midnight," and the spirited all-white female,

212

"Midday," since at midnight the heavens turn black, while at midday they turn to white light.

The name "Frost" suited the curious, spunky gray husky, his coat giving off a soft glimmer of new-fallen snow.

One dog still didn't have a name. Anya couldn't think of a name for the gray and white, the smallest in the group. The blue-eyed husky would be a runt in any wolf pack. That was it. She would name the gray and white male "Little Wolf."

All nine belonged to Boris the bear, but not for long. They belonged to the Chukchi, owing allegiance to their breed and no one else. Anya owed her allegiance to them and would protect them with her life.

Such is the power of love.

Rune had made it back to Nome. He scrutinized every dog he could find, hunting for the huskies from Siberia. He didn't know what he'd do when he found them, but he needed to find them, for Anya's sake. Upset that he hadn't come across the right undertaker yet where Anya's washed-up body might have been brought, he refused to give up his search for her or her dogs. So far no one had word of a girl's body washed up on the beaches, and most advised him to give

213

up looking.

"She's shark food by now," one of the undertakers had said. Rune wanted to punch the man right in the mouth, and draw blood — enough to ruin the man's clean, boiled, white shirt and wipe that smug look off his face.

Rune had to find Anya's body. He had to bury her properly. If he didn't, this wouldn't end. His search would never be over. As it was, he'd always carry her death on his conscience.

Since he'd arrived back in Nome he'd given no thought to hooking up with his shipmates or checking to see if the *Storm* had anchored again offshore. Ordinarily he would have, but he didn't live an ordinary life anymore. Nothing around him felt normal, and hadn't since he'd met the unearthly Siberian girl. Changed by their brief time together, he didn't understand why he'd felt so protective of a stranger, a stranger from a different world.

Well, he didn't protect her, did he? Now he meant to find her body and bury her. This sad fact followed him up and down every one of Nome's crowded streets.

Wherever Boris Ivanov went, he'd taken the nine Chukchi huskies. Nine dogs to find amid nine hundred, or so it felt to Rune.

He wished he remembered the exact colorings of all nine dogs and not just their small size compared to Alaska's heavier freight dogs. The markings of the Alaskan husky mixes looked too much alike to Rune.

No one dog stood out to him, before or now — except for the Siberian husky he'd pulled from the jaws of the sea. He remembered the drowning black and white, with its bluest of eyes and distinct look about him; he had believed the animal would die, the sea had such a strong hold. But for the moment one husky blended into the next. Confused and frustrated, he wanted to find Boris Ivanov.

Nome was a big place, Rune had discovered, with saloons, stores, churches, newspapers, schools, and a hospital. The frontier boomtown even had a hothouse on the other side of the Snake River, for growing vegetables year-round. Rune had been up and down Nome's streets enough to have every business, every hotel, and every home nearly memorized.

Right now he was standing on the same spot where he'd begun, in the middle of busy Front Street, no closer to finding Anya's remains or her dog team than when he'd started out.

The sea roared from the other side of the

215

shipping warehouse, a white, stretched-out building that sat between Rune and the Bering Sea. Gulls swooped and called. His neck ached. He had an odd notion that if he just walked around to the other side of the warehouse, Anya would be sitting there, alive, pretty as you please, waiting for him. He brushed the back of his neck much as he would swat a fly away, to get rid of the eerie notion.

He'd been away from the sea too long and couldn't think straight anymore. He stood still and let everything pass him by, almost convinced that if he did go around to the beach side of the warehouse, he'd find Anya's body washed up on shore just as he'd pictured. He wasn't accustomed to being afraid, but he was afraid now. He was afraid to see her lying dead, afraid to see her dark, lustrous, ice-seal eyes open, accusing him, condemning him. He couldn't face her. His fear took him all the way across Front Street, then around the next corner before he stopped and looked up.

Two ravens squawked at him from the roof of the Board of Trade Saloon. At least he imagined they squawked at him. No matter. He turned around and headed straight for the beach side of the warehouse.

This was no time to show fear.

"Ahoy, Rune!" someone shouted from behind him.

Rune turned to find Gunnar, one of his shipmates, approaching. He bristled at the interruption.

"Rune, glad I found you." Gunnar slapped him on the back. "I got us on crew at the Wild Goose Creek Mining Company. Where've you been since we brought the Russian and his dogs to shore? I've been looking everywhere for you. Karl and I came back down the Penny River to Nome to fetch you. That mine is busier than any *skepp* at sea, Rune. Gold is ready for the taking — *pengar* in our pockets. C'mon to the Discovery Saloon and we'll fetch Karl and get going." Gunnar talked fast, and grabbed Rune's arm to lead him back across the street.

"Nej." Rune shook off his shipmate.

Gunnar's weathered face showed true surprise.

"But Rune, you have to come with me," Gunnar said.

"Nej, I don't."

Gunnar's heavy brow furrowed. He turned serious.

"Look, your father ordered Karl and me to keep an eye on you until the *Storm* returns from the North. We need to work

217

until then, and so you *do* have to come with us."

Rune didn't miss the implication that Gunnar and Karl had to work but Rune didn't, since his father owned Johansson and Son Shipping. He also didn't miss his father's message to the crew that he was too young to be left on his own. Hah, Rune thought to himself. According to his father, he'd never be old enough to handle anything on his own. For the first time, this thought didn't anger Rune. He had more important things to worry about.

"Listen, Rune, if you don't come with us, your father could fire Karl and me off the *Storm.*"

Gunnar didn't lie about that fact. Rune didn't want either of the crewmen to get fired. They'd be left with no money, no *pengar* in their pockets. Gunnar and Karl had nothing to do with what was between Far and him. Stuck between wanting to help his shipmates and wanting to see if Anya's ghost waited on the other side of the warehouse, Rune made his decision and started to walk in the direction of the Discovery Saloon. He'd take his time. He needed to figure out what to do so his mates wouldn't pay the price for his actions.

Someone *was* waiting for Rune on the

other side of the warehouse, a ghost most assuredly — just not Anya's.

The dog corral, one of several at the outskirts of Nome, sat empty. Soon enough it would be packed with loaded freight sledges used for transport to and from the goldfields through the winter months. It was the best way for supplies to reach the mines. Dog teams had to be kept outside the corral and away from any opportunity to get at the provisions.

US Mail dog teams reaching Nome used a network of trails covering over a thousand miles of Alaska territory. Overnight roadhouses situated every thirty miles or so along the trails served mail-team drivers, freighters, and others traveling by dogsled or horse. Mail carriers always had first seat at the roadhouse table and first shot at fresh hotcakes. They were given the best bunks, too. Their dogs ate and slept in the open when no shelter existed, on straw if they were lucky.

In summer the mail came by stern-wheeler from St. Michael to the goldfields. In summertime also, Eskimo village dogs from the interior and coast wandered free to hunt and breed. Miners had inside and outside dogs: inside dogs being native to the North and outside dogs coming from the lower states. Outside dogs had a harder time of it, as they'd not been bred for the harsh northern climate. Miners kept their dogs tied when they weren't working; the animals were too valuable to chance losing.

The two months of summer light provided a respite for most of the dogs, but they still worked as pack animals when needed. Miners worked their fill, able to do so under the midnight sun. The race season would begin soon. With no ability to do paddy work, no shovel able to pierce the frozen ground, the sourdough miners had to find other work or other means to survive in such isolation — proving themselves through more than one winter in the North.

The end of mining season and the beginning of racing season meant more money, more *mazuma* in their gold pans, if the right bets were placed on the right dog teams. A good wage was considered eight cents to the pan, a prospect worth following up. A good bet was considerably more. The men who drove freight teams were not always the owners and not always skilled when it came to racing their dogs. If they wanted their team to measure up against the competition, they had to find a dog driver who could drive.

Boris Ivanov had just such a problem. He'd brought a team of what he thought was eight, but ended up being nine, Siberian huskies to America, to Nome, to race in the upcoming sweepstakes. Figuring on an easy win, already spending the ten thousand dollar purse, he hadn't figured on Frank Lundgren swindling him. He hadn't planned on being stuck with the girl, either. Adding insult to injury, no one wanted to race his Siberian huskies, and called them rats.

People said no one would bet on the little wolves. *Malinkiy sobaka,* Boris mentally scoffed. *Da,* they might be small dogs, but they *bystriy,* they fast.

"Make sure you keep *sobaka* tied!" Boris thundered at Anya, angry all over again at Frank Lundgren and forgetting she might not understand him.

Anya flinched at the sudden noise, reminded of Grisha. Grisha would yell at her like this. She was powerless to do anything but listen to Boris the bear because he owned the dogs. She had to try to understand and obey him, just as she'd had to do when she lived in Grisha's yaranga. Grisha had let her live with his family and had let her help raise and train the dogs. She needed to convince Boris to do the same: to

221

let her stay with him and the dogs long enough for her to make a plan of escape. She didn't have one yet.

Boris wheeled around and yelled at Anya a second time.

Zellie and Xander whined. The rest of the dogs watched but kept quiet.

Anya showed the ties to Boris. She realized that's what upset him.

He studied the ties in her hands and then inspected every dog, to make sure they couldn't run free.

"*Da, da,* gud," he said, his tone softened.

Anya tried to smile at him, wanting him to accept her. She didn't need him to like her, just to accept her enough to let her stay.

Boris's heavy brow unfurrowed. He gave Anya a gruff nod, then turned around and started back down the trail, at the front of his rag-tag team. Like it or not, he was stuck with the girl for a while yet.

Maybe she wouldn't call Boris a bear anymore, or stupid. If he didn't know much about the Chukchi dogs, maybe that wasn't so bad. She could tell he didn't mean to hurt the dogs, but she still didn't know what he intended to do, why he'd brought Chukchi dogs to this place.

Many dogs already lived here, Eskimo dogs, mixes of other village dogs, and some

222

mixes with wolves. The short time she'd been in this big village, this Nome, she'd seen enough to guess that dogs worked hard here just like in Siberia, especially during the cold months of snow and ice. Then their work really started. Right now a number of native village dogs roamed free, but the white man worked their dogs even in summer.

The dogs here looked different from Chukchi dogs. She'd seen enough dogs in Nome and outside the unfamiliar, crowded village to notice the differences.

Anya looked at the eyes first. The eyes of the Nome dogs were shades of brown, not blue. No watch eyes, at least that she'd seen so far. Set wider apart, more slanted and sly, the eyes of these village dogs reminded her of large wolves roaming the wilds. Dogs or wolves, she saw mixes of both and couldn't pick out any one kind that set them apart from each other. Whatever their start, Nome dogs were much bigger than Chukchi dogs. She didn't know how much bigger exactly, because she had no means to weigh them. She guessed they were at least twice as big.

Broad and heavily muscled, Nome dogs had double-coated fur like Zellie's, but their fur stood longer. The color of their fur varied much like the fur of the Chukchi dogs, but she saw more shades of sable-to-red color, more light gray color, and more in-between black color than the broad mixings of color in her dogs. Now that she thought about it, she hadn't seen any pure black or pure white dogs yet. Come winter, when all the dogs returned, she thought she might.

Anya's spine straightened.

Come winter . . . What would their fate be, come winter?

The sober thought set hard. Something had tried to get Xander two times, but failed. She prayed to the Morning Dawn to help her protect all nine of the innocent huskies, no matter how many times they were attacked. Their lives depended on her. Nana-tasha foretold the great burden she'd been given. Anya knew she had to keep the dogs safe. But could she?

Did she truly hold great powers, or was her grandmother's prophecy wrong? Doubts still ran through her.

Rune was the one who'd saved Xander the first time. She'd helped save Xander, too, but this wasn't because of any magic. Xander's own strength, combined with her fear for him, gave her the muscle to help him.

Hah, so Rune was strong, so what? Thinking of him made her mad, and she wished all over again she'd never met the mean-spirited, not-to-be-trusted Viking boy!

"Nome dogs are not pure in color but mixed in color," Anya repeated in an agitated whisper, to help throw off Rune's image. "Their paws are like snowshoes. Their legs are long. Their bodies are well-muscled and strong."

It wasn't working.

She couldn't shake Rune from her thoughts.

The warm sun beat down. The collar of her heavy, cloth shirt scratched her neck. When she reached up to loosen it, her fingers brushed Vitya's necklace. She clasped the ivory carving in her hand, wishing Vitya were close. Just then the hair on the back of her neck stood out.

She heard *gitengev* come across the winds. She was covered in goose bumps. It couldn't be! Then she calmed down; of course it couldn't be. Vitya was back in their home village, across the great sea. She missed him, that's all. That's why she imagined him calling to her, calling her *gitengev,* "pretty girl."

Feeling a fool, she let go of the husky carving Vitya had given her and unfastened the neck of the heavy shirt she wore. Boris had

225

stopped up ahead. Anya saw a group of men gathered.

Boris talked to them.

Her nerves set on end.

The dogs stirred, sensing her upset.

Anya didn't want to be traded, especially not now. She had to stay with the dogs and keep them safe. She thought of Vitya again. If only he *were* here to help her. If only she'd listened to him when he tried to help her leave their village and escape Grisha's punishment. Maybe Zellie and Xander would have found her and they could all have escaped Markova.

Gitengev. Gitengev.

This time when Anya heard Vitya call across the winds, she believed it. Scared and wary of the group of men up ahead, Anya shut her eyes and saw only tall, dark, handsome, and strong Vitya before her. A Chukchi warrior would beat any Viking warrior, she told herself. Vitya would best Rune in any fight! At that certainty, Anya opened her eyes and sent a challenging look to the group of men.

The men all had on clothes like hers, the ones she'd taken from the miner's camp. She'd picked up more English words along the way in and out of Nome, enough to help her better understand the language. She

226

picked up new words as she'd watched men work in great piles of dirt, and heard them talk of "gold," to understand that miners in Nome dug deep into Native Earth for the shiny rocks. She didn't think it was wise to harm Native Earth.

The Creator god and the Earth god watched. There would be a price to pay for angering such powerful gods. With every shovelful of dirt the miners took from Native Earth, the gods keep count, deciding their fate. No, it was not wise to harm Native Earth, Anya believed. She kept her eyes on the group of miners still talking with Boris, and decided they risked too much for "gold." None of the men looked her way. But wait; one did. He was tall, dark, handsome, strong-looking, and dressed in a fur kerker . . .

"Vitya!" she called out.

Everyone in the group looked at her then.

Vitya . . . where had he gone? She tried to keep her eyes on him but couldn't see him anymore! Sobs welled in her tight throat. Staring at each man in turn, she realized Vitya wasn't among them. Her heart sank. Her mind, and not bad spirits, had played tricks on her. She'd conjured his image because she missed him so much. Dropping her shaky hands to Zellie and Xander, she ran her fingers through their fur, needing comfort, needing to make sure they stayed close.

Two of the men broke from the group, along with Boris, and walked toward her.

Upset at what this could mean, Anya focused solely on the three men who approached and didn't see the shadowy shape move past her.

Chapter Eight

"I'll give you ten dollars each for the red and white pair, Ivanov," one of the men said, and squatted down to examine them more closely.

"Nyet!" Anya yelled. *"Nyet* trade *haskis!"*

All the dogs got stirred up at her shouts and barked excitedly along with Magic and Mushroom — already stirred.

"Hey, now, Ivanov, what's going on with your young'un?" The gun-shy miner stood up, then backed away from the upset pack of dogs.

Anya signaled for the dogs to quiet.

Boris stared at her accusingly. The girl understood the miner, and had probably understood most of what he'd said, too. He was surprised. Still, none of this was the child's business. She wasn't his *young'un.*

"Ivanov, I asked what's going on?" the miner grumbled, his tone irritable, his impatience apparent.

"*Haskis,* dogs, not for sale," Boris made clear. "I need dog driver, race driver for my team." Boris got in the man's face, irritated himself. "You not understand me," he challenged.

The miner blinked first. He backed farther away from the big Russian. The other man with him had already rejoined the group that headed away, their murmurs and laughter trailed behind them. The miner looked around and saw that he stood alone. He didn't look peeved anymore, but was hesitant. He didn't laugh as his friends were doing. Glad the dogs and the girl stayed quiet, he wanted to get going, too.

"Listen, Ivanov, I don't want the dogs. I don't want to drive them in any race, either. Clear?"

Boris stared hard at the shorter man. The miner knew dogs enough to want two of his, when everyone else he'd approached so far didn't.

"You race dogs? You know dogs?"

The wary miner eyed Boris carefully, as if trying to size him up and size up the situation.

"I know something about dogs."

"Racing dogs?" Boris questioned again.

The miner nodded his head yes.

"That why you wanted the red and white

ones here, for racing?"

The miner shook his head no.

"You bet on dogs in races here?" Boris shot his question quicker than any pistol.

"Well, yeah," the miner answered before he thought better of it. Race-betting was serious business — private business if you were smart. A man could lose his shirt or hit the mother lode, depending on how he placed a bet. When a bet was placed, it was also a bet on each and every dog on the team, as well as the driver. The miner didn't want to give anything away about his strategy in racing dogs or betting on them.

"Listen, I wanted your dogs for my kids. I didn't want 'em for racing. They're too small and puny-looking. Why, they'd never make it on the tough race trail, much less cross the finish line back in Nome." More than ready to leave, the miner turned and did just that.

Boris let him, still trying to decide if the miner had been truthful with him.

Anya relaxed. Magic and Mushroom weren't going anywhere but with her. The pair had calmed to a sit; their eager faces watched the stranger walk away. Anya watched with them; she would remember the word, "racing."

"What is racing?" she all of a sudden

231

asked Boris, getting right in front of his path with her question.

"*Nyet, nyet,* girl," he tried to shoo her and her question away, picking up his step on the dusty dirt road. "Bring *haskis.* Come on," he clipped, then waved his arm for them to follow.

Anya pulled the dogs up short, stubbornly waiting for Boris to turn around and answer her. When he did, he looked angry. His furrowed brow and toothy expression reminded her of a great whiskered walrus with broken tusks. She tried not to laugh.

"We go now, girl," was all he thought to say . . . all he thought he needed to say to the girl. His racing business was none of her business.

Anya stood her ground, her mouth set firm.

"Racing?" she asked again.

"*Nyet* racing!" he barked.

"*Da* racing!" she barked back.

Boris had to get the girl and his dogs going. The time for the big sweepstakes race to start wasn't that far off. He still needed the girl to help with his dogs, frustrated at the truth of it.

"Girl —"

"An-ya," she corrected him.

Boris heaved a sigh.

"Anya, racing is running dog teams against each other to finish line."

"*Da, da.*" She nodded. "I know racing. It is fun. It is game."

Boris's bushy brow turned into the great whiskered walrus again.

"*Nyet,* Anya, racing not a game." He shook his head. "Here, no game. Here, dead serious."

Anya stomach turned over at the word *dead.* She knew that word and what it meant.

"Why dead?" She had to ask.

"*Rubles,* little Anya. Many *rubles* bet on dog races." He had to answer her, he realized; especially when he saw how upset she looked. He wanted to tell her the truth.

"Do dogs die in races here?" she asked outright.

"*Da,* it can happen."

"*Nyet, nyet!* You *not* race the Chukchi dog! I see what you do now with the *haskis.* I see you." She tried not to cry as she pulled the dogs' ties closer to her.

"These *sobaka,* these *haskis* not die. They strong. They tough. They faster than big dogs here. They not die. They win races. They win, Anya," he tried to explain, upset himself at the girl's tears.

It is time. It begins.

233

Anya quieted the moment she heard her grandmother's words across the winds. Her throat ached. Her heart hurt. Nana-tasha's message was clear. Anya must stick to her purpose. The evil after the dogs wasn't Boris the bear . . . He wasn't trying to hurt the dogs.

But he wanted to *race* them, and they could be hurt, even die from that. Why did her grandmother want the dogs to race? That's exactly what Anya believed Nana-tasha tried to tell her when she'd whispered, "It is time. It begins."

What if she were wrong and that wasn't what Nana-tasha meant? Anya would be risking the dogs' lives by letting them race. As if Anya were not upset enough, a new fear struck. She didn't have total charge of the dogs. Boris did. He was the one to decide if they would race, not her and not any power from the spirit world. The dogs' fate was in Boris's hands, and his alone.

"*Da,* Boris." Anya tried to give him a bright look. "You can race the dogs." She didn't wait for him to say anything and didn't want him to, until she'd pointed each dog out to him. He should know their names.

"This is Zellie. This is Xander. Here is Magic and this is Mushroom." She quickly pulled in Flowers, Midnight and Midday for identification, then Frost, and finally the gray and white, Little Wolf. All of the dogs cooperated as if they knew they should.

Boris shook his head in regret — regret that the Siberian girl had named his dogs. He didn't know their future, but it was never a good idea to get too attached, to people or dog teams.

"I stay with dogs to race?"

The innocent smile on the pretty child's face prevented Boris from answering honestly. Maybe he could find a family to take her in . . . maybe a white family in Nome . . . maybe an Eskimo family in the village . . . maybe a missionary school somewhere.

"For now, *da,*" he muttered uneasily.

Anya brightened inside and out. Boris the bear was not a bear or a walrus. Boris was not stupid, either. Even though he wanted to race Chukchi dogs, he meant them no harm. It was up to her to make sure no harm came to them. Let the Raven try. Let the storms come. She'd fight them. She'd fight all the bad spirits armed against them.

Let them come.

Let them.

Rune stepped outside the Discovery Saloon. He still hadn't figured out exactly what to do. His shipmates stayed inside, belting down one more whiskey before they'd all leave for the gold mines. Gunnar and Karl always enjoyed their saloon time at trade stops between sailings. The saloons in Nome suited them fine for such celebration.

Rune didn't feel like celebrating, with sarsaparilla or "belly-wash" coffee or anything else. For the past hour, he'd tried to convince his mates to go on without him. His father wouldn't be back in Nome for weeks. By then they could tell his father whatever they wanted, that he'd run off, or that he'd signed onto another vessel. He didn't think his father would fire the crew over it. By then his father wouldn't be so worried about him, anyway. Rune's spirit sank a little at the truth of it. His father might have told Gunnar and Karl to keep an eye on him, but it didn't mean much more than that. It was his father, after all, who had left him in Nome.

Gulls called out over the street noise. Rune watched the seabirds swoop low over rooftops then fly back toward the water. The familiar sight eased his upset, a little anyway. The sea always brought him ease, everything about it.

Maybe things weren't so bad. Maybe Anya wasn't dead. Maybe her dogs were all right,

236

even in the hands of Boris Ivanov. Unaware he'd done so, he rubbed the back of his neck, annoyed by the sudden ache there. Ravens cawed loudly overhead, drowning out the gulls. Rune refused to think the birds could be the same two that had spirited him back to Nome. His mind played tricks on him.

He had been on land too long. It was changing him, confusing him, weakening him. He didn't belong here, but at sea. Only one thing stopped him from leaving Nome. In a quick move he threw his duffle over his shoulder, then charged toward the beach side of the warehouse on Front Street. He needed to face his fear; he needed to see if Anya's body lay dead at the water's edge and face her accusing eyes.

The moment Rune rounded the corner of the warehouse and set foot on the dark, cloying sand, he scanned all up and down the beach for any sign of Anya's remains. Waves crashed at his feet, causing him to step back. Disappointed, downhearted, he blamed himself all over again for her loss. Of course her body wouldn't just wash up on the beach! Of course the sea had taken her! He was a fool.

The back of his neck felt on fire. Ignoring the odd sensation, he looked up and down

Nome's shoreline, but he saw nothing. That's just it . . . he saw *nothing* . . . no seabirds, no people, no boats, no dogs, or any signs the beaches were ever mined. He shook his head hard. His mind played tricks again, dangerous tricks. Rune's thoughts went to a place beyond fear.

With slow and steady steps, he walked the deserted beach, watching for any clue that might help him understand what was going on. He carried no weapon. All of a sudden he realized he might need one. Putting his duffle down, he drew his hands into tight fists and set his jaw hard in readiness. Almost to the end of the warehouse, he thought he saw shadows around the corner. Something was there.

Ravens suddenly cawed and then alighted on the rooftop of the warehouse. The same two ravens he'd seen before, Rune thought suspiciously. Before he could react or think more on the ravens, two huge gray wolves rounded the corner of the building and stopped in front of him like predatory statues, their ice-blue eyes dead on him. This wasn't the fight he'd expected. He had nothing but his bare hands to do battle. His heart thudded, signaling the trouble he was in.

Unlike Viking warriors in days of old, he

had no sword in his hand so that he could die a true warrior and go to Valhalla. Until this moment, he didn't think he believed in the ancient Viking gods and Valhalla, but now that he faced death, he did.

Out of the corner of his eye Rune saw more shadows, more wolves waiting to pounce. His fists tightened more. *Let the wolves come.* Fight coursed through his veins. The instant he began his charge at the ferocious animals a large timber fell in between, blocking his way.

"Wh—"

Rune's fists landed hard on the timber. His eyes stayed on the wolves, ready for the fight, praying for a good death. His heartbeat numbed to silence. He tried again to charge to his death, past the fallen timber, but it suddenly lifted in front of him! The timber appeared to shift its shape, changing from thick timber to a thin staff. Rune couldn't believe his eyes.

He shut them against such magic, despite the wolves that waited to devour him. When he opened his eyes the timber changed again, and shifted its shape from a staff to a spear! Rune forgot about the wolves. They hadn't come at him yet. Magic or not, on impulse Rune reached out to touch the spear. What were the strange markings? He couldn't make them out. That's when he realized there was someone holding the spear, someone strangely familiar.

Expressionless, the man looked old, even ancient, in his musty travel robe and long gray hair and beard; his one good eye showed beneath the brim of a timeworn hat. Rune could just see where his other eye had been blinded. The oddly dressed traveler said nothing. Uneasy about the spear in the old traveler's hand, Rune waited for it to strike. What else could this mean but death coming for him, not ripped apart by wolves, but speared through the heart! Agitated by the fact that he had no spear of his own so he could die a Viking warrior, Rune raised his fists to Death and charged forward.

The razor-sharp point of Death's spear stopped him, puncturing his chest to draw blood, but not kill.

Rune stepped back, mindless of any pain, helpless to do anything but stare at the ghostly figure holding the spear, with its strange markings clearly visible to him. The old man's ice-blue eye pierced where the spear had not. Then the ghost began to speak.

"I hung on a windy tree nine long nights, wounded with a spear, myself to myself. I took up the runes — screaming I took them."

Rune didn't cower at the thunderous echo. Instead, he tried to pick apart what the old man said. He'd never heard anybody talk that way, like they were reading from some ancient book. And his name was mentioned? The ghost said "runes."

That was *his* name.

The birthmark at the back of his neck burned hot, the same mark of the Viking gods for which he was named, his father had told him. Rune had never thought about this before — that his name held any real meaning.

"The Gatekeepers have summoned me," the ghostly figure whispered secretively.

Rune strained to listen.

"From nine seas you are born, and nine serpents you must slay. Gungnir has found you and the wolf is awakened. In one hand you hold wisdom and in the other, war. But beware. *Hel* is coming. The wolf and the dog battle as one. The power of the runes is cast in human hands. It is time. It begins."

"What begi—"

Rune stopped talking and stood in disbelief as he watched the old man's ghostly shape fade into nothing, the spear along with him. Rune instinctively reached out to where the ghost had stood, and waved his arm through the dead space. He darted a look at the two wolves and saw *three* now, all with ice-blue eyes targeting him, before the three wolves mysteriously vanished into thin air.

Time stood still for Rune. He couldn't get his bearings; he had no sunstone in hand. Everything shut down around him. He couldn't see or hear or feel anything in the dead space surrounding him. All had vanished, leaving nothing but a dry void. His parched throat irritated him. When he reflexively ran his tongue over his dry lips, he tasted the salt of the sea.

Then he smelled fish, freshly caught and gutted. The sounds of the sea had returned. Gulls squawked. Men yelled out from their boats. The buzz of miners working hammered through the sunshine. Dogs barked. People walked by him. Everything was back to normal, Rune thought matter-of-factly, his neck no longer bothering him.

He reached down for his duffle where he'd left it on the beach, then flung the heavy canvas over one shoulder. If he'd been upset and confused a minute ago, he wasn't anymore. He thought of Anya. *She wasn't dead.* She was alive, and so were her dogs. They were all alive. Someone or something was after them. Their lives were in danger. He had to help. He had to stop whatever was coming for them.

Passing a hand inside his shirt, he wiped away the few drops of blood left from the point of the old man's spear. Rune studied the bloody residue left on his fingertips, and knew it hadn't been any dream. But he wouldn't think any more on the mysterious encounter he'd just had.

Every step now took him farther away from memories of his past, his family, and his life at sea, and toward the dangers that waited ahead for Anya and her dogs.

Hel is coming.

The wolf and the dog battle as one.

"We sleep here tonight," Boris told Anya the moment he walked back out the door of the Village Missionary School.

The school comprised one longhouse-style cabin and two smaller cabins, one with bunks for boys and one with bunks for girls. Two Christian missionaries ran the school for the dozen native children whose parents had died in the last influenza attack. The children had already gone to sleep, as the hour was late. Dressed in black homespun and wool, the missionary couple had just come outside, behind Boris.

Anya had been waiting with the dogs, all of which she held loosely tied. She shot Boris a questioning look, not sure what he'd just said.

"We sleep here," Boris repeated.

Anya nodded her understanding, but she didn't like it. She looked around the space outside, then led the dogs over to a crop of trees not far from the cabin and began to settle the dogs down. Satisfied they were set, she crawled in between Zellie and Xander to rest but not go to sleep.

"No, no, my gracious." The minister's wife came over to where they'd lain down. "Land sakes, child, you must come inside for a bath and proper clothes," the friendly woman declared. She tugged on Anya to get her up. "Come on, no more dilly-dallying."

Anya stared blankly at the intrusive woman. What was this all about?

The dogs stirred and started to get up.

Anya motioned for them to lie back down, then she looked around for Boris. When she'd caught his eye, she waved him over. By now she'd freed her arm from the nuisance woman.

"What is 'land sakes'?" she asked Boris as soon as he'd approached. "What is 'dilly-dallying'?" Anya was irritated. The woman meant no harm, she thought, but Anya didn't appreciate being bothered at the moment. Bad spirits didn't sleep. She had to stay alert and remain with the dogs.

"Anya, you go with lady inside," Boris said, and pointed to the main cabin.

Anya stayed put on the ground with the dogs. She followed the direction of Boris's finger, puzzled over the situation, and shook her head no.

"Child, look at you. You must be hungry as a grizzly." Mrs. Hutchins ignored Anya and Boris, seemingly intent on her own purpose. "You need to get clean and wear something proper," she scolded, then promptly clutched Anya's arm again; this time she succeeded in bringing her new charge to her feet.

The dogs had all gotten back up. They whimpered and whined at the disturbance.

The way the woman poked at her clothes and pointed inside to the cabin, Anya started to figure things out. Some of the English words made sense; she understood more each day she spent in this new land. She heard "child," and thought of Nanatasha, softening a bit toward the stranger.

"Come, child," Mrs. Hutchins coaxed, gentler now.

The "child" still inside Anya did just that, but not before she signaled to the dogs to lie back down. She could rely on Zellie and Xander to keep watch.

Boris followed Minister Hutchins to the lean-to by the main cabin, where he was told he could "bunk on one of the straw-summer-beds" for the night under a reindeer sleeping blanket.

Anya followed Mrs. Hutchins through the doorway.

A fire burned bright inside the home of the white man. The cabin light in the room was dim compared to the light outside. A large pot hung over the cook fire, which was set in the wall of the cabin. For the first time in weeks, Anya thought of sitting inside Grisha's yaranga, warming herself around its central fire. Nothing in this cabin looked like the home of the Chukchi.

This was a large space, but half of it was filled with raised wood slabs and long wood seats. The other half had raised sleeping boxes covered with reindeer blankets and a large pot set on the cabin floor, big enough for a person to climb into. Water steamed up from the pot. Anya looked accusingly at the woman she'd thought to be kind, close to panicking over the sight. The woman didn't mean to cook her, did she?

Mrs. Hutchins started to pull off Anya's dirty, baggy clothes, thinking to make use of the warm water before she offered the child any food.

Anya slapped Mrs. Hutchins's hands away then backed away herself.

"*Nyet. Nyet.* No. No!" Anya protested, daring the woman to touch her again.

Mrs. Hutchins smiled in exasperation.

"Child, you need a bath," she tried to reassure the girl. "Come on now." She motioned for Anya to follow her to the washtub. When the girl didn't follow her, Mrs. Hutchins tried another tactic.

"I am Mrs. Hutchins," she said, touching her thick homespun blouse-front. Then she pointed to Anya. "And you? What is your name?"

"An-ya," Anya answered right away, emphasizing the correct pronunciation. She understood "Missus Huttch-inz" to be the woman's name well enough but she was wary of the big pot of hot water behind the woman.

"Anya is a lovely name, child. I can see you have white blood and native blood in you. No matter, you are a lovely girl just like your name."

The rest of the conversation was lost on Anya, who was still busy trying to fend off Mrs. Hutchins's attempts to get her over to the pot of hot water!

247

"Now let's get these off, child." The missionary kept up her conversation, doing whatever it took to rid the poor girl of her dirt-infested clothes. "Mukluks, too," she insisted and managed to drag off each hide legging before Anya realized it. "There." Mrs. Hutchins put her hands up, all done. She'd finished getting Anya ready to bathe. "Your parka is on the bed. Do not fret over it. You can have it back as soon as you get all clean."

Stripped naked except for Vitya's necklace, Anya paid no mind to what the woman was saying. She kept her eyes on the stew pot in front of her, disregarding her tossed-away kerker, forgetting it held her knife — the only weapon of any kind that she had.

"Oh, for pity's sake, child!" Mrs. Hutchins exclaimed, then rolled up the sleeves of her blouse and dipped her own arms fully into the water, seeing Anya's hesitancy. "See? It's not too hot. Now come on and get into the bath. The water will get cold waiting for you. And don't you worry any over Minister Hutchins coming back inside. He'll stay out a goodly proper time. Now come on," she finished, finally successful in getting Anya to step into the water.

The next thing Anya knew, she'd been pushed to a sit in the pot of steamy water.

Never in her life had she experienced anything like this. She'd always washed in cold streams or rubbed herself with seal fat or whale oil to clean her skin and keep warm. Her first instinct was to climb right back out of the water, but it felt so good. She lowered herself even more and rested her head against the side of the wash pot.

"Here, Anya." Mrs. Hutchins reached into a nearby drawer and pulled out a sliver of soap. "I have a bit of lavender left from Kansas, and it will do nicely for you. No lye for you, young lady. Go on, child," she insisted. "Take the soap and wash."

Anya looked at the pretty piece of soft stone in her hand but didn't know what to do with it.

"Now wash." Mrs. Hutchins snatched the soap back and began rubbing Anya's face and arms with the sweet scent. She doubted the girl had ever had a proper bath.

Anya accepted the soap and knew what to do with it this time. She washed herself all over. The soft stone smelled good and it felt good to lather her body with such riches. She reluctantly handed the soap back.

"No, not yet, Anya, now for your hair. My, my, you do have lots of it," Mrs. Hutchins noted right before she plunged Anya's head totally underwater.

Anya came up sputtering and laughed. The experience of washing in the white man's world came as a surprise, a good one.

"You could be a mermaid, Anya. Don't suppose you came here right out of the sea?" The minister's wife laughed at her own silliness. A true believer in the gospel, she knew there were no such things as mermaids, of course. Hefting a full water bucket, she poured the warm water over Anya's head to rinse her hair and then set the bucket down to grab up a large square of muslin.

"Step out and let's get you dry." She clucked over Anya just like a mother hen. "Over by the fire now so you can warm yourself better."

Draped in the soft muslin Anya stood in front of the bright fire set in the wall. The heat felt good, still soothing and relaxing her, making her think of the way she always felt when near her loving grandmother. How she missed Nana-tasha! Even with Zellie and Xander and the Chukchi dogs close, she still missed her. Mrs. Hutchins seemed nice and reminded her a little of her grandmother. That was the real reason Anya cooperated with the bath.

"Step into these." Mrs. Hutchins bent down in front of Anya, struggling to pull long underwear on her.

"No!" Anya stomped out of the unwanted garment.

"Child, you have to wear necessaries. I insist. Do not tell me no, young lady." Mrs. Hutchins set her jaw and grabbed each of Anya's feet, stuffing them into the underwear bottoms and forcing them up enough to insert each of Anya's arms into the upper body portion. The missionary was stronger than she looked.

In one jerky motion, Anya reached for her hide leggings and pulled them up, on top of the funny clothes. She glared at Mrs. Hutchins, her black-lashed, seal-brown eyes filled with mutiny.

"Next, your dress," Mrs. Hutchins said, unperturbed by Anya's stubborness, as if used to rebellious children. Without another word she pulled a cotton long-sleeved dress over Anya's wet hair then down over her body. The loose native calico fit easily. The dress came just to Anya's knees.

"Why, it looks wonderful on you," Mrs. Hutchins clucked.

Anya smiled to herself. She liked the dress, too. It reminded her of the soft hide of her grandmother's dress in times gone by. Anya felt pretty, just like Vitya said when he'd called her *gitengev*. If he could see her in this "dress," would he like it? Would Rune?

Her smile disappeared at the thought of the traitorous Viking, and she was mad at herself for even thinking of him. Her odd underclothes chafed everywhere. She'd rather go bare under her pretty dress, but she kept the nuisance underclothes on. She didn't want to upset kind Mrs. Hutchins.

"Your hair won't be dry for a time yet, Anya," Mrs. Hutchins fretted. "You'll have to go to sleep with wet hair. I'm sorry, child."

Anya knew Mrs. Hutchins talked about her "hair" and heard the word "sleep." That understood, Anya reached for her kerker and started for the front door. The dogs slept outside. So would she.

"No, no, Anya. You can sleep in here. The minister will sleep outside." The gray-haired minister's wife headed Anya off at the door. She pointed to her husband's bunk, then took Anya's arm and pulled her over to it. "You sleep here, all right?" Mrs. Hutchins thought to wait until morning to offer any vittles.

Anya didn't want to sleep in anyone else's sleeping box and didn't want to sleep away from the dogs. Zellie kept watch along with Xander, she knew. One of them would call out if something went wrong — but still, Anya didn't feel safe inside this white man's yaranga, away from the dogs. These strange surroundings set her on edge.

No matter that Anya had protested, Mrs. Hutchins had managed to get her tucked in the odd sleeping box, bedded down for the night, with her mukluks off. The pretty dress Anya fought to keep on. She couldn't understand why Mrs. Hutchins wanted her to get out of something she'd just had her put on? Too exhausted to do otherwise, she would stay in the white man's yaranga on this night, but she wouldn't sleep.

Shadows danced in the imagined moonlight. Anya's lashes fluttered; she tried her best to stay awake. Her lids grew heavy. She fell asleep before she could see or hear them — the dark elves coming to whisper their plans.

"It's going be an early winter, Mr. Ivanov," Minister Hutchins told Boris, the moment he took a look at the cloudy, early morning skies. "Temperature's dropped ten degrees if one. Don't think we can count on much more summer, no sir," he added, shaking his head regretfully. He climbed out of his straw bed situated near Boris's outdoor bunk.

Boris grunted. He'd just woken up. Winter meant racing time. Winter meant he needed to find a dog driver. He had too much invested in his *Sibirskiy haskies* to quit now and go back to trapping and trading in the Yukon. He'd reach Nome today and find a dog driver. *Da. Da.* He would.

Shouts rang out in the morning quiet. The mission children were up, laughing and chattering as they scurried inside the main cabin for breakfast.

"Best we hurry, Mr. Ivanov," Minister Hutchins chuckled out, "or there won't be anything left after the young'uns are done."

Boris sat on the edge of his bunk. He rubbed his face hard, still trying to wake up. He didn't feel like eating with a bunch of people, especially children, but he didn't feel like trying to hunt himself up something on his own. Anya was inside, anyway. He had to fetch her, like it or not. And he had to fetch the dogs, like it or not, he complained to himself, worried that nobody wanted to drive his team. He looked in the direction of his dogs. They were *gone.*

"Anya!" he roared.

The Hutchinses came running outside, along with all the children.

Boris didn't see Anya among them.

"Where is Anya?" he shouted at the entire

group. "Where are dogs?"

"I thought she'd come outside with you," Mrs. Hutchins said. "Land sakes, isn't she with you?"

"Where are the dogs?" one of the boys asked, then took off to look for them.

"We want to play with the dogs," one girl said, then ran after the boy. The rest of the children scattered out to look, too.

"Who is Anya?" an older girl asked, standing next to Mrs. Hutchins. She was the only child who didn't run off.

"I find Anya myself," Boris muttered, before he stormed past the missionaries and headed inside the cabin. His search turned up nothing. There was no sign of the Siberian girl. He stormed back outside.

"You not see my dogs?" he asked suspiciously. "You see nothing?"

"No, Mr. Ivanov," Minister Hutchins answered clearly. "I think you'd do well to worry over the child and not worry over any dogs," he chastised.

"Dogs special," Boris barely answered.

"The girl is *not?*" Mrs. Hutchins didn't hide her shock.

"No, not like dogs," Boris answered honestly. He looked the couple straight in the eye.

"Mr. Ivanov, I am a Christian, but I'm

255

sorry I gave you shelter," Minister Hutchins said, his tone preachy.

"You go and find that poor girl, or you'll pay the price with your Maker." Mrs. Hutchins shook her finger in Boris's face.

"*Da,* I go, but you keep Anya here if she comes back," he told them.

"Of course we will, but not for any reason to do with you. We'll keep her with us to go to school and be raised with us in the proper Christian way. If she comes back, I'll see that you have nothing to do with the child. Is that clear?" she huffed. "Even if I have to go to Fort Davis to bring the law, I will!"

Uncomfortable at any mention of the "law," Boris backed away from the missionaries and tramped over to his bunk. He grabbed up his things. He didn't trust the law, not in Nome where there were too many men waiting to take your claim and, in his case, take his dogs.

Anya must be with his dogs, or else she'd be here at the school. More afraid something would happen to the dogs than to Anya, he had to find them quick as he could. They couldn't have gotten too far. He was a trapper. He'd find them all right.

There'd be hell to pay either way.

Chapter Nine

Old scars opened. Anya's hands bled. She kept hold of her knife, wiping it against her dress to help wipe away the smell of death. The dogs were bloodied, but they were alive. Down on their sides now, stretched out and unmoving, only their eyes twitched open. They looked dazed, but they lived. Anya sent a silent prayer to the Morning Dawn and all the gods for blowing enough breath in the dogs to sustain life.

She'd found all nine huskies coiled in the tentacles of a grotesque snaking whip, just as her nightmare had foretold. The dogs were being dragged away to a sure, suffocating death, unable to cry out. Her crude knife overpowered the monster from her nightmare, cutting each lashing tentacle away and freeing each dog from death. It all happened in the time it takes for a heart to beat, giving life to all things and ending it just as fast. It all happened in the time it took for Anya to leave Native Earth a human and return a masterful spirit.

She was in her body, yet she was not. She was on human ground, yet she was not. The noise from the spirit world deafened her, yet she could hear everything. Light shapes blurred past in a clash with dark shapes, all shouting at each other in eerie whispers. Some spirits slowed to peck and paw and pull at her, while others stormed on by. More curious than afraid, Anya watched with her eyes wide open. Spirits slowing before her suddenly changed their shapes — so fast, she couldn't get a good look. Gulls, hawks, ravens, seals, whales, wolves, reindeer, dogs, and countless other things all shifted shape before her, yet only one spirit stayed long enough to come into clear focus: the spirit of the husky, the spirit of the Chukchi dog from which Anya was native born. "The first of your kind," her grandmother had said.

Glued to the moment, Anya had the oddest sensation she was looking at herself, gazing in a mirror of reflective ice, seeing herself as she appeared in the spirit world. Her insides tugged in all directions. She felt faint but did not. What was happening? The reassuring brown eyes of the unwavering husky in front of her met hers. On impulse,

Anya tried to touch the dog, but it faded from sight, only to return in the next blink of an eye.

Anya kept her hand away. She wanted more time to study the vision. The dog matched her in color. Its coat matched her hair, colored like the ice seal, with its mix of rich brown and dusky black fur, complete with a primarily white mask, paws, and tail tip — the contrast in colors unique, unlike any Chukchi dog she'd seen before. Dogs from her village were never coated with the rich brown of the seal. They didn't have brown eyes, either. This ghostly animal did. Anya didn't understand. Just then the dog's eyes shifted to watch-blue, to the eye color of the Chukchi dog.

In that instant Anya understood what she saw.

This was Spirit, *her* Spirit.

Her husky counterpart could shift in appearance and color in the spirit world, even disappear and reappear. It could not on Native Earth. It didn't exist there but . . . *she did.* Could she have such powers on Native Earth, able to disguise her human shape and fool dark spirits? Her heart raced at the possibility, refusing to slow, refusing to disbelieve ever again that she was a medium, a shaman honored by the ancestors and guided by the gods.

When the spirit before Anya broke its bounds and nuzzled Anya's hand, knife and all, licking away the rest of the bloody residue, Anya was shocked by the contact — by the fact that she felt it.

You can't *feel* spirits.

She'd just tried and failed. Confused by the spirit's ability to reach out to her when she could not do the same, Anya tried again to stroke the dog's fur. The animal vanished, gone in the blink of an eye, leaving Anya to wonder where her "Spirit" had gone.

"Anya! Where you go? What you do to my dogs? What happen here?" Boris thundered, coming up on the obviously injured pack. His dogs all lay down as if they'd been struck by something.

Anya faced Boris, knife in hand, still unsteady on her feet over meeting her Spirit, and in a panic over how to explain the blood on her dress, and around the dogs' necks, to Boris. She couldn't tell him the truth. He wouldn't believe her anyway. The dogs needed more time to rest from their ordeal, time to fill their lungs with the breath of life. They would be all right, but they needed time. Boris had to give them time, especially Little Wolf. She knew the runt suffered the most, and was close to death when she cut the snaking whip from his neck.

"Dogs sick, look at them!" Boris stomped around their circle, gesturing at each one, agitated.

Anya did look at them, not believing what she saw.

Zellie's intelligent eyes met hers. There was no blood on Zellie, or on Xander — or the rest? She ran her fingers across all their necks in turn. No blood? Not a drop? Out of habit, she wiped her hand on her dress, discovering there were no bloody marks on her clothes, either. The knife in her hand glistened, and made her think of Spirit. *Spirit* had washed away the blood from all of them, she realized.

"Dogs can't race like this. Dogs sick," Boris stated flatly, and shook his head in disapproval.

Fury welled inside Anya that Boris the bear only worried about his race and his rubles. He only cared about her and the dogs if they could help him win the big race. Upset that Boris wasn't really kind after all, she wanted to take the dogs and get away from the Russian, but she remembered Nana-tasha's voice signaling across the arctic winds, telling her the dogs must race in this new land. Anya wouldn't question

261

her grandmother's wisdom again — not with Spirit showing herself to Anya on this day.

"The dogs ate bad food. Give them time and they get better. They race," Anya said firmly, in her newfound English. She wouldn't favor Boris anymore by using Russian words. Ignoring him, she put her knife in the pocket of her dress and crouched down to Little Wolf. The gray and white runt had yet to open his eyes. Her simple blade had mastered the beast, this time. A gift from the gods, she remembered.

Boris grumbled something Anya didn't understand. She watched him pace back and forth, and knew he was mad at her and the dogs. Boris reminded her of Grisha, seeing how angry he was and seeing how unkind he could be. She thought of Rune's father, Keptan Lars. He'd been kind, but his son wasn't. Rune left her for dead. And so was Rune to her now, *dead*!

Arctic storms gathered force. An early winter hit Nome. Temperatures dropped to freezing. Rainstorms turned to ice storms that pounded the coast with ferocity unlike any in years past. The beaches eroded more than ever, their dark sands swallowed by the Bering Sea as if a great serpent fed there, hungry and mad. Daylight dimmed to twilight.

Everyone talked of the sudden, unexplained change in the weather: miners, townsfolk, and Eskimos alike. Some grabbed their Bibles, while others held on to their shovels. Miners didn't like their work cut short for any reason. If they were on the gold, they wanted to stay on it, filling their pans and sluices. Businesses in town thrived in summertime with activity and trade all along the coast. Winter meant bad business. No one looked forward to shipping and transportation shutting down, to being cut off from the rest of the world by impassable ice and by snowstorms. Supplies could run low and run out. An early winter meant hardship and isolation.

The Eskimos studied the darkening skies, anxious about the mysterious change in weather, enough to seek out their shamans for answers. The gods must be angry.

Albert Fink called an emergency meeting of the Nome Kennel Club. Preparations for the big sweepstakes had to be stepped up. The abrupt change in weather meant a forced change in schedule, the club president decided. Albert thought it necessary to set the sweepstakes earlier and not wait for the end of the season. Eight months seemed too long a wait for people's interest to hold up. He wanted word spread throughout the District of Alaska and to the Outside; bets were already coming in from the Outside to the Bank of Nome.

Winter would be long and lonely, thanks to the sudden storms. Ice already coated rooftops, telegraph lines, their new electric lines, and it blanketed the streets in accumulated slush. Fierce rain pounding down this time of year he could understand, but not ice storms. No matter though; snow would soon follow with no letup in sight until next summer.

Miners would be anxious to fill their empty hours with the excitement of dog racing and fill their empty hands with bets won. Sled team owners would be anxious to find the right dog driver and put the right dogs in place. Time was short. Albert was concerned about getting word to all the sled team racers, notifying them of new race rules and reminding them about existing ones. Every dog driver had to abide by the rules or they'd be disqualified. They couldn't use whips anymore. That might be hard for some of the drivers to accept, but the rule would be harder still for Albert and the Nome Kennel Club to enforce.

The gavel banged loudly on the table that had been moved into place for the emergency meeting.

"Friends," Albert said loudly. He needed to be heard over the din of conversation about the odd change in weather. "Looks like racing season will be starting a little early this winter, since Mother Nature has decided it so." He tried to joke but didn't see any smiles among the club members. "A superstitious man might think something is trying to keep us from having a successful racing season, but I'm not given to superstition. You can all see from looking outside that this is going to be an early winter, but I'm betting the odds are in our favor for a good run of our big race. I don't care who or what might have brought this first winter storm on us. Since we're stuck with it, we'll deal with it and get through our season."

The members murmured among themselves, conversations beginning all over again about what might be going on with the weather.

Albert brought his gavel down.

"Friends, let me have your attention." He banged the gavel once more.

The room quieted.

Albert saw his opening.

"I'm thinking to run our sweepstakes

before the end of the winter, for this season at least. Folks are already jittery enough over the unexpected weather, and I don't want anything to dampen interest in the race. A lot is riding on it, and not just money. For us to wait eight months through a long winter sounds risky to me. Besides, it will be a boon to miners' spirits, having something to look forward to in the middle of such a desolate winter. Evidently that's exactly what's in store for us all. So what say you, yea or nay?" Albert looked out over the membership and waited for their response.

No one had anything to say — which was a phenomenon as odd as the weather outside — but they stared mutely at their club president as if still making up their minds.

"Raise your hand for a nay," Albert threw out to them.

No hands came up.

"All right then, you agree with me." He brought down his gavel on their decision. "First of the year we'll run this race. With the help of our newspapers and all of you, we can spread the word and have the rules ready to hand out when the drivers register. Some might register early. We have to get things set up and ready. Any questions so far?" Albert paused to scan the room.

"All the money will be on Scotty Allan for sure," one of the members blurted, someone at last speaking out.

"Hold on, Charlie. I'm sure the Bank of Nome appreciates your mention of their potential holdings, but I don't. We're not here to talk about who's going to drive which team, but getting the race planned and run on time. Got that?" Albert said, dead serious.

"Yeah, got it," the worried miner mumbled.

"I know we still have four months before the sweepstakes, but dog drivers will likely want to register their teams as soon as they get them together," Albert explained. "We have to be ready here at the Board of Trade. Harvey, can you get the telegraph apparatus all set up so we can receive up-to-the-minute-reports from the trail when time comes?"

"Sure enough," Harvey threw back.

"Bartholomew, still have that big chalkboard from last year?"

"Yep, I do, Albert," the mercantile owner replied.

"Good. Bring the board and lots of chalk, and set up here to keep track of each team. I want you to record each result and guard the board with your life," the kennel club president warned.

The room quieted to a whisper. All eyes focused on Albert Fink, and all the club members heard the words "guard the board with your life." Everyone in the room was brought to the same realization at the same time. The sweepstakes would be a life-and-death struggle to the finish, whether it was held midseason or end of season. There were no guarantees of survival in Alaska, racing or otherwise. Life-and-death situations should be commonplace to them all by now, but they were not. Uncomfortable with the odds, to a man and woman, they all knew the lives of the dogs and their drivers were in jeopardy, start to finish. The room stayed quiet.

"All right, let's talk about the judges." Albert moved the meeting along, even though he knew what was likely on everyone's mind. Too late to turn back time and cancel the only pastime in winter that gave men something to look forward to and help them forget, for a time, their loneliness and isolation.

Rune plodded through the deep snow, getting deeper by the minute. This was August. Where did this weather come from? Even for the arctic north, this was unusual. He'd exchanged his sea jacket for a hooded fur parka back in Nome, and he had on his serviceable mukluks. Able to trade at the native mercantile for his parka and boots, he spent almost all of his money on fur mitts and food supplies. He had a few dollars left if he didn't trade or buy a gun or a knife, although he thought he should have. He'd kept his duffle to store his provisions and what belongings he had.

Predators roamed the hills and wild outside Nome. Losing daylight, he had to stay sharp. He wasn't at sea anymore. At sea he'd be ready for the hunt. Here, he wasn't so sure.

Rune put his cold fingers to the back of his neck to chase away the ache that had plagued him for too long. Tired of the nuisance, he reached up out of habit. The pain had gone? When he thought about it, he hadn't experienced any since his encounter with the ghost, the stranger at the edges of the Bering Sea. Rune didn't take his hand from his birthmark. Funny, he'd never noticed until now that the mark of the ancient rune — how he got his name — felt raised like a scar. He let his hand fall away from the spot.

Maybe the scar had always been there, maybe not. It wasn't important to him.

Finding Anya and her dogs was.

Their enemies were his enemies.

The wolf and the dog battle as one.

Wolves howled, the sound far off. Instead of turning back, Rune kept on the path into the hills and the wilds beyond. The cry of the wolf didn't worry him, but rather stirred his blood. His fists tightened; every muscle in his body was tense and ready for what might come. His survival depended on more than his fists, and he knew it. Experienced locals were used to this; he wasn't. As he headed into such fierce weather, Rune knew he didn't have enough skill to combat the cold and keep from freezing in these ever-worsening conditions. He'd better figure a way to survive, and quick. The icy winds already tore through him. His body ached from the pain. He secured his heavy mittens over his stiff fingers and set his jaw for the path ahead.

The cold clouded Rune's thinking. Had he left Nome yesterday? The day before? Numb head to foot despite his hooded parka and mukluks, he held onto his duffle and kept it clutched to him as if it were his only hold on life. He hadn't seen another human being for hours.

Ravens squawked and circled overhead. The skies darkened even more. The tem-

270

peratures fell far below zero. Rune's teeth rattled. He couldn't open his jaw. When his vision blurred to blackness, he had to stop, unsure what to do, which way to go. Before, he'd been certain of his direction, or at least he'd thought so. Everything around him seemed to shut down. He'd die if he didn't keep going, but he couldn't see. He tried to take a step anyway but abruptly fell to his knees, then into a snowy grave, face down, unconscious.

The swarm of ravens stopped circling overhead and stole away the moment Rune fell, then disappeared into the night skies.

Wolves called across the arctic winds, but Rune couldn't hear them anymore.

Two ravens suddenly appeared out of nowhere and perched on an icy branch over the spot where Rune's body lay buried in snow. They stayed only moments before they flew off in the direction of the sea.

Anya didn't care what Boris might do to her. She set all the dogs free when the ice storm turned to snow. She stood rebelliously and waited for him to strike her, caring only that the dogs ran free. She was hesitant to be parted from them — she knew something bad could happen any time — but she believed they desperately needed to exercise, to hunt, to find their way in the unknown countryside where they would learn to survive as a pack. She needed them strong for the coming race.

Her grandmother's prophecy rang clear in her head. The dogs must race. They must endure. The season of Middle Summer had turned to the season of New Snow over-night, so fast there was no time to release the dogs in the days of summer. Then again, the dogs needed to run on the arctic winds and breathe life back into their weakened, wounded bodies. They would stay together, their instincts sharp, and look to Zellie for guide. Anya was sure of it.

Wolf packs would not harm them. The Chukchi never sent their dogs to hunt the wolf. It was forbidden to kill the wolf. The wolf understood. The wolf would not harm the Chukchi dog, or so she believed.

"You messed up, girl," Boris bellowed "*Sobaka* run away and never come back!" He raised his arm as if to strike her, then cast it outward in upset, before lowering it in defeat. "I lose all my money, girl. What you did lose me all my money," he said, his voice strained.

Anya softened a little toward the big Russian. He could have hit her, even killed her, and deservedly so over such valuable dogs, but he did not. Boris was like Grisha, she realized again. Grisha could have run her through with a harpoon, but he had not. Still, Grisha had left her for dead — trading her in Markova. *Like Rune.* He'd left her for dead, too.

Howling cries called across the winds. The sound brought Anya back to the moment. These weren't the cries of the wolf, but of dogs, *her* dogs, Zellie and Xander signaling to her all is well.

"Dogs will come back," Anya said, before she looked at Boris.

"*Shto?* What you say?" Boris blurted. He grabbed Anya by her arms, kerker and all.

"Let go," she demanded.

"*Da, da.*" Boris dropped his hands from her. "I not mean to hurt you. I must know what you say? *Pozhalujsta.*"

"Dogs will come back. Dogs will race. They need to be away, but they come back. You will see," she finished, and had nothing more to say on the subject.

She trusted Boris with the truth only as far as the race would take them. After the race, she would find a way to get the dogs away from Boris and back home across the great sea, safe again. But the more she thought of taking the dogs back to Siberia, the sicker she got to her stomach. What in

273

the world? She gagged and then vomited. Boris shouldn't see her like this. She quickly scooped up a handful of snow to clean herself, grateful his back was turned. What could have made her so sick? She saw no shapes, and didn't hear any whispers from the spirit world. All she'd thought about was taking the dogs back to her village in Siberia.

Spirit *raced across time and back again, restless, unsettled.*

Anya's stomach refused to calm. She got sick again.

Boris shifted back around.

"You gud?" He seemed concerned.

"Yes," she said, not believing his concern.

Snow flurried between them; the storm was over. The darkness lifted slightly, yet left an eerie dimness to the winter air. Still below freezing, the temperature kept its icy hold on the day. Anya felt the cold but at least her stomach started to feel better.

Boris watched her.

Humph. She turned her back on him and brushed the snow from her. She was glad for the warmth of her seal-fur kerker. Its fox-trimmed hood covered her long, thick, bound hair, kept so by a hide tie at the base of her neck. She wore her kerker over her dress, in spite of thinking she should have thrown the impractical garment away,. But she'd kept it. It was pretty. She also had on her "necessaries," as Mrs. Hutchins had called them, beneath her dress, yet she didn't think them pretty at all. She'd never worn underclothes before. They felt funny, but they warmed her skin. She was used to being naked beneath her kerker, and the funny layers of clothing felt just that: funny.

Anya reached inside the deep pocket of her kerker to make sure of her knife. She ran her fingers over the crude blade, comforted by having it. That knife was all that stood between her dogs and death. Bad spirits brought the whip to the Chukchi dogs. The Dark would strike again. She didn't know why bad spirits hunted the dogs, but she was becoming used to not having answers to impossible questions. No matter; she must be ready. Her knife would help protect her. So might her Spirit. In her human hands, she could hold the knife, but it was up to the Gatekeepers to send her Spirit.

The Gatekeepers listened and summoned the Morning Dawn.

So did *Hel* listen, and summoned its legions.

"When dogs come back, Anya?" Boris suddenly thundered his question, breaking the winter quiet. "We stay here or we go find them?"

Anya put her fur mittens over her ears. She hated the thunder of angry men. The dogs had to race. They had to endure. She had to put up with the noise for their sake.

"Dogs come back when they ready," she whispered in the Chukchi way.

Boris neared, obviously trying to hear what she said.

"How long they stay away?" He kept on with his questions but in a more reasonable tone.

"They stay away until they come back," she replied simply.

Boris threw up his hands in frustration and then walked off, only to return to face her.

"Race comes soon, Anya. I need dogs. Dogs need driver!" He raised his voice again.

Anya watched his mustache twitch over his broken teeth, reminded once more of a great whiskered walrus. She imagined all nine Chukchi dogs circling the walrus, hunting him down on the frozen seas, keeping him quiet. Gentle by nature, they would not kill. Men would do that. Then again, the dogs were capable of a kill. She shook her head to clear such thoughts; Anya didn't want to see Boris dead, just *quiet*.

"We wait here, Boris. Dogs come back here when they ready," she explained — for the last time, she hoped.

The big Russian threw up his hands again and trudged back and forth in the snow, grumbling under his breath about listening to a "little girl" when he had a "big problem."

Anya watched him pace. At least his thunder silenced.

Lars Johansson had another nightmare, this one worse than the last, this one deadly. Old superstitions haunted him. He climbed out of his sleeping berth on the *Storm* and did something he'd never done before when he woke on shipboard. He poured a shot of schnapps and downed it, then another. His worry over Rune hit hard. The stiff drink didn't help.

Shoving the glass away, he reached for his thick sweater, needing to go on deck to the wheelhouse to clear his head. He'd never given in to superstition before, but he suspected that's what troubled him. Viking legend had followed him in dreams right after Rune was born, when Lars had thought to name his son after the magic runes of Odin, master of all the gods. As

277

he'd been born with the alphabet mark of the gods, the name "Rune" seemed fitting at the time. Now Lars wasn't so sure — not with dark elves whispering their ghoulish deeds in his sleep.

He'd had bad dreams before, enough to cause him worry about Rune, but ever since he'd left Boris Ivanov and the Siberian huskies on Nome's beaches, his nightmares had stepped up. Lars didn't understand why. He shouldn't be having nightmares. He'd left his son in Nome to protect him, so he'd thought. On land Rune would be safe. Lars's nightmares were always of harm coming to Rune, harm from the sea. With Rune on land now, Lars should feel his son was safe. But he didn't. The dark elves visited every night, foretelling danger.

Viking legend had become reality to Lars, at least in his dreams. Ancient legend spoke of a powerful sea serpent encircling all the waters of the world, destined to kill the greatest of the gods at Ragnarok, the final battle at the end of time. In his latest dream, the dark elves foretold Rune's death at sea, slain by the powerful Midgard serpent, whispering to Lars how Rune's death would happen.

Rune bore the mark of the Viking gods, but he was a simple boy, not a warrior engaged in any kind of battle with enemies of the gods! More alarmed than ever about his bad dreams, convinced his long-held suspicions were correct — that Rune should no longer navigate the oceans and seas — Lars desperately wanted to keep Rune from the sea and the mystic serpent that waited for him in its depths.

Lars reached for his radio communications, thinking to contact Rune in Nome. He wanted to make sure his son was all right. Then he withdrew his fingers from the transmitter key because he wasn't within range, and he had no idea how to get in touch with ship-to-shore.

He tugged the irritating collar of his heavy sweater away from his neck. Perspiration coated his fingers. He wiped the nervous sweat away, afraid for his son. Dreams or not, real or not, at least Rune was safe for now, on land and not at sea. With the ice already moved in, Lars couldn't get the *Storm* anywhere close to Nome's beaches. Rune would have to be all right. Didn't he have the blood of Viking warriors in his veins, strong and able to brave any new frontier? Lars's chest caught.

Yes, but he is only a boy, my only son.

His chest hurt as only a father's can. He wanted to protect his son. He wanted to tell him how much he loved him. At least Rune had money with him, Lars knew: five hundred dollars in his duffle for food and shelter until Lars could return for his son when the ice melted. Rune's shipmates had already caught up with the *Storm* in Kotzebue, and had told Lars that Rune had decided against mining with them and had stayed in Nome. Lars didn't give Gunnar or Karl a hard time about this. He knew Rune had a mind of his own.

Grudgingly Lars set the *Storm* toward Seattle, hating to leave Rune and wondering how he would explain his actions to his wife and his daughter. The collar of his sweater scratched against his skin at this thought, chafing to the point of pain.

He didn't think Rune's mother or his sister would worry too much about Rune not coming home this trading season. Margret and Inga were caught up in Seattle's elite society, spending money and attending parties. He suspected they loved Rune, but they had an odd way of showing it. Rune never said anything, but Lars knew his son was bothered by their snub of him. It would do Margret and Inga good to live like Rune and work hard for what they had.

An idea struck. The chafing at his neck eased. In the spring when he returned to

Nome, Lars would bring his family to spend the summer season in the frontier city. It would do them good to see how ordinary people lived. Maybe he would build them a home where they could all be together as a family under one roof. The idea brightened Lars's flagging spirits. He reached for the nearby cord and sounded the ship's bell for home port, momentarily forgetting about his latest nightmare and worry over Rune.

All nine of the Siberian husky team ran across the frozen tundra, running fast and hard, running together in a fanned-out style in the Chukchi way. The territory might be unknown to them, but their sharp canine instincts served them well, and they were able to find the open ground and run on the arctic winds. They'd been pent up for so long that, but for few stops, the dogs ran through the day into the night, uphill and down, over ice and through snow; steering clear of the bear, the wolf, and any sign of human shapes.

They ran as a pack, instinctively knowing they must. When Little Wolf would slow, panting hard, the whole team slowed, sensing the runt was still weak. Xander, like a big brother might, stayed by Little Wolf while the rest ran off to hunt, nudging him to lie down, as if he gave Little Wolf permission to rest. The little gray and white runt whined and did just that; quickly curling into a circle in the snow, he shut his eyes and abruptly fell asleep. Xander was still weak from the fits he'd suffered but he didn't sleep. He stayed alert, his senses trained on the landscape.

Hours later Zellie returned with a half-eaten white arctic hare in her mouth, her jawline still bloody. Frost, "frosted" gray as his name, ran back at almost the same time. His kill was a ground squirrel about to go into hibernation, and he'd brought what was left to Xander and Little Wolf. Little Wolf fed on the leavings of the hare, and Xander finished off the squirrel and anything else.

All four dogs, their husky masks blood-tinged but their stomachs sated, then waited for the rest of the pack to return. Howls called across the tundra. Zellie's ears pricked at the call of the wolf, and she stirred to keen alertness. Jumpy, Xander broke into a run, but he turned around and came right back. Frost greeted him with a short bark, the spunky male on edge, too. Out of instinct the four stayed together, alert, nostrils twitching, ears pricked, watching and waiting for the others to reappear.

Twilight to dark, the skies overhead

changed into swirls of color. The dogs saw the motions of light but not the colors. They whimpered at the sight but still waited patiently for the other dogs to return. Their instincts told them the light in the skies didn't belong, that the season was wrong. Their instincts had already told them the cold was early, the season wrong. On impulse, their eyes and ears trained at ground-level, looking to all Directions for the others in the pack to come back — they waited as they had for centuries — they waited to pull their sled across and into heaven, together.

The multicolored piebald husky at last came onto the horizon. She ran up with nothing in her mouth, but with bloody smears on her face and neck. Flowers had evidently eaten something. All of the dogs stirred at her homecoming, excited she was all right. Settling into a sit, each dog watched and waited expectantly in the eerie quiet for the return of the rest. The skies still swirled light and dark, but Zellie, Xander, Frost, Flowers, and Little Wolf were used to storms and didn't look up, their sharp focus kept ahead. None picked up any scent of danger; their senses were intent on the horizon.

Miles away, the remaining four dogs had located one another when they found themselves hunting the same prey, an arctic fox. Instead of fighting over their kill, they all fed in turn, pulling apart what they needed to satisfy, to survive.

The blood of their kill attracted the beasts of the wild. A grizzly picked up the scent. With winter coming suddenly and early, the grizzly had yet to hibernate. The bear found its prey.

In a standoff with the gigantic grizzly, and with Midnight already badly hurt by the bear, Magic and Mushroom snarled and barked at the predator while Midday sank her teeth into its thick neck. The grizzly easily threw off the white husky.

The dogs would instinctively fight to their death.

Death was close.

Midday, injured and stunned, crawled over to where Midnight lay and managed to curl close. She would wait for death with him. When the grizzly turned to the downed huskies, the copper-red and white pair charged the great beast, drawing the bear's attention to them. In one swipe from the bear, Magic fell to the ground. The only one left, Mushroom charged full into the face of death.

But death did not come.

Wolves did — three of them, big, gray, and

with blue eyes. In the time it takes for a heart to beat, giving life or ending it, the wolves struck. They killed the giant grizzly and sent it thudding to the ground. Snow ruffled in the air where it fell.

Arctic breezes stirred, whispers of spirits carried on them.

Mushroom faced the wolves now, expecting them to attack him next. He saw only death coming, his instincts telling him to kill or be killed. He didn't see any difference between the bear and the wolf. Midday got up on shaky legs, her white fur red with blood. Like Mushroom, she faced the wolves. Midnight tried to get up but couldn't; the black husky was too injured. Magic shifted and stood up, then growled low at the enemy, the fight to the death still on.

No fight came.

The wolves vanished in a swirl of snow, leaving no sign, no trail to follow

Magic, Mushroom, and Midday, more able now, raced to the spot where the wolves disappeared. They sniffed and pawed at the ground and then did the same to the dead bear. In unison they trained their senses on the Directions, alert to the winds for any sign of the wolves and more danger. No sign came.

The wolves had gone.

On some level the dogs imprinted the fact that the wolves killed the bear to protect them.

With the danger past, Magic, Mushroom, and Midday scuttled over to Midnight and did what came naturally. They licked the injured black husky's wounds clean and lay down with him. They would wait for him to get up. They did not howl to the Gatekeepers, giving any signal of death. Instead they howled across the wild, signaling to their pack.

Zellie heard them. So did Xander and the rest. They started to run despite deep snow, and headed in the Direction of the howls. They ran far and fast, and found Midnight and the others in two hours by human time. When they reached the scene of the dead bear, they saw Midnight wobble to a stand. The injured husky still bled from the deep claws of the bear, but he could stand. He took one step and then another, trying to walk.

Xander and Zellie both paced over to Midnight, and took turns nudging his hurt side. Midnight let them come close and lick his wounds. The other dogs danced around each other in greeting, with curled tails wagging, noses touching noses, and sniffing in the friendly air.

Together again, their pack mentality set, the dogs started for home, for their guardian.

They didn't run, since one of them could not. They headed through the deep snow one in back of the other, quitting their fan hitch. By virtue of moving forward, with Zellie at the lead, each dog helped clear the trail for the next, with Midnight the last in line behind Little Wolf. An intelligent breed, the dogs knew the best way to travel narrow trails, made by the snow-walls formed on each side as they moved. Such travel came naturally to them, and their progress was slow but sure. The freezing temperatures didn't faze them.

Alert for more predators, all nine kept their eyes sharp and their ears pricked. Zellie abruptly stopped in her tracks, sniffing the air in short intakes, then took off in a run. They all followed except Little Wolf and Midnight, who were still too weak to do so. The two left behind, curled in circles on their carved-out trail, rested where they lay. Their pack would return for them. They lay quiet, waiting.

It had begun to snow. The evening wild took on a glimmer, the icy flakes gently sliding through the air not unlike tiny stars might fall from a winter sky. Birds called through the quiet shimmers of light: the owl, the ptarmigan, the raven.

Zellie followed the call of the raven; its cry pierced the twilight over any others. The smell of danger flared her nostrils and sharpened her senses, drawing her to the spot where one of her own lay. Her paws and nails tingled and sharpened even as she ran, the instinct to dig overwhelming. Xander ran behind her; the same instinct had taken hold of him. The rest of the pack followed them, and stopped to dig in the same spot Zellie and Xander did.

With all seven Chukchi huskies digging away, it wasn't long before Rune Johansson's body was uncovered. His head rested face down on his arm, his duffle next to him. A sizeable air pocket had been created by this, enough to keep Rune alive if the temperature hadn't killed him. Zellie licked the ice off Rune's frozen-cold face. Xander nudged him repeatedly, first with his nose, then his paw. Frost and Midday kept digging at his feet, piling up snow behind them. Flowers pawed at Rune's body much as Xander did, while Magic and Mushroom ate snow and ice away wherever they found it.

When all else failed to bring life back to

288

Rune, Zellie and Xander lay next to him, to heal him. The rest stopped what they were doing and curled close, like Zellie and Xander. The body heat from the seven provided a double-layered blanket of thick fur to warm Rune on this deadly cold arctic night.

Rune came to and gasped for breath. He coughed in spasms against his arm. He felt frozen solid. Was he in Valhalla or *Hel*? He felt dead. He had to be. No one alive could feel like this, blinded and buried in pack ice. In a place beyond fear, he was puzzled over his circumstances. He didn't try to open his eyes because his lids seemed seared shut. Breathing in sharp cold air made him cough more, and so he tried to lift himself to find an easier breath. The moment he moved his body, he forced his eyes open to see for himself what could make the ice that had buried him melt away.

What could make him feel warm, feel alive, when he *had* to be dead?

CHAPTER TEN

Anya stretched out facedown in the snow to pray to the Morning Dawn for the return of the Chukchi dogs. She did this out of habit and believed the gods could better hear her in this posture. She'd worried through the night after picking up the dogs' howls the day before; they were mixed with the cry of the wolf. Had the wolf attacked after all? Zellie and Xander should be back by now.

Afraid for them and for the rest, she called to the Creator god and the Earth god to send the spirits, to send her Spirit; to send any who might help give the dogs Direction and bring them safely home to her. Her prayers went also to the Gatekeepers: that they keep watch over them and not close the gates of heaven on any of the loyal nine.

Upset and alone in the snow-covered clearing, Anya hadn't seen Boris for hours. He'd stomped off to track the dogs, rifle in hand, more angry than ever at her that the huskies stayed away. "You messed up, girl," he'd kept telling her to the point of pain. What if she had? What if she'd freed them only to have them torn apart by prowling bears or attacked by wolves on the hunt?

Chukchi dogs cannot survive the bear.

Chukchi dogs are strong and fast, but so are wolves.

Worries shot through Anya like shards of ice; every thought hurt. She got up off the ground, too upset to pray anymore. It felt like that's all she did: pray. Why should any of the gods listen to her anyway, a mere girl, a stupid girl, a girl lost to the spirits, especially her own. Feeling utterly deserted by all in the spirit world and all on Native Earth, Anya reflexively put her hand to her necklace, her gift from Vitya, to not feel so alone. The necklace stayed cold. She did her best to conjure Vitya's image but all she could see was . . . *Rune.*

Rune! He was all right!

He appeared out of nowhere, and so did the dogs: all nine rushed up to her, all nine competing for her attention at once. Flushed all over, her cheeks mainly, Anya used the dogs as excuse so not to face Rune, embarrassed head to toe over her reaction to him. Shocked to see him and surprised to react *like a girl,* she hoped he didn't see.

Her prayers had been answered, all nine of them. The dogs were home safe. She gave each husky what attention she could, and kept her gaze off Rune. She had no idea what she'd do after the dogs settled, what she'd say to him.

"An-ya," Rune carefully pronounced, "are you all right?"

She felt herself flush again at the rich tone of his greeting. He was a boy; why did he sound like a man? She was a girl; why did she feel like a woman? She had turned fourteen years, old enough to marry in her native village, but not old enough to cover her unexpected reaction to Rune. She'd never reacted to Vitya like this. Being attracted to Vitya, she could understand, but not this.

She shouldn't be attracted to Rune, no matter how good-looking he was — not to Rune, who'd left her for dead. Her anger and upset at Rune suddenly fueled, and saved her further embarrassment.

"You go to the shamans," she blurted before thinking better of evoking spirits.

"I think I have," he joked, despite his belief that shamans might well have brought him back to life. Even though he'd been convinced Anya hadn't died, the ghost of the Vikings foretelling as much, Rune was

292

relieved to see her alive and well.

"Then go back to the shamans and leave me alone," Anya snapped at him. "I don't need you here. The Chukchi dogs don't need you here." She'd said enough, more than Rune deserved to hear.

"Your English is better, Anya." He couldn't believe the change in her — not just her speech, but her appearance. She looked older than he remembered, and prettier. Her seal-brown eyes sparked with anger at him, yet he saw something different under those thick, dark lashes of hers. There was sadness, yes. He'd seen her sad, but never so determined, or so on guard. This made her seem older to him, when she was really just a lost little girl.

Then again, she didn't look lost or like a little girl at the moment, the way she faced him, standing tall, her thin shoulders square.

"Where did you come from?" she accused more than asked.

"Let's just say your dogs found me," he joked again. It wasn't a lie.

Although it was on the tip of her tongue to ask Rune why he'd left her for dead in Nome, she kept quiet. She didn't want to know and shouldn't care. But she did, about both. Still, she bit her tongue. The time had passed for her to think of her human feel-

293

ings, especially now with the dogs under constant threat from dark spirits.

Admittedly she was glad to see Rune, glad to see him alive and wishing he truly were a Viking warrior. The way his watch-blue eyes gently trained on her, the way his straw-colored hair ruffled in the arctic breezes, and the way his strong body tensed: he looked every bit like she'd imagined the Vikings of old. She doubted any were as handsome as Rune. He looked the same to her as before, but she sensed a change in him. She shouldn't care about what might have happened to him, but she did. Still, she held her peace.

"Last I saw, Boris Ivanov took the dogs away," Rune said matter-of-factly. He really wanted to explain what had happened between them on the beach in Nome; that he hadn't left her; that she, in fact, had left him. He'd gone back to wake her and she'd disappeared.

By magic she hadn't died.

Rune believed in the ghost who'd saved Anya, the ghost who'd traveled from the time of the ancients to warn him of *Hel,* and to send *the wolf and the dog into battle as one.*

Rune would fight for Anya, and for her dogs.

He wondered if Anya noticed any change in him, the way he'd noticed something different about her. He'd have to keep wondering, knowing he'd never put such a question to her.

"So what happened to Boris?" Rune asked Anya instead.

"He's gone hunting," was all she said.

"That's it? That's all you have to tell me?" His voice rose.

"Do not use your thunder on me," Anya warned.

"Anya," Rune said quietly. He wanted to ask her questions, but he didn't want her to ask him any. He would not give up the secret of the runes, even to her. "Anya, how did Boris find you?"

"I found him," she answered, before she realized she'd said too much — that she'd almost told him how Zellie's pointed cry led her to Xander — that she knew why Xander was in a fight for his life and that she'd found them all because of voices from another world. She would keep that secret from Rune. She would not tell Rune about her Spirit, either. Rune would never accept such mysticism and magic, but think her a "messed up girl." She shouldn't care what Rune thought, but she did.

"You found him?" Rune repeated indifferently, more focused on Anya and the dogs than on the Russian. Determined to stay with them, he needed to convince Anya that he should. Something was after them, but it wasn't Boris Ivanov.

"Boris wants to race dogs. I help him." Anya was surprised she'd said what she did. Then again, maybe the news would make Rune go away. Wasn't that what she wanted? He did not like the land. She could tell, and had from the first, that he didn't want to go with her and the dogs to the new land, to Nome.

She'd like to send him back to the sea and away from her and the dogs!

She didn't need him. The dogs didn't need him.

"No, Anya. You and the dogs must return to Siberia. I can help you get back home." Rune loomed over her, using every bit of his height to press his point.

Zellie and Xander lowered to a sit on either side of Rune; their eyes looked from Rune to Anya, as they followed their voices.

So intent was she on what Rune said, staring up into his glacial blue eyes, Anya didn't notice Zellie and Xander's traitorous action as they stood with the enemy Viking. Anya longed to return home. It was all she wanted, but the thought made her sick to her stomach. Homesick — that's all it was. No spirits haunted her. Yes, she was *homesick*. That's all.

Little Wolf slept next to Midnight now, both dogs needing more time to heal and regain their strength. Magic and Mushroom lay nearby. The copper-red and white pair didn't sleep, but watched the two human shapes — their guardians — whimper and whine back and forth. Flowers and Midday tumbled in the snow, diving at each other in play. Frost piled on; the spunky gray male easily joined in, frisky and rough-housing with the two females, as if they were all puppies again.

"It is time. It begins."

"What was that?" Rune stepped away from Anya and scanned the clearing, thinking he'd heard someone call out.

"I didn't hear anything," Anya said quickly, when she knew full well that she had. Her grandmother warned across the winds. The dogs must race. They must endure. This is the message Anya heard, the one she would heed. *The dogs will race and they will endure, Grandmother. I will make sure of it. Without Rune's help!*

She didn't need him. The dogs didn't need him.

Rune faced Anya again. He eyed her

297

suspiciously this time, sensing she kept secrets. He did, too, he realized.

"I will not go home to Siberia. The dogs will not go home. The dogs will race. I will stay with Boris," Anya said, more to herself than to Rune.

"Then I will stay, too." Rune found the nearest spot upon which to sit, then did just that.

Anya came back to her senses, and stared incredulously at Rune.

"No, you go!" she snarled at him.

At just that moment, a snow-covered Boris traipsed into the clearing.

"Gud. Gud. *Sobaka* back. Gud, Anya," he repeated, and shook the snow from his parka, stomping his feet like a bear coming out of hibernation. He set his rifle down, then noticed Rune sitting nearby.

"Rune Johansson! *Privet. Privet.* Gud to see you," the big Russian greeted Rune and went over to him right away. Boris put out his hand in welcome.

Rune stood and shook Boris's hand, thick mitts and all.

"You and dogs, gud, gud, very gud," Boris repeated, his smile so broad his mustache resembled that of a barking walrus. "You stay with us. Gud."

"No. Not good!" Anya suddenly charged

298

over to the men and broke their handshake with the stroke of her arm. "Rune is not staying. He is going!" Anya said in a raised voice.

"Oh, but I'm happy to stay." Rune removed his mitts and gingerly tapped Anya on the head with them, smiling in satisfaction.

"Rune has to go." She turned to the big Russian. "Rune does not know about dogs. He does not know about racing dogs. He cannot stay. He cannot help us." She tried to make her point to Boris the bear.

"Yes, I can," Rune said in a sure voice. "I can stay, and I can help."

"No, Rune." She turned on him, in a panic over her grandmother's prophecy. That was really what bothered Anya. Danger lay ahead. As upset as she was with Rune, she didn't want to see him dead.

"Do you know dog driving?" Boris put his question directly to Rune.

"Sure," Rune said. "I know enough to get by." He smiled mischievously at Anya, knowing he'd put her on the spot.

"Do you know about big race in Nome, big sweepstakes to Candle and back?" By now Boris had elbowed Anya out of their way, and was in Rune's face with his question.

All of Anya's previous upset at Rune turned to fear for him. She prayed he'd answer Boris honestly, that he didn't know the first thing about dog racing, and give Boris little reason to let him stay. Her necklace suddenly burned.

Forced to, she reached inside and pulled the ivory carving away from her skin, thinking of Vitya and not Rune. A shadow raced by, but she didn't notice it. If she had seen the ghostly shape, perhaps she would know if it brought good spirits or bad.

"Sure," Rune told Boris. "I know about Candle. It's the halfway point in the sweepstakes, at the two-hundred-and-four-mile marker."

Anya forgot Vitya and let go of the necklace. She was fixed on Rune's answer to Boris. *She* didn't know about Candle! *She* didn't know about the miles between Nome and whatever or wherever this *Candle* was! How could Rune know? He had no Direction on land; only at sea. The ancestors didn't guide him as they did her. The Directions were for her People, not Rune's!

"Gud," Boris enthused. "You know dog driving. You know the big race. I say you drive my dogs. What you say?"

"Sure," Rune said. "I'll do it."

Somewhere beneath his mustache and

whiskers the big Russian smiled.

Anya, however, did not. She stared open-mouthed at the two of them, not believing any of it — what Boris asked or what Rune answered. Zellie and Xander had moved next to her, one on either side. Anya needed their comfort more than ever, and she threaded her fingers through their fur, stroking behind their ears and along their necks.

How she loved them. How much more afraid she was for them now, as they faced such a race for survival . . . *with Rune guiding them.* Not believing Rune knew anything about Direction on land, she certainly didn't believe he knew anything about sleds and harnessing dogs!

Boris and Rune continued talking about the big race coming up.

Anya didn't listen, but went to a place inside her mind where thoughts are most private, with no one to hear but the gods. Doing her best to conjure her Spirit, Anya prayed hard for guidance. This must be a part of the "great burden" from the gods, of which her grandmother spoke: she not only carried the burden of keeping the dogs safe, but evidently the Viking, too!

They all faced death.

Anya knew her Spirit already traveled the other side of life, but Anya did not. She might be a medium, a shaman, but she was native-born and subject to mortal injury. She couldn't count on Spirit to save her from death on Native Earth. Anya realized death could come not only from human hands but also from the evil touch of spirits.

Until recently, she didn't think anything in the spirit world could really harm on Native Earth. She'd been proven wrong, when she saw what the dogs had already faced. Like her, mortal on Native Earth, they might have survived thus far, but they could be killed.

They must race. They must endure, her grandmother whispered softly in the Chukchi way.

At once envious of Spirit, Anya sensed her grandmother embrace her husky counterpart in the spirit world. This made Anya impulsively reach up to the heavens; her arms mentally embracing them both, and felt their love returned to her.

"They will race. They will endure," Anya promised silently, then self-consciously took down her arms.

"Anya, go, go," Boris ordered her offhandedly. If he noticed anything about her, he didn't comment. "Rune and I must make plan. You go hunt food for dogs like good girl."

Being dismissed "like good girl," flared her anger.

"No! I stay and hear your plan," she said rebelliously, shooting daggers at Rune, including him in her anger at Boris the bear. Both of them were creating bigger and bigger problems for her.

"*Nyet,* girl," Boris thundered.

"She stays, Boris, or I won't," Rune spoke just loudly enough for the Russian to get the full meaning of his words. Rune hadn't missed Anya's earlier action — her arms outstretched to the Almighty, he thought.

Boris grunted his displeasure, but didn't argue. He didn't need Anya except to feed the dogs. He had his dog driver. Now his team could race and win big. The only thing the dogs needed from the girl was food. The rest, the keptan's son would provide.

"What will it be?" Rune's agitation with Boris grew.

Boris appeared to contemplate what to do.

Anya glanced from Rune to Boris and back, not believing this new conversation any more than the last. Did Rune actually say she had to stay or he would not? As concerned as she was over Rune's welfare, still, what he said made her happy, even flustered, "like a girl."

303

"*Da,* the girl stays," Boris muttered disapprovingly.

"Anya stays," Rune corrected.

"*Da,* Anya," Boris repeated, shrugging his big shoulders enough to toss off the snow still coating them.

Anya's insides fluttered when she heard Rune say her name with such care. This was *no* time to feel "like a girl" around Rune or think of Vitya, either! Confused by her body's reaction, she didn't have time to worry over it. The dogs didn't have time.

They must race. They must endure.

Storm clouds regathered overhead. The winds picked up while temperatures dropped.

"Anya, get dogs," Boris snapped his order. "Weather is bad. I know place we can go. I have trapper cabin this way." He pointed his intended direction and started out of the clearing.

"Let's go then," Rune said, and tossed Anya an encouraging smile. "It is time. It begins."

Anya's spine stiffened at his words.

"Yes, it is time," she repeated hesitantly, doing her best to smile back, unnerved by what he'd just said. It was as if she and Rune had some kind of silent understanding, some reason they sometimes thought the same thing. It *couldn't* be — yet he'd said the words, the same words calling across the arctic winds that brought her and the Chukchi dogs across the great sea to this unknown land.

It is time. The race begins, she thought, dismissing her earlier concern, and thinking of the race ahead. She signaled for all the dogs to follow, and couldn't help but wonder if this was the only race they'd have to run for their lives or . . . only the first.

The storm brewing overhead at last unleashed its fury.

Boris, Anya, and all nine dogs filed through the blizzard in a single line, with Rune at the end. To leave each other in the sudden whiteout would mean certain death. Boris knew the way. He'd been through many a storm before in the Alaska wild and wasn't deterred in the least. Nor were Anya or Rune. They were both determined, both with their minds set on what they had to do, neither of them aware of the other's great burden.

The storm raged.

The seas roared. The Raven cawed. The wolf howled.

The battle engaged.

"We must take down our yaranga pole and

pack up our home!" Grisha roared to his wife and sons. "We must hitch our dogs and leave!"

"Why must we leave, husband?" Grygyn stood in between Grisha and their sons, not wanting Rahtyn or Uri to be hit with Grisha's latest thunder. "Please sit, husband, so we can talk."

"Sit? Like a dog you tell me to sit!" he roared, his bronze complexion steaming with anger.

Grygyn had run out of ways to calm her husband during these explosive episodes. He'd started having bad dreams since his return from Markova, since he'd traded Anya away. Then when his mother left this world, his dreams got even worse. Grisha was a village leader, a dog breeder, a man of means. Grygyn didn't understand why he'd changed so. She'd asked the shamans for their counsel, but they refused to have anything to do with anyone who gave shelter to "a child possessed of evil spirits. Bad luck follows bad spirits," the holy men told her; unwilling to admit their jealousy of Anya's perceived magic.

"Husband, our sons must care for the dogs. Do you not want to see their good work?" Grygyn motioned for Rahtyn and Uri to quickly exit out the door flap of their yaranga.

"They are not as good as Anya with the dogs. Anya, my daughter," his voice quieted to a whisper. He paid no attention to his sons' exit. "She was my rightful daughter by Tynga, no matter that she was not of my blood."

Grygyn stiffened at the mention of Grisha's dead wife. *She* was wife to Grisha now, not Tynga! She refused to share him with another, in life or in death. She refused to share any of their riches with Anya, either. Glad the undeserving girl no longer abided with them, she was upset to learn Grisha now claimed the child as his own. Anya was not his true daughter and wasn't going to get anything from him that rightfully belonged to her, as Grisha's wife. Grygyn smiled every day, knowing Anya had been traded away, never to return.

She thought nothing of Anya, but believed she and her sons alone should benefit from Grisha's wealth. Anya should get nothing. Unlike the majority of Chukchi People, who to a man and woman considered greed the most contemptible of offenses, Grygyn did not — though she hid this from the rest in her village. Perhaps the shamans saw through her, but if so they stopped short of bringing punishment, because she was the

307

wife of an important man, a breeder of dogs.

"Tell me of your dreams, husband." Grygyn feigned interest, when really she just wanted him to calm down.

"The gates of heaven will close to us all," Grisha said to himself. "The Gatekeepers cannot keep them open," he whispered, as if he were telling secrets.

With her husband beginning to quiet, Grygyn fussed over her cook fire, happy the latest storm had passed.

Grisha said no more and took down his harpoon, the one he'd almost used on his own daughter the year before. He thought of Anya, wondering where she was and how she was doing. He did love her. He always had. He'd always been proud of her, too. She was born with a gift, skilled with the Chukchi dogs, and had helped him acquire means and position in the village with her natural-born skills. Maybe if she still lived under his yaranga, the bad dreams would no longer haunt him. He'd wronged her.

Maybe that was why spirits plagued him. Spirits warned him to leave the village before it was too late. He'd heard the whispers in his dreams. The ice storm would come. The gates of heaven would shut. An ocean of blood would rise up from the great Bering Sea and seal them all in a tomb of ice! They'd be gone, forgotten for all time!

Nonsense, Grisha had thought. This would never happen. He shouldn't listen.

Grisha always saw a figure in his dreams — turned to nightmares — but he could never make out the distorted shape. What was it? Who was it? It was a faceless shape, an imagined spirit that faded quickly away. If only his Anya were still here. She'd told him all her life about seeing and hearing spirits. Maybe she really did. Maybe she could explain his dreams and keep them from haunting him. He didn't believe they meant anything, but could he be sure?

How he missed her, his little Anya.

"Hide? What you mean we have to hide?" Boris yelled at Anya.

Anya worried that she'd said too much. Desperate to keep Boris from taking the dogs into Nome early and revealing their whereabouts, she'd blurted her fears. She was afraid the dogs would be in danger.

They'd arrived safely at the trapping cabin and had no more come in from the storm than Boris the bear growled about needing to enter the dogs in races right away. The race for the big prize was coming in the new year. He wanted the dogs to start earning him rubles, *now.*

"How about we wait for this blizzard to quiet down first?" Rune stepped in between the Russian and Anya. "Anya and I need to tend to the dogs. Later we can hear your plans for them." Rune didn't wait for Boris to answer, but grabbed Anya's arm and took her outside into the storm. Boris's grumbling followed them both out the door.

All nine huskies greeted them outside, shaking snow off their backs in the process. Afraid for the dogs all over again, Anya dropped to her knees and reached for the closet to her, which happened to be Zellie and Xander. She hugged them tightly, feeling the bite of arctic winds along with them. The blinding storm hadn't let up. She almost wished it would not break, to prevent Boris from racing the dogs in Nome. They couldn't, not yet. It was too risky to expose their whereabouts until race time. Better to keep a low profile. She had to keep the dogs hidden, not just from the whip in the hands of so many humans, but safe from the lash of dark spirits after them.

Somewhere along the trek to the trapper's cabin Anya had decided to let the dogs race only once, and only for her grandmother, out of respect for and belief in her prophecy. Anya must fulfill the prophecy and race the dogs, and she would, but only once. Any more exposure would be too dangerous. Her knife was the only weapon she had to help protect the dogs — her knife and her Spirit. Would they be enough? She had nothing else, no one else.

"You have me, Anya," Rune said to himself. He knew she couldn't hear him through the loud whistle of the winds or over the moan of the giant evergreens creaking in the storm. More sensitive to her than before, he imagined how she must be feeling — alone, he thought. He knew she feared for the lives of her dogs. He knew something had tried to stop them, to kill them. That's why he'd been sent across the Bering Sea to Nome: to help protect Anya and her dogs. Rune couldn't remember much else but this purpose at the moment.

The weather, as if by magic, cleared. The snow diminished to flurries, and the winds died down. Sunlight even tried to peek through the thin layer of clouds in the twilight sky. An unearthly sensation misted through the air, and brought the music of the ancestors — the Chukchi and Viking together — whispering of times to come and making plans, inaudible to the human ear.

In the time it takes for a heart to beat, for worlds to collide and interlock, the whispers silenced; their plans were made. The passing of time for the Chukchi and the Viking stood still on Native Earth, as their ancestral spirits joined for the battle ahead. The Gate-keepers and the wolf returned to their own worlds, both feeling the ghostly burn of *Hel* travel through time, giving chase.

Zellie instinctively tossed her head back and howled; her call echoed across the tundra. Xander, Magic, Midnight, Flowers, and the rest howled along with her. Their combined calls turned to thunder, their echoes creating uproar.

Anya got up off her knees. She saw that the blizzard had passed. But how could it disappear, just like that! Amazingly, she didn't hear the dogs, being deafened by her concentration on the unexplained, *instant* change in the air. On impulse she reached inside the pocket of her kerker, making sure of her knife. Then she counted all the dogs, making sure of them.

The dogs were quiet now, too quiet.

Rune had listened to the dogs howl and the wolves answer, pack calling to pack. That couldn't be. It didn't make sense to him. Dogs and wolves calling out to each other? His mind must be playing tricks on him. The weather had let up. He didn't worry about its sudden change, but tried to figure what might have stirred the dogs

312

besides the call of the wolf. His senses sharpened, on guard for predators more than only moments before, he turned around full circle and scanned the surroundings. Then he remembered the ghostly call to him: *the wolf and the dog battle as one.* He didn't let down his guard.

Boris threw open the door of the cabin.

The dogs reacted to the commotion, jumpy yet on the alert.

Caught by surprise, Anya and Rune stayed mute, staring blankly at Boris as if seeing him for the first time.

"You finish with dogs?" Boris asked. He came outside and put himself in the middle of the group gathered.

The dogs scattered out of his way, yet kept an eye on him.

"The storm is over," Anya said in a whisper she hardly recognized. She felt strange but didn't know why.

"*Da,* I see," the big Russian smiled and chuckled. "Gud, gud. Was bad blizzard. Slow down training for you," he went on, eyeing the dogs, trying to approach each one for a better look. "I see you train in bad weather. Gud. Dogs look gud. Harness still on. Gud."

Rune looked at Boris, stupefied.

Anya's expression mirrored his.

They both kept their eyes on Boris, intent on his words, yet not understanding what any of them meant. They knew Boris but they didn't have any idea what he was talking about. What did he mean, "training"? What "harness"?

"I like this sled you make." By now Boris had made his way over to where a long, brush-bow basket sled waited; its birch runners were smooth, and its towline was already secure and ready for the dogs' individual tug lines to be hitched on.

Rune and Anya mechanically followed him over to the sled and inspected the light-weight, wood-and-hide-framed sledge along with Boris, but they had no idea how the sled got there.

Zellie came up to Anya.

Anya stroked the animal's neck and back, needing the comfort and security of her forever-friend. When her fingers slid over smooth hide straps and not fur, Anya jerked her hand away as if she'd been bitten. She looked at Zellie's harnessing but couldn't believe it. Yet there it was — smooth, wide, leather straps set in the way she always hitched her dogs in her home village: around the chest, across the withers and back, then around the rib cage. The familiar pattern proved best for the dogs to run easily and at full strength; this way the harness wouldn't rub or injure them over the long distances they needed to travel. Anya immediately ran her hands over the entirety of Zellie's harness, the touch familiar, comforting.

Zellie whined low and licked Anya's hand when Anya was through with her inspection, seemingly to want her guardian's comfort, sensing change in the air. She sniffed in quick intakes, and smelled danger coming close. Xander's harness was identical to Zellie's. He stood next to Zellie now, his senses trained on the same danger coming. He was just as stirred, just as discomforted. The two huskies licked each other's faces in acknowledgment, and then briskly headed back over to the other dogs.

They'd all been harnessed in the same way, and by now they instinctively reacted in the same way as Zellie and Xander, to the heightened danger in the air. No howls resounded. The dogs didn't hear the call of the wolf, yet they picked up the scent of the wolf. This didn't alert them, but something else, something unknown, did.

"Anya," Rune began, turned to the sled and not her. "I helped you build this." He knew he'd helped her but he didn't know how or when?

Boris had gone back inside the cabin and

had food ready on the table.

"Is gud. I make venison stew," he'd told them.

The last thing on Rune or Anya's mind was food; both wrestled with their own gods, with their own beliefs over what kind of magic could have caught them up, spun them around, and then, all of a sudden, let go. Time had obviously passed — yet, *it had not.*

CHAPTER ELEVEN

Anya struggled for Direction. What was going on? She took her time and pivoted slowly around to look at everything with a suspicious eye. She felt her arms and face to make sure she hadn't traveled to any dark spirit world. Hit with panic, afraid of what might have happened to them all, she was scared of bad spirits that might have overtaken them. Instead of praying to the Morning Dawn for help, she shot a look at the ancient heavens, to find the Pole Star, the portal to the worlds beyond.

She desperately needed a sign telling her bad spirits didn't master *her* Spirit! If she found the Pole Star maybe she could find the answers she needed. Maybe she'd get a sparkle of reassurance that everything was all right. The drums of the ancestors pounded inside her chest. She couldn't catch a good breath, she was so anxious over who was master now: bad spirits or good?

"Rune, do you . . . believe . . . in your gods?" Anya whispered in between shallow breaths, still searching the twilight skies for the Pole Star.

"Wh-at gods?" he asked warily.

"The gods of your ancestors . . . the Viking gods," she said, so focused on the skies she didn't notice the catch in Rune's voice.

"No, I don't believe in legend and superstition," he lied. He did believe in the secret of the runes. He wasn't about to give up such a secret, even to Anya. She was already in enough danger. She didn't need more.

"It's not legend and superstition!" She looked at him, challenging his words. She didn't have any trouble finding enough breath to answer him and didn't whisper anymore. "The gods of both of our ancestors live still; they always have and always will. How else do you think *we* live still, if not for our gods?"

"Your English gets better and better, Anya," Rune said, partly to throw her off the subject. She had a point, a very good point, but he wasn't about to agree with her and keep on such dangerous ground.

Anya's glare at Rune softened. He was right, not about the gods but about her English. She couldn't explain the change,

318

but she knew the gods could. She smiled to herself, thinking of the Morning Dawn and thanking the powerful Directions. It helped her calm a little, knowing the ancestors were with her and the Gatekeepers watched over them all, even Rune the Viking. If only Rune knew her gods were with them, and his, too.

"Let's get back to this," Rune said, and looked at the parked sled. He didn't know what she was up to, smiling so prettily, talking of the gods that sent him to her in the first place. He'd realized by now that they had. Why else would he be here, moving through time like a shooting star, "born from nine worlds coming to slay nine serpents"? Why nine serpents? Why not slay ninety-nine? He already knew the answer. Because there were *nine* dogs to protect — the serpent would come after them *nine* times over.

Nine was a magic number to the Vikings. It wasn't an unlucky number, as he'd thought; it had been a lucky number to his ancestors, an *important* number. More of his memory returned.

"Rune, you said that you helped me build this sled." Anya crouched down to their supposed handiwork to examine it more carefully.

Forced away from thoughts of the ancient

past to the hard reality of the present, Rune knelt next to Anya.

"Yes. I helped you build this, and you helped me learn to be a dog driver," he said, still a little confounded. He waited for her to react, expecting upset. Something had definitely just happened to the both of them. He'd begun to sort through it, but he didn't know if she had.

Anya stood up.

So did Rune, looking down into her cautious, seal-brown eyes, their dusky lashes shielding little. Her soft expression surprised him. In that moment, he decided she was the bravest girl he'd ever met. She'd stowed away and come all the way across the Bering Sea to be with her dogs, only to lose them, somehow find them again, then face danger upon danger, knowing more would come.

On top of all that, her world had just spun her around in time, no doubt scaring the life out of her, yet she'd accepted the reality of the moment. She must have, the way she appeared calm in the face of so much confusion.

"That's good then." She smiled up at Rune. "We don't have to waste time on any more lessons, do we?"

Relieved by her attitude, by the fact she'd

worked through the upset of the moment, Rune didn't want any more discussion about the gods, hers or his.

"Just to make sure, maybe we should take a practice run," she suddenly suggested, her smile mischievous. "Let's see what the dogs think of you. They might not like you anymore. We'll find out," she teased.

Rune couldn't appreciate her humor. He was too worried about whether the dogs *would* like him anymore, and whether or not he could control the strong, enduring, and fast-as-lightning huskies. It might prove easy to get the Chukchi dogs started, but getting them to stop could create a whole other set of problems. If he didn't do a good job driving, if he showed any uncertainty or confusion, the dogs wouldn't respond to him and things could get dangerous in a hurry. It wouldn't be their fault but his, if anything happened.

The lines between him and the dogs needed to stay taut, with the dogs leaning out. He mentally repeated these instructions. Dogs don't make mistakes. Drivers do. Oddly, he remembered he'd made more than one mistake, and imagined which ones: he'd run into trees, he'd pulled muscles, he'd fallen off the sled and had to chase after the team, and then had been too exhausted to keep on. Maybe it all happened as he remembered, maybe not. Either way he had a job to do. He "mushed" the sled and walked over to where Anya waited with the dogs.

Anya checked every harness and collar on every dog, worried about how they'd take to a double team hitch in pairs when they'd run in a fan style all their lives. To race, they'd need to run side by side in twos, with Zellie as their leader. Lines would be set differently. Chukchi dogs didn't fight and get all tangled up in their lines, but how would they take to the new hitch? Would they still get along?

For that matter, how would she take to any new hitch? How would Rune, who'd never taken to any hitch?

Concerned yet determined, Anya mentally went over the position of each dog, knowing how she'd place them to run the safest and best, at the same time wondering how she'd come to learn about the double-hitch and new commands in Nome. She didn't question how she knew to best position each dog on the team; she relied on her skills in raising and training them. If you knew your dog, you knew exactly what they're capable of, what they're afraid of, and how to run them without creating unnecessary injury.

She already knew Zellie and Xander, and at this point, she believed she knew the heart and spirit of the rest of the dogs.

In the lead position, Zellie would steer the team and set the pace. She'd be the one following commands and listening to direction. Since she was a pup, Zellie had shown the qualities of a good leader, with her natural-born ability to find her way in the worst of conditions. Used to the fan hitch, always running right in the middle, Zellie directed the pack naturally, even if there were no commands specifically given to her. Intelligent and resourceful, she also had good common sense. She'd be leading a smaller team when she was accustomed to running with larger teams, usually twenty dogs in all. Even so, with her natural instincts, she'd be the best to lead in the coming race. The team would follow her lead into the unknown, and give her their complete trust.

The copper-red and white pair would run behind Zellie to help swing the rest of the dogs behind them. Magic and Mushroom would keep the team pointed in the direction of their leader, around turns or curves along the trail. Anya hadn't raised or personally trained all of Boris's dogs, but she relied on what she'd observed in the pair since getting to know them better, ever gauging their heart and spirit.

Right behind Magic and Mushroom, she needed to place dogs for added power on the team. The strongest would run last, but in between, she needed power and co-operation. Frost and Flowers, combining their spunk and friskiness, would run hitched behind the copper-red and white pair, with energetic Midday and hard-working Little Wolf directly in back of them. The gray and white runt had gained back his full strength. She hadn't noticed any lung problems in him, not since the attack on him that had tried to suffocate him. Shivers shot through Anya when she remembered how all the dogs had been caught up in the tentacles of the same monstrous whip.

Immediately her hand went to her knife. Let the monster come again, let it try: she silently sent out a battle cry to the dark spirits, daring them even while knowing it was unwise. Her anger got the better of her. She'd cut down the monster from her nightmares, but she was still mad over letting it happen in the first place. Xander had been attacked three times before, nearly drowning, thrown into fits. Anya knew why: Xander was the strongest, the most durable of the Chukchi dogs. Dark spirits wanted him dead first.

Well, so far the Dark had failed! Anya intended to keep it that way.

She ran her fingers over her knife again, making sure of it one more time, thinking of the bear that had caused such severe injury to Midnight. The black husky seemed recovered, yet Anya wondered if he'd suffered from the lash of the dark spirits *or* the claws of a grizzly. Maybe they were one and the same?

No matter from where an attack might come, she needed to be ready — for the next attack and for the race. Something had tried to stop them from racing. Something wanted them dead. It did little good to remind herself of such threats. Right now she needed to think of Xander and Midnight and how she'd pair them in the last position on the team. They'd run directly in front of the sled and closest to the driver.

This position called for calm dogs that didn't startle easily. With the sled moving at their heels, the dogs in this spot needed to keep steady. Xander and Midnight were the largest on the team, both steady and strong and with the right instincts to know how to wheel the sled around tight, troublesome curves. Anya thought again of the grizzly and the fact that Midnight had some of

Xander's same qualities, which made him more of a target to dark spirits.

She needed to caution Rune about this, since he'd be driving the sled. Rune needed to keep an extra sharp eye out for Xander and Midnight. How to give Rune direction without alerting him to her Spirit and her native-husky-born instincts presented a problem. If he knew she communicated with spirits, he might decide to shun her, just as most everyone else in her home village had done all her life. No, she couldn't chance Rune leaving, not when she, and especially the dogs, needed him the most.

Frustrated, Anya realized she couldn't be with Rune and the dogs every step of the way, every mile, all 408 of them. She hadn't thought about this before, that she'd have to trust the Viking boy completely, because he held all their lives in his hands.

She prayed they might be the hands of a warrior after all.

"Here we go." Rune took up the towline and attached tug lines from off the sled, and looked at Anya. The main towline had individual tug lines coming off it, one for each dog.

"Let's get these guys hitched," Rune said.

Anya agreed and held out her hands for him to give her an end. Together they spread out the towline, which was the line running the length of the sled, onto the ground. Once all lines were set and the sled moved into place, Anya secured the towline Y connections to the front of the sled. She and Rune walked the length of their handiwork.

Anya would have to make sure each pairing of dogs would have enough room to run freely without running into each other; she was surprised to discover she was calculating in a new way: in feet. There needed to be nine feet between the dogs, nine in front, and nine in back. Funny, she thought, it just so happens there are nine dogs.

Arctic winds began to stir, as if the gods, Chukchi and Viking, could hear her thoughts. Anya hardly noticed, she was so concentrated on measuring everything accurately for the dogs.

The dogs!

She'd forgotten all about them. Ashamed of herself for her poor guardianship, she looked up from her line measurements to find all the dogs waiting nearby, frisky and excited to be hitched and have the opportunity to run. They not only looked anxious to get started but willing to be hitched in the new way. Surprised at first, she realized she shouldn't be — not with spirits about.

She looked to Rune then started to match each dog with their position along the towline and mentally counted out how long each tagline for each pair — one dog running on either side of the towline — needed to be. Each line would differ, according to need. If the lines were too short, the dogs could get hurt. If too long, the dogs could become entangled. As wheel dogs, Xander and Midnight's tug lines needed to be five feet. The distance for the dogs helping power the team, Frost, Flowers, Midday, and Little Wolf, needed to be shorter, about four feet. Zellie would need three feet of line to run well. Once Anya had the tug lines set, she signaled this to Rune and then turned to the waiting dogs, motioning for them to come.

Rune collected Xander by the collar first and hitched him to his tug line, as Anya instructed.

Anya then hitched Midnight on the opposite side.

The four team dogs came next. Anya couldn't believe how cooperative they were in letting Rune work with them. He'd hitched Frost and Midday on the right even before Anya told him where they should be positioned and on which side of the towline they should run. The spirits must be directing him, she thought as she secured Flowers and Little Wolf on the left. She couldn't think of any other explanation for Rune's sudden knowledge of sled driving — or hers, either, in this new way.

Zellie stood in the lead position, and waited for her hookup.

Anya went to do just that while Rune stepped to the back of the sled. He needed to check the gee-pole for steering and the snow hook for stopping. There was no place for a whip on this sled — neither a long whip for striking nor a short one for guide commands. Rune knew the damage a whip could do to dogs, beating them into bloody submission, and he'd have no part of it. If he couldn't control the sled and command the dogs by his skills, alone, he had no business running or racing any dogs, especially these. He had a lot to do to prove himself on this practice run. His nerves picked up. He didn't want to disappoint.

"Wait. Let me check their harnesses," Anya called to Rune, starting with Zellie's. For her part, Anya didn't want any harness to be too tight or too loose, because either condition could rub and possibly injure the dogs. Then, too, the dogs could back right out of their harness if it wasn't fitted properly. She also ran her fingers over every inch of strapping, making sure of padding to cushion the chest, and making sure there were no weak, worn spots in the leather. The dogs' paws, naturally tough and thickly furred, should stay the course, no matter how icy and rough. Moving from Zellie to the next dog, Anya made sure of all their harnessing before she looked at Rune again.

"All right —"

"Mush!" Rune cut her off with his command for the dogs to go.

Startled, Anya jumped out of the way so fast, she fell backward in the snow. Up on her feet again in the blink of an eye, she anxiously watched the sled disappear into the thick wood. Did Rune even know where to run in the evening light? Anya settled a little. Zellie would know where and when the trail would open. Anya trusted Zellie to lead the sled safely even if she wasn't so sure of Rune.

"Gee!" Anya heard Rune call out in the distance. Rune must know the way, too, if he was commanding Zellie to turn right. Maybe Rune had the commands of a warrior going into battle, after all. Still Anya thought to pray to the Morning Dawn and all the gods for the safe return of the dogs. Now that she couldn't see or hear the dogs or Rune anymore, she'd no choice but to

trust the Viking. But did the Gatekeepers trust him? He had the eyes of the Gatekeepers, the same glacial, watch-blue eyes. That had to count for something.

"Come! We go register team for sweepstakes," Boris suddenly announced the next morning, having witnessed Rune's triumphant return on his practice run the evening before.

The next thing Anya knew, she was being ushered out the door.

"Wait!" Anya easily wriggled her arm away from Boris. "It's not time. I say when it is time, when it begins," she said, unaware she used the very words of her grandmother's prophecy. She felt on edge and anxious, and her heart pounded inside her chest. She wasn't ready to enter the dogs in the race for their lives! She needed more time. They all did.

"*Is* time, girl. It is time for big race. *I* own dogs. I say is time!" Boris's brow furrowed, and his mouth was tight under his bushy mustache.

Rune opened the door and came inside. He'd been out seeing to the dogs, all the while looking forward to a "gold-rush-grub" breakfast of sourdough bread smothered in clover syrup, seagull eggs, and canned beans. Hot coffee, too. He was surprised he'd come to like the miner's drink of choice, at least in the early morning. Gold miners preferred shots of schnapps, and drinks of hard liquor later in the day. Rune felt a twinge inside at the word "schnapps," but ignored the unwanted memory that stirred from his past. He needed to keep his focus on what lay ahead. Right now that was — Anya!

She glared at him, then at Boris, then back at him, and she had anger and upset written all over her pretty face.

"Rune, you tell him," Anya ordered.

"Tell him what?" Rune shut the door. Cold air and a brush of snow rushed in behind him.

"Boris says it is time to race. It is *not* time. Tell him, Rune. Tell him," she pled; the anxiety she felt was obvious.

"Sure it is," Rune said quietly, his breakfast forgotten. "It *is* time, Anya." He gazed straight into her upturned face, open-wide seal-brown eyes and all. His heart went out to her. She was just as scared as he was. But this was no time to show fear, not to each other or the gods.

Anya gaped at Rune. She didn't understand him at all. He didn't look one bit upset.

"You don't think we need more time to train and practice?" she accused more than asked. Trying not to panic, she forced her voice to stay steady.

"No." Rune impulsively ran a finger lightly along her soft cheek, then gave her a reassuring chuck under her chin. "No, Anya, it is time to leave and begin this."

She stared into his mesmerizing eyes, wanting to believe what he did: that they were ready to race. But she wasn't as confident as he by a mile — by 408 of them, actually.

"*Da,* gud, we go now." Boris, packed and ready, had a hand on each of their shoulders, pushing them toward the door.

Anya turned to fetch her kerker and make sure the knife was safe inside its pocket. She pulled her fur coverall over her dress, the dress she'd kept on over her long underwear. With her hood drawn up, she made sure of her necklace. *Vitya's gift.*

If only he were here with her. Vitya, she felt certain, could race the dogs, not injure or lose one, and bring them all across the finish line to win. She supposed she shouldn't doubt Rune, but she did. Everything still felt strange and unreal, except for the danger ahead. There was nothing unreal about that. Digging her toes deep inside the tips of her mukluks, the action helped her get a better footing. She needed one. She needed to find her confidence for the challenge ahead.

Rune already wore his parka and mukluks and only needed to fetch his fur hat and mitts. He'd leave his duffle behind. His sunstone he kept tucked away in his head. If his ancestry bore out, despite being on land, he'd manage to find his way along the grueling race trail with the advantage of the ancient sunstone of the Vikings ingrained in him — innately helping navigate him and the dogs back to Nome and across the finish line, alive.

Once outside, Rune and Anya had the team hitched in no time. Rune gave the command to mush. Zellie responded, and the dogs started out. Rune and Anya took turns pedaling the sled along, one foot on a runner and the other foot helping push in the snow, going at a slow enough speed for Boris to catch up. The big Russian exerted effort and managed to keep in their sights. Neither Anya nor Rune voiced their fears: the ones racing through their heads about the days to come.

Sometimes their eyes would meet when they'd look behind for Boris, but they said nothing. Neither one spoke of the threats they faced or how they might fight them, determined as they were to keep their ties to their gods a secret.

Zellie kept her ears pricked, her senses alert, and kept a slow pace, since she heard no commands to take her off the path ahead. Magic and Mushroom quietly trotted behind their leader, with the four dogs in the team position just as steady. Xander and Midnight leaned out, one to the right and one to the left, and paced soundly in front of the sled.

All nine dogs mushed along as if marching to battle.

The Gatekeepers marched with them.

Dark spirits gathered in angry clouds over Nome, waiting for *Hel*.

Christmas had come and gone quietly in Nome. No one felt much like celebrating, what with poor light in the sky and the weather staying sour. This year more than last, Nome's residents looked forward to the new year and the sweepstakes coming early. It was the one event bringing light to the sky for all. Smaller races had been run throughout the season when the weather allowed. With the big race approaching, everyone held their breath and hoped nothing would interfere, especially Mother

Nature. A violent blizzard could eliminate teams from competing, disappointing them all. Bettors were ready with their wagers, waiting for all the competing teams to report to the Board of Trade Saloon and register.

Bets were already heavily on the side of the well-respected dog driver Scotty Allan. Bets were flooding in from the Outside, as well as from locals. The *Nome Nugget* had done a good job publicizing the early sweepstakes. The newspaper couldn't do anything about the fact that the race would have to be run under darker skies than if it were the "true" end of racing season. Albert Fink couldn't do anything about the weather, either.

"The All Alaska Sweepstakes of nineteen-oh-nine is officially open for business," the Nome Kennel Club president shouted over the din inside the Board of Trade Saloon. Crowds had already gathered inside and out, wanting to see for themselves every dog team, owner, and driver who had registered, as well as those who had yet to register for the biggest race of the season. It would be the race of a lifetime for many. Every team would line up on Front Street, and every owner and driver would report inside the saloon for their official papers.

All the people in the crowd would have an opportunity to look over the teams and place their bets, if they hadn't already done so. Street lamps blazed up and down Front Street, shedding what electric light they could on the scene below. The skies began taking on a glow that the crowd welcomed, happy they had electricity. For a time, no one noticed the arctic lights that were beginning to swirl across the heavens, their red, green, and blue colors finally settling in a soft glow of yellow, illuminating the skies to the daylight of early spring.

The first person in the crowd to become aware of the arctic lights was one of the Eskimo children, a little girl who nudged her mother and pointed to the heavens. Native Eskimos had come to take part and watch the start of the big race. To a man, woman, and child, they knew the signs above. The gods were at work, bringing the light.

"Well I'll be damned," muttered Albert Fink, the Nome Kennel Club president, amazed, as he stepped outside. A hush fell over the crowd, inside the saloon and out. Everyone else was equally amazed by the change in the sky.

Reminded of the eerie start to winter, some wanted to run for their Bibles, while others tried to comprehend how Mother Nature could change so quickly. And that's what they wanted to think: that the weather had decided to change on them again, period. Nothing would interfere with the start of the All Alaska Sweepstakes of 1909! Their minds set on the day ahead, a portion of the crowd moved back inside the Board of Trade Saloon to get down to business.

Boris collapsed in a heap, his sudden heart attack fatal. He didn't call out. He hadn't felt any pain or received any warning. In the time it takes for a heart to beat, his stopped. He was winded from excitement over the upcoming race and exerting more effort than usual to traverse the long trail back into Nome. Perhaps the big Russian's death had come naturally . . . then again, perhaps not.

Zellie pulled up short. The rest of the dogs stopped reflexively behind her, then stayed in place, unmoving but for the arctic breezes ruffling their fur. Light snow fell in the dead silence.

"What's wrong, girl?" Anya called out to Zellie, scanning everything in front and to the sides of the sled for trouble. She didn't see anything wrong.

"Boris is not behind us," Rune warned.

338

Anya turned around so fast, her foot slipped off the runner where she'd been taking her turn pedaling the sled. She didn't see the big Russian, and became immediately alarmed. Inside her mitt, her hand throbbed, the same hand marked by the lash of dark spirits. Instinctively she pulled off her mitt and saw what she'd expected. A thin line of blood oozed from the scar across her palm.

"He's dead," she pronounced to Rune.

"Maybe he just went back to his cabin for something. We're not that far away. Let's go back and find him, Anya," Rune said, not wanting to believe her.

"Come haw!" Anya took the handle bar of the sled and helped turn the team left and back around on the wide trail. She hoped Rune was right. In a desperate hurry to find out, she made a kissing sound with her lips to speed up the team.

Rune kept up with the team. Luckily the trail had been packed down enough for him to do so. Only then did he notice the daylight. They'd left Boris's cabin under an arctic, winter sky — not bright, like this one. He hadn't wanted to race under dark skies. Now he didn't have to, apparently. Weather at sea could change in an instant. Maybe the same held true on land. Maybe that's all this was. No matter. Rune ran with the speed of a Viking warrior, trying to make a plan, worried that the Midgard serpent, land or sea, somehow already lay in wait ahead.

"Whoa!" Anya's command for the dogs to stop thundered through the tense atmosphere. She didn't need to dig the snow hook, the sled's brake, into the ground to help them stop. Intuitively, the dogs seemed to know the very spot where Boris lay dead in the middle of the trail. They'd already begun to slow down before Anya's command came. Her mitted hands slipped from the handle bar, but she didn't approach Boris's body. She stared and struggled to comprehend what had happened to him — who or what had killed him.

Not for a moment did she think Boris the bear had died of natural causes. He was too tough and too accustomed to the ways of the Arctic to die following them along the trail. Besides, the blood on her hand told the tale.

"He's dead for sure, Anya," Rune called out. He knelt next to Boris's stiff, cold body. Rune couldn't take his eyes from Boris's. The way they stayed open wide in alarm, even in death, unnerved Rune. Quickly, he scanned his surroundings for any more signs of trouble. When he didn't see any, he looked again to Boris and ran his fingers over Boris's lids and closed them. Whatever killed the Russian could still be there, lying in wait.

Wolves howled from far away.

The Chukchi huskies responded with howls of their own.

Unseen and unheard shadows whispered in the trees, content for the moment. The next arctic breeze swept them away.

Anya joined Rune next to Boris's body. She hadn't seen the look in the dead trapper's eyes that Rune had, so she was unaware of the sign. Yet she believed something or someone had killed Boris. Even if she weren't suspicious on her own, the howling dogs seemed to underscore her thoughts. She swallowed hard, and waited for the dogs to quiet.

"We should honor Boris the bear in death, Rune. I don't know why the dogs have to be here to race, but I know they must. Without Boris, the dogs would not be here, but across the great sea in Siberia. Without Boris, I would not be here, either. He could have killed me for what I did, because I released his valuable dogs more than once. He had the right, but he did not. We must honor him," Anya said again in a whisper, in the Chukchi female way of speaking.

"Yes," Rune agreed. He stood. He needed to walk out his worries.

Anya got up, too, and watched Rune pace back and forth. She had a good guess what troubled him besides deciding how best to honor Boris in death.

The dogs quieted and stayed in place, watching them.

"We have to make a new plan for the race, Anya." Rune stopped pacing. "We have to register the team in Nome without Boris. The race might start any time. We don't know when."

"You have to do it then, Rune." Anya looked up at him.

He kept his gaze on her and listened to what she had to say.

"You have to say the dogs are yours and register them like Boris would have. You have to say you're the dog driver, too. Some people already know about Boris and our dogs. Miners we passed would stop and laugh at us, and say our dogs were little. They called them 'Siberian rats.' Some of the miners know dogs and dog drivers and owners. They will notice when Boris doesn't come to the race start. What should we tell them happened to Boris?"

"The truth, Anya, I will tell them the

truth." Rune said, sure of his words.

"What truth?"

"That Boris the bear died of a heart attack. That he'd agreed to sell me his team after the sweepstakes race, because he was so grateful that I'd agreed to be his dog driver, when he couldn't find anybody else who would be." Satisfied with his made-up explanation, Rune didn't wait for Anya to say anything else. He bent down and put his arms under Boris's shoulders to get the Russian's body loaded onto the sled.

Anya immediately took up Boris's feet to help. She had second thoughts about Rune's claim of ownership.

"Rune, why should anybody listen to you? You're only a boy." She winced inside at her description of Rune. She didn't think of him as a boy anymore, not really.

"Be . . . cause . . ." Rune huffed at the dead weight in his arms. "I'm the son in Johansson and Son Shipping. My father is known all along the coast on both sides of the Bering Sea. No one in Nome will give me trouble, I don't think." No sooner had memories of his father come to mind than Rune pushed them out again, unwilling to think about anything but the race ahead.

Keptan Lars, Anya remembered — *Captain Lars,* she mentally corrected, using her newfound English proficiency — had been kind to her. She wasn't used to kindness, which was why Rune's father stayed in her memory. She supposed Boris the bear had been kind to her, too, but not in the same way. All her life she'd longed for a father just like Rune's. Suddenly she envied Rune, and dreamed of the life she'd never have.

"Mush!" Rune commanded the dogs as soon as Anya cleared the sled.

"Wh—" Anya took off behind Rune and the team, doing her best to forget about the life she might have had and thinking instead about the one she'd been given. Nothing mattered, really, to her but the dogs and keeping them safe.

She hoped Spirit ran with her, especially seeing how in the blink of an eye, night had become day.

Anya and Rune watched Boris's cabin go up in flames, then quickly smolder to the ground. They'd lit the funeral pyre themselves. Anya had made sure Boris had all of his things inside the cabin with him he'd need for the next life, as was custom to the Chukchi, while Rune trenched outside the cabin, carving the outline of a ship in the snow. It was a stone ship, and it was akin to the Viking custom of setting a burning ship out to sea. In their own way, each of them mourned for Boris, believing he deserved a proper send-off to the next world. Anya imagined the Gatekeepers welcoming him into their heaven, at the same time Rune wondered if Valhalla would make an exception and open its golden doors for Boris.

Zellie whined. The other dogs moaned in chorus.

"Yes, we know it is time, girl," Anya said to Zellie, then started to put her things in the basket of the sled. She stopped what she was doing to make sure of the knife inside her pocket. This was motion made religiously on her part, done many times a day. The knife was a gift from the gods and she didn't want to lose it. Finished now, Anya felt ready for what might come.

Rune picked up his duffle and tossed it in the sled atop Anya's scant bundle, then went to his position behind the sled, planning to pedal first and give Anya a rest. She was still the bravest and most capable girl he'd ever met, yet he wanted to take care of her and protect her. If anything happened to her, he'd blame himself. Same with her dogs, he thought soberly.

"Mush!" he called out. He wanted to get going and forget his fears. He couldn't af-

ford to have any, not now, not with *Hel*
coming.

"*Mush!*" he called again, this time razor-
sharp. Who was he kidding? *Hel* was already
here.

Chapter Twelve

Frank Lundgren sneered at the "Siberian rats" in front of him then spat juice from his tobacco plug at the ground. The splat just missed a woman's booted foot. Frank didn't care. He was good and mad. The goddamned, husky rats had no business running in any race with Alaskan huskies, and especially not in this one! They were in line in front of him, pretty as you please!

Spitting mad, he let go another splat of tobacco juice. The woman had already moved well away from him. Frank stepped out from behind his sled to find the son of a bitch Boris Ivanov and see who he'd found who was stupid enough to drive the Siberian rats. He knew he could leave his sled for a moment, as Boris's team was just ahead of him, so Frank could keep an eye on his own team and lead dog. He didn't want anybody messing with Brutus, no sir. Anyone tryin' would be lookin' at dyin', he joked to himself.

The thick crowd had been there most of the day, and still lined the street three and four deep along the way to the Board of Trade Saloon. They'd be out again tomorrow morning at ten sharp, in full force for the race-day start. So would all the children in the isolated boomtown. School was let out for the four days of the race.

Twelve teams had registered, and two had yet to sign in and pick up the rules. Many bettors had already put their money down for their winning choice at the Bank of Nome. True to prediction, satisfying their favorite frontier passion, gamblers bet heavily on the known and experienced Scotty Allan. His sled had the best odds so far, but bets were still being made, with shouts ringing back and forth across Front Street as to who liked whom to win, and who would be sure to lose. Betting wouldn't close until the first race team crossed the starting line. Rumor had it the betting totals would hit the hundred-thousand-dollar mark!

Rune's turn came to go inside the Board of Trade Saloon. He'd waited in line a long time now, listening to jeers and laughter at his team of Siberian huskies.

"Whattcha got there, little wolves?" someone yelled.

"Nice of you to bring dinner for the malamutes!" another gibed.

"Say, boy. Reckon you don't belong here with yer rats all the way from Si-by-golly-beria!" This taunt brought a lot of laughs from the crowd. "Yer rats won't take to our trails, being so puny and scrawny! No way will you be back in any kind of time to win, if you find yer way back at all!" More laughs erupted at the man's shouts.

Rune would turn and look at Anya; hers was the only opinion he cared about now. She was confident the Chukchi dogs could run well against the Alaskans. Rune estimated the weight difference to be at least thirty pounds. Anya's dogs weighed forty-five to fifty pounds on average, and the mixed malamutes had to weigh over eighty. Some topped one hundred pounds; they had to, the way they were muscled.

The teams ahead of theirs also had more dogs hitched than theirs did. The typical number was sixteen. Rune's thoughts raced. Nine smaller huskies against sixteen larger, more-powerful-looking huskies didn't seem like very good odds. Then he would look at Anya again, find her standing with her dogs, confident and sure, and he'd feel better about his own chances — a little anyway.

The odds were already stacked against him, he knew. Other dog teams were not the biggest threat. Something unknown was. *In one hand you hold wisdom and in the other, war.* Rune hoped the ghost of the ancients spoke true. Rune might be a human with the mark of the gods, but he was no Viking god with the power to change the wind and turn the tide, no matter the trouble faced.

He wanted to believe that in his human hands he held enough power to drive the sled, find his way, and bring the dogs back safely across the finish line. He wanted to believe he had enough power to fight the forces of *Hel.* Rune fisted his hands then relaxed them again and again, willing the powers he'd need for the coming days into his taut fingers.

Just then someone jerked Rune's arm, keeping him from going through the saloon door and taking his turn.

"You don't really think yer gonna race with us, now do ya?" Frank Lundgren snarled at Rune. "Not with yer rats here, anyways."

"Get your hands off me, mister," Rune said to the man.

Xander growled. So did Zellie.

Anya stared hard at the pock-marked stranger — ugly in looks and actions — and knew the dogs didn't like him. She listened to her own instincts, and she didn't like him, either. *He used a whip.*

"Aw, poor kid," Frank mocked, looking back at the crowd, expecting them to join in the fun. "Looks like he don't want my two cents here." At this remark, some folks laughed, but others stayed silent and waited to see what would happen next.

"I said" — Rune shoved off the offensive man's hold — "get your hands off." Though younger than the offensive stranger, Rune thought he could easily best him in a fight. Still, he didn't want to fight. He didn't want to waste any energy he'd need for the race. "Go back and wait your turn," Rune said dismissively, then twisted around and went inside the saloon.

Left with egg on his face, hearing some in the crowd poke fun at him, Frank stomped back to his team. He tried to scare some of Rune's dogs along the way by raising his arm and pretending to come at them. On the race trail he'd take care of the upstart and his rat dogs. There'd come a time and a place. No one would know what happened. No one could follow every mile and every move made by every team and driver. He would take full advantage of that and take care of the kid and his poor excuses for dogs! All's fair in love and dog racing, Frank thought deviously as he planned when and where he'd make his moves so no one could see and accuse him of anything.

For now, he'd wait for Boris Ivanov to come outside. As the team's owner, he must be inside. Frank knew how to use a whip, and the Russian fur trapper knew it. Boris would back down, no matter what he said, Frank thought. The Russian had done as much when Frank had threatened him with a whip before. Boris had scat in no time. Frank would look like the better man to anybody watching them spar. Yeah, he looked forward to Boris Ivanov coming back outside. The upstart kid, he'd take care of on the trail.

The 408-mile All Alaska Sweepstakes would start in one hour. Excitement built in the icy air over Nome among the frontier townsfolk, gamblers, and racers alike. Very few people were concerned with plummeting temperatures or the winter storm that threatened. Race day had arrived! The chalkboard at race headquarters had the odds and race lineup posted. Scotty Allan's team would leave first, with Rune's team last. The Siberian huskies were given a hundred-to-one betting odds. Most bettors obviously thought little of Rune Johansson's "Siberian Wolf Dogs," as they were officially listed, and they expected a poor showing.

Rune had slept all night in their stable quarters on his bed of straw. His needs were the same as the dogs': strength and endurance for the days ahead. Anya had stayed up to keep watch. Every other possible accommodation in Nome, whether inside or out, had already been taken. With the money they had left after paying for shelter in a chilly stable corner, Rune and Anya purchased what food they could for the dogs, mindful that the dogs were used to running on little and still going long distances for long periods of time.

They would need a four-day supply of food. Because they ran out of money to finish buying their supplies, the owner of the native trade store donated the rest; he wanted the Siberian team to win. Surprised at the Eskimo's good opinion of them, Rune and Anya didn't question their luck; they'd had luck twice now.

Earlier in the day Rune met a man in the Board of Trade Saloon who was a friend of his father. The man guessed Rune didn't know the trail, and he told Rune that the racers had already stashed caches of food for their teams along the race course. He drew Rune a map to show the trail and rest stops, pointing out danger where he could, especially in the valley of blizzards. "This spot is always stormy and always dangerous. Good luck, son. You'll need it," he'd said after they'd gone over his map.

Anya had carefully packed the provisions needed in the sled's basket: enough dried meat and fish for Rune, too. She'd included the water skins donated at the Eskimo trade store, not relying on the rest stops and roadhouses to have fresh water. Rune could refill them at the stops when possible. The gods had been kind to them, she thought, while she pulled the reindeer fur blanket over their provisions to safely stow them on the sled.

That was last night. The race would start soon, and she had promised to wake Rune. Watching him sleep so peacefully, she hated to wake him up. Over the next four days he'd get little rest, much less actual sleep. If only she could help. If only women could race, she would. Maybe her youth or her native-born blood wouldn't disqualify her. At least Rune hadn't been disqualified. He'd had no trouble at registration the day before; the judges accepted him as the team owner and dog driver. Anya wished she had a role to play, and she longed to leave with him at the race's start. But if she ran alongside or helped pedal the sled, she'd break race rules.

Rune had shown her the race map drawn for him and explained most of the rules to her. Two rules stood out: the same dogs starting the race must cross the finish line, and drivers were not to use whips on their dogs. She immediately thought of the dog driver who had waited in line behind them the day before — *he used a whip* — and she warned Rune that she didn't think the ugly dog driver would abide by the race rules. She wondered if that driver could even read, and she wished she could.

Anya wanted to be able to read the rules herself. She could speak good English, thanks to the magic of shamans, but she couldn't read the English words, or write them. Rune could. Rune was smart, smarter than she'd realized when she'd first met him. Vitya was smart. When she caught herself mentally comparing the two, she quickly let go of Vitya's necklace and forced her attention back to the moment, still not wanting to wake Rune. His handsome face and well-muscled body spoke of strength, endurance, and capability. Rune had all three, she admitted to herself. He did have the heart of a husky, after all.

The dogs lay in quiet circles on their beds of straw, eyes closed yet aware, somewhere between awake and asleep; they waited as they had for centuries for their guardians to command them. To a dog they sensed danger. Unlike most inhabitants of Nome, they could smell the next ice storm brewing. None were tied. None tried to run. Their leader would give the call to run. Until then, they would stay put. Their pack bond, like that of the wolf, connected them; it was a bond broken only by death.

Boris Ivanov's death hung in the chill air. Anya tried to push the image of his dead body from her thoughts. Bad spirits had found him and killed him. Could the dogs outrun the bad spirits that might be after them? Very slowly, so as not to rouse Rune or the dogs, Anya lay down on her stomach, her face to the straw, hands outstretched on the frozen earth. She needed time to pray to the Morning Dawn and to the Directions, and ask for guidance on this day.

The drums of the ancestors sounded throughout her tense body. They *must* help her find a way to help Rune and the dogs. What good would she be to them if she waited in Nome? *None!* There was something else that troubled her: why was it so important for the dogs to race now, and in this race?

Why, Grandmother? She called out silently to the ghosts in the air. Her grandmother was listening. She had to be.

Why must they risk their lives now? Why?

Tears stung her eyes. She shut them tightly against the straw poking at her and against her pent-up emotions. The spirit world wasn't talking to her, and neither was her grandmother! Choking back sobs, she didn't think either would visit her again, and she doubted her powers as a shaman. Perhaps she had possessed those powers once, but no longer; otherwise, she would hear her grandmother's answer to her question. Heavy with doubt, Anya forced herself to rise off the straw.

It is time. It is time to save us all, child.

Anya froze. *Nana-tasha!* It was her grandmother calling to her from across worlds! It took Anya long moments to grasp her grandmother's answer; she didn't want to hear the truth of it. The dogs must run now and in this race . . . *to save us all.* Full of more questions, Anya dared not ask them, especially now with no time to waste.

"Rune," she whispered and gently shook him awake.

"It is time. It be . . . gins," he said, and yawned sleepily, slowly opening his eyes as

357

if coming out of his dreams.

Taken aback by what he said, by the now-familiar words, Anya didn't say anything. She felt it again, her unmistakable connection to him.

Wide awake, Rune scrambled to a stand.

The dogs stirred when he woke up. Zellie rose first. The rest followed, all briefly touching nozzles and whimpering in turn, to signal their readiness.

Anya went to each one of the dogs and checked their harnessing a final time before she gave each a tight, devoted hug. She'd come to love them all in the time they'd been together as a team, not just her own Zellie and Xander. She'd developed affection and deep respect for each one, especially Little Wolf, the runt of the pack. He might weigh the least, but he had as much heart and spirit as the rest. Anya came back to Zellie one more time, and knelt down to her, hugging her close.

"You must find the way, my beautiful girl," Anya whispered. "This hunt is like none before it. Your task is great. I love you more than life itself. Know that I will be with you in spirit every step of the way."

"Anya," Rune said softly. "You must let her go."

Suddenly frightened by his words, she

clutched Zellie even closer.

Zellie let go first, gently twisting away from her guardian, ready to face into the ice storm already gathering.

"Anya," Rune said. He read her thoughts. "I know a storm's coming. Help me hitch the dogs. We don't have any time to lose."

Anya said nothing, mutely signaling to Zellie and the dogs to follow her. Once outside, their breaths steamed in the frigid air. The dogs automatically stood in their trained places in front of the sled, and waited for their hitch. Anya and Rune went down the line, connecting each dog in turn. Xander was the last to be connected to the towline, right in front of the sled and paired with Midnight. Anya reluctantly let go of Xander's fastening, the last connection holding him to her. She tried not to panic.

Xander nudged her hand with his cold nose, then put a playful paw to her mukluk leggings, and pushed her a little as if in play.

"I love you, my strong, brave boy," Anya dropped down to him and whispered. "You must save your strength for every turn. Much depends on you." She gave him a quick kiss on his head then moved away. Like Zellie, she had to let him go . . . *to save us all* . . . as her grandmother foretold.

■ ■ ■ ■

"Last?" Anya yelled her question to Rune. It was all she could do to hear over the roar of the cheering crowd reacting wildly to the start gun. The sound cracked through the air, barely audible over the wind and deteriorating weather. The latest storm had arrived. Anya's face, pelted with snow, burned from its sting. She worried about Rune and the dogs starting out in such bluster.

She didn't have to scan the crowd for menacing shadows. They were there, ready, waiting to start right with her dogs. What good would it do to share her suspicions with Rune? He already knew he faced into danger. Her gods would watch over him, wouldn't they? The Gatekeepers could see the dark shadows that armed together on Native Earth and would be with him. Anya took some solace in believing the Creator god and the Earth god would not desert them. If Rune had any belief in his gods, surely they would watch over him, too.

"Yes, I'm in last position!" Rune yelled back at Anya, as he readied for his start. "Don't worry. We'll catch up!" He tried to joke, but he didn't know if he really could catch up, not in all this bad weather. Rune had time before his start: time to wait for the weather to worsen, he thought. The seas could be just as rough. Rune was used to rough seas, but he didn't look forward to heading into this snowstorm.

The race start judge told Rune his team would have the last fifteen-minute-interval start since they had the poorest odds. He also gave Rune one more chance to pull out, telling Rune his dogs were too small to handle the tough trail like the Alaskan huskies. His dogs could *die* on this run. Surely Rune didn't want that, and as a judge, he didn't want that! If Rune wanted to save face and pull out of the race, no one would blame him or make him a laughing-stock. Hah, Rune remembered the laughter from the day before from the locals, and he was well aware they didn't think much of his team. Mocking didn't bother him now, though. The weather did — the weather and the dark shadows hiding in the crowd. The judge didn't need to advise Rune his dogs could die on this run.

At first Rune thought his eyes played tricks on him. He saw murky shadows shoot through the thick crowd of men, women, and children lining the race start. He blinked hard to get rid of the shadows that flickered across his line of vision. He needed a clear view of the trail if he was to have any chance of keeping the dogs alive and winning this race for Anya. Nothing worked; not rubbing his eyes; not opening and shutting them. The suspicious shadows lurked and didn't disappear.

Reflexively he glanced at Anya. She sees them, too, he realized in that moment. The back of his neck pulsed. Was it possible she and he saw the same ghosts? He believed they did. He couldn't shake off this peculiar feeling any more than he could shake off the shadows in clear view. *The wolf and the dog must battle as one.* Rune set his jaw and tightened his fists for the fight ahead. He repeated the now-familiar battle cry to himself, then tried to turn his focus back onto the race.

He knew what the shadows were.

The ugly shadows snaking through the throng of onlookers were legions of the great serpent, ever lying in wait for any Viking warrior. Rune scanned the crowd again, glad he could spot the enemy, glad that it was finally showing enough courage to reveal itself. He just hoped he could outrun it. Danger waited over ice but not land, Rune thought. The serpent could only strike in water. He would keep the dogs off the ice as much as possible, determined to keep them safe from the serpent's poison lash.

Zellie yelped in obvious pain.

Rune and Anya both rushed to her at the same time.

Xander barked wildly, still hitched in place and unable to go to Zellie. The rest of the dogs barked, too.

Frank Lundgren's team had just passed by. No one saw his lead dog, Brutus, lash out at Zellie and bite her. It happened too fast for anyone in the crowd to witness. No one paid any mind to Zellie's painful wail or the reaction of her upset team. Many of the dog teams already barked excitedly while they waited to start their run. Standing out in heavy snow, most in the crowd had their eyes trained on the next team started.

Frank Lundgren snickered to himself. Works every time, he thought maliciously. He'd have more shots at the upstart kid's team before this race was over.

Zellie stood still and whimpered but didn't move while Anya examined her.

"*Blood,* Rune. Look." Anya pulled her fingers out from beneath Zellie's collar. "The holes are deep. She's been bitten."

Rune thought of the serpent. He thought of the snaking shadows.

Anya spied the team in front of theirs, thinking of the mean dog driver who used a whip. His lead dog looked just as mean as he did, and he was a mix of breeds she didn't recognize. She didn't trust the dog any more than the man. The dog snarled at her when she caught its eye. It had to be the dog that attacked Zellie. It wasn't bad spirits that hurt Zellie. The shadows had no bite, not like this.

"Is she all right?" Rune asked quietly, worried about Zellie. It had to be a dog bite and not a serpent, but still, he wasn't convinced. Ghosts lurked, he was sure.

"She will be. I have something I can use." Anya reached inside a pocket for her medicine pouch, for the paste she used on wounds. She opened the container of homemade salve and rubbed medicine into the holes made by the teeth of the dog.

"There, Zellie girl," Anya cooed as she treated Zellie's neck. Then Anya ripped a strip of soft hide from the inside of her kerker, and wrapped it over a portion of Zellie's collar, to help prevent rubbing and further injury.

"Anya, do you want her to stay with you? Maybe we can —"

"No, Rune!" Anya didn't let him finish.

Zellie jumped at her upset.

"No." Anya softened her tone. "We can't win without Zellie. She's the leader dog. We need her." Anya put her cheek against Zellie and hugged her close. "She's my brave Chukchi girl. She knows what she must do." Anya held onto Zellie until the dog felt steadied.

The rest of the dogs watched, Xander especially, then steadied despite the race activity all around them. Arctic winds gusted and surged through Nome, blunting some of the noise made by the cheering crowd.

"Take this." Anya eased away from Zellie and handed Rune her container of salve. "You might need it again."

Rune pocketed the salve, glad to have it, expecting more trouble ahead. He petted Zellie reassuringly, then looked at Anya.

"What, I mean which dog bit her?" He had to catch himself from saying anything about his earlier suspicion of ghosts.

"The leader dog from the same team I've warned you about. Their driver uses a whip. I know it. Their sled is just ahead of ours."

"Did you see it happen?"

"No, but I didn't have to. I know which dog. I know," Anya said.

Rune believed her.

"I'll be right back." He started for the sled

365

and team she'd pointed out.

Anya caught his arm.

"Save your anger and your strength for the fight ahead. We can't risk being disqualified from the race. You don't know what the judges might do if they see you fighting with another dog driver. It might break rules. Please, Rune," Anya implored.

Rune struggled to relax his fists. He knew she was right. In one hand he held wisdom and in the other war. His wisdom won out, at least for the moment. This was one more reason to keep his guard up; he had to watch out for Frank Lundgren's whip and his dogs.

He'd heard Frank Lundgren's name called out when he was inside the Board of Trade Saloon to register. Rune wouldn't forget the name, the face, or the sled. He knew Frank Lundgren wouldn't play by any rules, and he knew he'd never get an "on by" from the likes of the lowlife dog driver. If Lundgren tried to make another move against any dog on his team, Rune didn't think wisdom would win out a second time.

Just then Frank Lundgren's team shot down the street and was quickly out of sight in the heavy snowfall. Startled, Rune exhaled sharply then watched the sled disappear into the storm before calmly taking his position behind his own team and sled. Fully dressed for the race, he had on a hooded, knee-length fur parka over a layer of pants, shirt, and long underwear. Mukluks would keep his feet and legs warm. He'd brought his fur hat and hand mitts, both needed for protection. Making sure of his dogs, he mentally went over each position, each dog's abilities, and the dangers each one faced.

He would check Zellie's wound during rest periods and give her the extra care she needed, watching her for any new problems. He then mentally calculated all the goods loaded in the sled's basket, the food and supplies they'd need over the next four days. Next he went over the race trail in his mind, telegraph lines and all, having memorized the stops and the mile markers along the trail. He would rely heavily on his natural-born navigation skills to guide him, and he prayed the sunstone of the ancients would be with him. And all the gods, he underscored in his prayer.

It was only when he realized the dogs might not return, or him, either, that he remembered Anya. If he failed her in any way, he wouldn't see her again. The thought upset him enough to force him to look at her when he'd rather not face this particular fear. He didn't think he could take seeing those long, dusky lashes close over those sparkling seal-brown eyes for the last time.

Their glances met, and they were both filled with confusing, unexpected emotion.

Anya hadn't been able to take her eyes from Rune, much as she'd tried. Her focus should be on the dogs and the dogs only, but for the life of her she couldn't control her feelings. What if . . . what if something happened? What if this was the last time she'd see him in this life; the last time she felt his strong presence; the last time she saw his ice-blue eyes; the last time she heard him say her name; the last time for everything, for *any* more time with him?

Vitya's necklace heated against her skin, which made her reach for it and think of him. He was far away, in their home village. Vitya was gone from her life but not dead. At least she hoped nothing had happened to him. She dismissed the idea this was any kind of sign and let go of the husky carving.

Her anxious thoughts went back to Rune. He might die.

Even through the snow, Rune could see tears welled in Anya's expressive, sad eyes. They reached out to him the same way they had months ago on his father's ship. He'd let her down then. What if he let her down again? His chest suddenly felt heavy for an altogether different reason. What if he never saw her again? He had to look away from her.

Crestfallen, Anya fought new tears when he did. She pulled the hood of her kerker down far enough to hide her upset from Rune. It hurt when he looked away from her, especially at this moment when they had to part.

"May the Creator god and the Earth god and all the gods be with you," she whispered, not expecting him to hear her over the sharp whistle of the arctic winds.

"And you," he whispered softly, willing to give up Valhalla to win this race for her.

Anya felt a shudder.

"Go!" The starting judge suddenly called out.

Rune gripped the handlebar, forcing himself not to look back at Anya.

"Mush!"

Zellie took off, with all the dogs instantly pulling in turn, and they disappeared in a flurry down the street, head-on into the storm.

Anya watched them.

A thin crowd cheered for Rune, but many folks had already left for home to escape the weather, while others moved inside the

Board of Trade Saloon to watch the chalk-board. Press from Nome and the Outside had already found a warm spot inside race headquarters. Admittedly, some onlookers didn't think enough of Rune's team to stay and watch its start. Bettors knew which teams had a good shot at winning. None of them thought "Rune Johansson's sled had a chance in hell" to finish, much less win. None of them but the Eskimo, that is.

The Eskimos stayed to watch Rune start; every man, woman, and child in attendance. Their native spirit spoke to them, telling them of the spirit within each of the Chukchi dogs. The Chukchi had once been their enemy, but were no longer. Now their spirits ran together in the All Alaska Sweepstakes of 1909. The Eskimos left after Rune did, worried over the fierce storm coming. They wondered what the next days might bring to them all. The gods must be angry.

Dark shadows and shapes collected in snowy swirls in and around Nome's streets and byways, coming together in whooshes and whispers on the wind as if gathering for a storm. The icy winds picked up and carried the ever-gathering storm out of Nome, then headed right onto the race trail in the direction of Candle.

Only Anya remained at the race start.

Rune was gone. She'd never felt so alone. She'd never been more scared for her dogs. Their fate was in Rune's hands and not hers. She felt helpless.

The snow and winds refused to die down.

Securing her hood and kerker against the weather, she reminded herself that Rune had capable hands to run the race and care for her dogs. The dogs trusted him, respected him. That meant everything in dog driving. Zellie and Xander and the team would run for him until they could run no more. For ones so gentle in nature, the Chukchi dogs were tough, fast, and enduring. This was the secret of the Chukchi breed. This secret held the power of life and death.

It is time. It is time to save us all, child.

Anya remembered her grandmother's words of warning; she would live by them or die by them. Unsure of what Nana-tasha meant, exactly, by her warning, Anya had no doubts about what she'd do: she'd protect the dogs at all cost. This was a race for survival, "to save us all." Anya whispered on the arctic winds, and hoped her message carried to Zellie's ear and to Rune's. May her Spirit follow theirs every day and every step of the way.

On that wishful thought, Anya turned in

the direction of their rented stable corner. She would pray, yet again. If she had any powers at all as a shaman, as a medium between worlds, she intended to pray for these powers to help Rune and the dogs — *to save us all.*

Starting at ten in the morning and leaving at fifteen-minute-intervals, all fourteen sled-dog teams had departed Nome by two-thirty that afternoon. All headed into the same storm. Eleven teams arrived back in Nome by nightfall, eliminated from the race due to the blinding blizzard. Some had gotten as far as Safety, twenty-two miles out, but the majority didn't even make it to the Cape Nome checkpoint, thirteen miles out.

Weary dog drivers checked back in at the Board of Trade Saloon with stories of "the most violent storm I've ever come across," and "I'm all in," and "my dogs couldn't see shit and I couldn't, either!"

The weather in Nome had cleared, but inside race headquarters things still stormed. Bettors argued back and forth as they saw which teams returned and they waited nervously for news of the rest. No one could hear much of anything above the hubbub. Those who didn't curse the weather cursed the dog drivers. Those who didn't curse the dog drivers cursed the dogs. Those who didn't curse either of those, cursed the day they came to Nome looking for gold in the first place!

Something wasn't right, they all agreed, despite their money worries, and despite knowing the Alaska frontier weather was always unpredictable. No one could say exactly what, but *something* wasn't right.

Unable to stay away from race headquarters herself, Anya hoped she'd be allowed inside to find out about Rune and her dogs. She couldn't read the results posted, but she could listen, and she could ask questions. Before when she'd tried to enter the saloon, she'd been tossed out, told, "No child, Eskimo or white," was allowed inside.

Plenty of young people had lined the street earlier to watch the race start. Shouldn't they all be allowed inside now, to learn the results? Anya thought so. In any event, she hoped that same woman wasn't inside to spot her.

Anya didn't have to worry over being noticed; she discovered that the moment she entered the Board of Trade Saloon. There was too much noise and commotion in the crowded room for anybody to worry about her age or sex or her race. Unlike before, when she'd hidden behind a wall of casks, Anya didn't try to hide. She made her way straight through the press of men gathered around the chalkboard. Hood off but still in her kerker, she elbowed her way through to the front, anxious for news of Rune's sled. Beyond upset with herself for not being able to read English, she watched a man rub words off the board, hearing shouts come from the crowd at the same time.

"Aw, hell, Percy Blatchford's been taken off," one man complained.

"Damn shame!" another seconded.

"What about Coke Hill or Fay Delzene?" someone yelled.

"Out, too, both of 'em!"

Disappointed murmurs sounded through the crowd.

"Who's left, then?" someone shouted over the din.

Everyone quieted at the all-important question.

So tense she couldn't breathe, Anya waited with the rest to hear Rune's fate. The dogs' lives hung in the balance of the faceless man's simple question.

As promised, and as a rightful member of the Nome Kennel Club, Bartholomew guarded the chalkboard with his life. He raised his shirtsleeve-rolled arms out to get everybody's full attention.

"There are three teams left in the All Alaska Sweepstakes, friends. They are Scotty Allan, Frank Lundgren, and Rune Johansson."

Anya let out the breath she'd been holding.

"What?" a man roared.

"That can't be!" another complained, just as loudly.

"All right, all right, folks. Settle down," Bartholomew said, and he turned to the board to rechalk the three drivers at the top of the board.

He put Scotty Allan's name at the top, since his sled had already checked in at the Topkok Roadhouse forty-eight miles out.

Next he listed Frank Lundgren's name, since he'd checked in at Solomon before Rune. At the checkpoints, watchers had already telegraphed the standings.

Rune Johansson checked in after Frank Lundgren at the thirty-three-mile checkpoint, so the board now indicated.

Finished with the current standings, Bartholomew turned back to the crowd of bettors.

Shouts fired at him.

"It can't be that those Siberian rats are still in it!"

"Must be some cheatin' going on, Bartholomew!"

"Scotty better watch his back, is all I got to say!"

"Johansson's sled ain't gonna make it back, I'm bettin'!"

Bartholomew raised his arms out again.

"Settle down. There's no reason to think anything is interfering with this race but this blizzard. You folks know better. You know what conditions are like right now. Settle down. We've got watchers at every checkpoint. Nobody has telegraphed here that anybody's cheating." Bartholomew stared hard at the crowd, daring them to shout any more rumors about cheating. He would stand by the chalkboard and guard it, and stand by every rule set down by the Nome Kennel Club!

Still, one bettor couldn't keep quiet.

"Everybody's got their money on Scotty! He'd better win, or we're coming for you, Bartholomew!"

A gun went off, and a bullet pierced the ceiling: Albert Fink's Smith & Wesson .44.

The entire room had his undivided attention. He didn't yell, but he spoke with enough voice for everyone to hear him clearly.

"No need for you guys to get as violent as

the storm. No need for threats. I know this is about money to a lot of you, but it better never be about anything else. It better never be about going after anybody, or I'll go to Fort Davis and any other place I have to, to bring the law down on you." Albert reholstered his pistol and sat back down at the table where he'd been having his supper.

Bartholomew broke the tense silence.

"All right then, you've all heard Albert and you know he's a man of his word. I'll keep current with all the results and checkpoints for you. Yes, sir. I'll be right here," he reiterated, nodding to the crowd.

With that, despite a grumble here and there, most people in the Board of Trade Saloon scattered about the room — all but Anya. As luck would have it, she'd yet to be noticed and tossed out. Good — she didn't want to be. Scanning the smoke-filled room, she spotted the familiar wall of casks and made her way over to it and hunkered down to hide. Then she stripped down to her native dress and long underwear. The saloon was hot, too hot. No matter, she had to stay and hear the results as they came in. It wasn't much, waiting to see what happened, but she had to be here.

She had to know if something went wrong.

CHAPTER THIRTEEN

Since Frank Lundgren's team reached the Topkok Roadhouse first, he and his dogs had the best accommodations, with Frank getting the warmest bunk inside and his dogs the thickest straw in the covered stable. All his dogs had been fed, watered, and secured so none could wander off.

With no one else having arrived, Frank didn't worry about leaving Brutus unguarded. Besides, if anyone tried to mess with his lead dog, Brutus would take care of 'em, he was sure. Frank had passed eleven teams going "on by" back to Nome before making his way to the Topkok checkpoint. He laughed to himself; he couldn't believe his luck with this blizzard. The weather had taken care of a lot of the teams, so he didn't have to worry over much competition now.

Scotty Allan had to be ahead of him, but Frank didn't doubt he'd catch up, no matter Scotty's reputation. Frank needed to best the expert dog driver. It was about time folks recognized him, Frank Lundgren, as an expert driver! Yeah, he'd best Scotty Allan by beating him fair and square. Most teams had already turned back. Maybe Scotty Allan would, too. Besides, it wouldn't do to go after the likes of Scotty Allan. He'd be done for in Nome if he were caught.

But as for the upstart kid, Frank had different ideas about how to best Rune Johansson. His ideas didn't have anything to do with fair and square. He'd make sure no checkpoint watchers would see what he did.

The ice over the Norton Sound proved too dangerous for Rune's sled to cross. Zellie would take off one way then the ice would crack and start separating. The same thing would happen when they'd try another path. Rune didn't doubt what was going on. Ghost or no ghost, the ancient serpent repeatedly butted its ugly head beneath the frozen layers, and forced the cracks and breaks. What else could cause this? It wasn't natural, what was happening. The glare from the snowstorm had blurred Rune's vision a little, but he didn't have to see through the ice to know what tried to stop him.

Maybe that was where all the shadows had gone; they'd disappeared like ghosts beneath the ice. He hadn't spotted any suspicious shadows since Nome. They lurked somewhere, cowards now, too afraid to show themselves and fight fair.

Zellie's skills and even temperament amazed Rune. She didn't react to the ice cracking other than to change direction. The rest of the team followed, with Xander and Midnight pulling their weight on each tight turn over the increasingly treacherous ice. Rune put his entire trust in the Chukchi dogs. He believed they knew the way to navigate the ice and find good footing against the enemy much better than he did.

Time became a blur, just like his vision, and he'd no idea how much they'd wasted already by dodging the serpent's deadly game. The old enemy of the Vikings had come out of hiding, at least enough for Rune to feel the wrath of the Midgard serpent. Any second the serpent might break through the ice and end it all.

Rune sent out a quick kissing sound to Zellie, signaling for her to speed up in spite of the impossible conditions. He knew he asked a lot of her, but he had no choice. He hadn't forgotten she ran hurt. Placing both feet on the sled's runners, he grasped the handle bar and held on for the bumpy ride. Heavy snow still clouded the path.

The dogs would run on instinct. He wasn't so sure of his own instincts at the moment, with his sense of direction and time blurred. Rune felt the dogs speed up, and he let them turn and go easily when they needed to. He wasn't about to interfere with them. The dogs were used to ice. He was used to navigating around ice, but not trying to race across it. Certainly, neither of them were used to fighting serpents — serpents from another world in time, that shouldn't be here! The sled suddenly lurched right.

"Haw!" Rune yelled reflexively for Zellie to turn left.

She'd already tried, with Magic and Mushroom struggling to help her. The ice was giving way beneath them. Xander and Midnight trod on ice and water, using all their strength to keep out of the frigid depths. All the dogs worked as one, and pulled with everything in them, trying to save their guardian. They all sensed his danger, and theirs.

Rune pulled with all his might, too, to recover the sled that was already partway underwater. Some of its provisions fell into the icy water. Rune grabbed hold of the main pack and kept hold of it along with the handlebar. Reaching for strength that none of them had, after expending so much energy fighting the storm no doubt brought by the serpent, Rune and the dogs managed to set the sled on thin ice, then thicker ice, and then off the ice entirely. They'd made land!

Rune thanked every god he could think of — Odin especially.

The wolf and the dog battle as one.

In the distance Rune picked up the cry of the wolf.

Zellie answered with her howl, and then Xander did with a howl of his own. Off the ice and out of immediate danger, the whole team howled instinctively as a pack, answering the triumphant cry of the wolf. Little Wolf howled the loudest and longest, instinct making him feel every bit the master on this day, in this battle.

Once the sled rested safely on the frozen shore, Rune carefully checked Zellie before the other dogs. He felt under her collar to make sure her wound hadn't opened, and was relieved to find it had not. She licked his cold fingers then nudged away.

"You're a tough girl, you are," Rune praised her, and gave her a soft pet behind an ear before going to Magic and Mushroom. Other than their harnesses slipping a little, they were all right. So was the rest of the team. Rune made sure to run his hands over Midnight's old wound from the grizzly to ensure that the injured place hadn't opened again, the same as he had Zellie. Relying more on touch than sight, Rune shook his head to better clear his blurry vision. Concerned about snow blindness, he made a mental note to try to keep his eyes shut against the storm as much as possible. He had known this race wasn't going to be easy. Well, it wasn't.

Relieved to have escaped the serpent this time, Rune knew there was no escaping the blizzard. Which one was worse? He wasn't so sure, in the face of this blizzard. The brutal weather had already taken its toll on the dogs. Now that they were back on land, he needed to get them past Safety and then on to Topkok. At the roadhouse he would be fifty miles out on the race trail, with over three hundred and fifty still to go.

Yes, he still had a race to run and a finish line to cross. In all this uproar, he'd almost forgotten.

It did little good for Rune to worry over anything but mushing forward. If he stopped to worry about shadows and shapes giving chase, they were all dead. This weather was a killer. He'd almost died before in just this kind of weather. The dogs had helped bring him back from certain death. He hadn't forgotten. They'd just saved him again, by pulling him across the dangerous Norton Sound, and beating the icy serpent at its own game. He owed the dogs his life, and he'd give it willingly, to save them.

Once he had the sled set right again and could see the dogs were eager to go, Rune gave Zellie the command to mush. He pedaled, then ran alongside to help speed them along. With no trail carved out in the deepening snow, they had to make their own. Although they had been thrown off course by the ice, Rune knew they were now headed in the right direction, toward Safety, then Solomon, and then the roadhouse in Topkok, where they would stop in about thirty miles, he calculated. Without the storm and without any more problems, the Chukchi dogs could make up the distance in an hour and a half. With the storm, it could take them twice as long.

At least they didn't have to cross any places where the serpent could attack again. Rune thought they were safe from that danger. He couldn't believe he fought demons in mist and magic now! But he did.

As for any other problems, Rune would

keep watch. His vision had begun to clear along with his sense of direction, as if he were holding the sunstone of the Vikings up to the skies. He thought of the race and the other racers. Having been out on the ice for so long, he'd no idea about the many teams that had already turned back to Nome and gone "on by." All he knew was he had miles to go before he and the dogs would see Nome again, almost four hundred of them.

When Rune spotted telegraph lines, he knew he was on course. His eyes burned a little, but his vision improved. It was no worse than during a rough day at sea, he told himself. Sea or snow, they'd keep on the trail and win this race. He had to for Anya. She had no one but him. He couldn't leave her alone again as he did on the beach that day, a lifetime ago.

His course in life had changed direction the moment he discovered her stowed away on his father's ship. Whoever he was now, Rune wasn't that same boy. To prove it, he saw ghosts, even talked to them! Before he met Anya, this impossibility never happened. He'd never found himself in the world of the ancients, either. There had to be a connection, but what was it? He didn't have time to think about anything but winning the race and keeping the dogs safe.

Answers would have to come later — if there was a later. He'd wasted time. Angry at the downturn of his thoughts, Rune shrugged them off.

"Come gee!" he commanded, seeing the quick twist in the trail to the right and through the trees.

Zellie responded immediately without slowing her swift, steady pace.

Magic and Mushroom led to the right; the copper-red and white pair helped swing the sled.

The four huskies in the "power" position shifted with ease.

Xander and Midnight brought the sled around the difficult turn without a hitch.

Rune felt the determination and heart in each dog through the unexpected turn, maintaining their speed, steady as you go. They seemed all right even after their tough run across the frozen Norton Sound. The dogs showed no signs of tiring, even though Rune was sure they must be exhausted from their struggle over the ice, if not from withstanding the storm or the injuries they already carried. But not one complaint, not one falter, not one sign of giving up came from any of the Siberian huskies. If they feared any demons, they didn't show it.

Rune felt renewed respect for these dogs.

He sensed something magic within them, something that would keep them going against all odds. They'd need that magic and more to get them across the finish line, he knew. He hoped he had some of their same magic within him; then he remembered the mark at his neck and the secret of the runes.

Rune checked in at Solomon in two hours with no problems other than outwitting the blizzard. He'd made good time. He learned that two other teams had already checked in and that eleven teams had dropped out of the race. He'd never thought of dropping out, but he understood why others had. The weather plagued them all.

Then again, he had a fight on his hands that the others did not. *Nej,* dropping out wouldn't be a consideration. He decided to press on and cover the next fifteen miles needed to make it to the Topkok Roadhouse before he fed, watered, and rested the dogs. With a portion of his supplies gone, he hoped to replenish them at Topkok. Until then Zellie, Xander, and the rest of the team seemed eager to keep going. After he'd checked the paws on each dog for any injuries from the jagged ice, Rune followed the dogs' lead and headed back into the storm, anxious to reach Topkok. He had no idea Frank Lundgren lay in wait.

Stony shadows hovered over northeast Siberia, stretching as far as Anya's coastal village — the grayest of shadows that seeded and formed near the edges of the Black Sea.

Thirty times over the evil is born.
Thirty years coming and all will mourn.

Cruel winds blew all across Mother Russia, set to reach the very edges of Siberia and the Chukchi Sea. Once reached, the breach in Native Earth would be complete, the time of the Chukchi marked. No gods from worlds past or present, fighting together or alone, would be able to do anything about it.

The time of the Gatekeepers would be over. Their watch eyes would close, and with them, the gates of heaven.

Unless . . . Worlds ever brush past, both human and spirit. Good and Evil are born into each. Some become master; some do not.

Only human hands could slow down the breach in Native Earth and buy time. The breach would bring death, nothing but death from the ice storm. In the hands of two guardians rested the fate of all and the hope for survival of any. The human spirit

must prevail. The gods could not, for they are not mortal.

Born of ancestral spirit yet mortal themselves, unknowingly, Anya and Rune must continue to gain in strength and power, and create enough momentum to crash through and leave their own mark — to slow the killing ice storm.

There was no one else, in heaven or on Native Earth, who could.

Numb with tension, Anya tried to stay hunkered down in her hiding place behind the liquor casks in the Board of Trade Saloon. She kept her eyes peeled on the chalkboard and jumped every time she saw the man in charge of the board walk past it, or try to change something he'd written on it. Nothing in her life to this point seemed harder than waiting for the next announcement about the three sleds still out on the race course.

Even though the storm in Nome had quieted, she knew the one along the trail had not.

It still lashed at Rune and the dogs, whipping at them and trying to beat them down. So did the ravens, keeping up their attack. The ravens would spiral and spit until the last dog brought the last sled across the finish line, Anya believed. Which dogs would cross first and which last? Fear hit her all over again. It didn't help to remember the rule that all dogs starting must finish. The rule didn't stand up as any kind of protection against evil spirits from dark worlds! Mortal rules didn't apply to them.

Desperate for some way to help Rune and her dogs stay alive, much less win the race, Anya lowered herself behind the casks and shut her eyes, concentrating hard. Maybe she could talk with spirits and travel between worlds. She was shaman. Why not? If she couldn't do anything on Native Earth, maybe she'd be of some use in the spirit world.

She silently called to her Spirit and willed her husky counterpart to hear her and call back to her. If she truly had any powers, Anya would find out once and for all. She'd already experienced odd sensations, as if her physical body could disappear from Native Earth. Determined her Spirit would come to her with news of Rune and the dogs if she made contact, Anya concentrated hard on just that.

Long moments passed, but no call from Spirit came to her.

Anya's sinking emotions weighted her down. Her grandmother had been wrong.

Other than wished-for mystical beliefs, Anya had no power, human or spirit, to help in this dark hour. All of her fourteen years on Native Earth counted for nothing! She angrily wiped away her tears with the back of her hand, and ignored the fact she had the shakes. Filled with disappointment and beyond upset at herself, she didn't worry over anything but this.

Zellie was out there and needed her. Xander was out there. Magic, Mushroom, Frost, Flowers, Midnight, Midday, Little Wolf . . . and Rune, too, needed her help. Anya's shivers hadn't quit. She was hot, *not* cold. What a nuisance!

She imagined the dogs' watch eyes on her, waiting for her to come. She'd trade her life to have Zellie and Xander close again. I've failed them, she thought pitifully. Her tremors subsided a little. In the next moment she fell into a dispirited, exhausted sleep.

The dark elves didn't hesitate to taunt her with their nightmarish whispers of the whip she so feared. They planted doubts, creating mischief. Anya could do *nothing* to save her dogs from the whip in this world or any other, they told her. She'd no powers to help them.

■ ■ ■ ■

The Gatekeepers kept their watch-blue eyes on Frank Lundgren. They'd already shut the gates of heaven to him. Cruel and unkind, he used a whip. Only on rare occasions did the Gatekeepers allow a second chance. Frank Lundgren had already used up too many chances. From their sentry positions they never missed any movement on Native Earth against their own.

Their guardians must beware. The ice storm grew. The Raven flew full against them now, strengthened by *Hel.* Time had been marked, running out faster than prophesied. Centuries had dwindled to precious years. There was much to be done. The Gatekeepers would keep watch over Rune and Anya each step of the way. Their trials were not over, and would not be, until the end.

"Whoa!" Rune called out to his team, as they finally arrived at the Topkok Roadhouse; the outline of the cabin and stable was barely visible. The storm hadn't quit. His dogs hadn't either. There were moments over the last fifteen miles when Rune thought he might. He'd already come back

392

from the dead in one storm, but he doubted he'd have the same luck a second time. His cold, stiff fingers refused to bend inside his fur mitts. His toes could be broken off inside his mukluks for all he knew. Each time he breathed in, the air caught and froze in his chest.

He worried about the dogs.

Throwing the snow hook hard enough to stick into ground, Rune fought his way through the weather to reach Zellie first.

"Look at you, pretty girl," he crooned, and quickly brushed the snow and ice from her husky mask.

Still at her sled position, Zellie licked Rune's frozen fingers.

Once Rune checked her, he went down the line of dogs, first to Magic, then working his way lengthways to Midnight and then around the sled to Xander. Working back up, he ended with Mushroom. They were fine, all of them. Rune had never felt so relieved. The sheer determination and heart within these animals impressed him all over again. Once he had them fed, watered, and bedded down, he'd make sure of their paws and webbing. The race depended on having heart, but it depended on having unhurt feet, too.

"Say there!"

Rune turned in the direction of the shout. A man in a hooded fur parka approached.

"Say there," the man said again and patted Rune on the back. "You must be Rune Johansson."

"Yeah." Rune said, a little suspicious and moving out of range of any more back pats.

"Then these fellows must be your Siberian rats. Eh, excuse me, your Siberian wolves," he said jokingly, and bent down close to Zellie for a better look.

"Keep away from my Siberian *huskies*," Rune warned, then stepped in between the stranger and Zellie.

"Son, I'm not gonna mess with your leader dog, and I didn't mean any offense. I'd heard about your dogs. That's all. I meant no harm." The man took a step back. "I'm Farley Smith, and this is my roadhouse. Come on inside and meet Seth Granger. He's the watcher here for the race and the one telegraphing things back to Nome." With that, Farley head back toward his cabin.

"Wait!" Rune yelled through the weather. "I mean to see to the dogs first."

Farley reapproached.

"Sure thing, son. Bring your dogs round to the stable yonder. There's plenty of straw, and I'll fetch water."

Rune nodded a thank you.

Farley plowed through the snow and went back inside his cabin for the promised water.

Rune yanked up the snow hook, then took hold of Zellie's collar and gently tugged her in the direction of the stable, to get her, the others, and the sled, closer in to their shelter. He didn't hear Farley Smith say anything about other racers ahead of him. Both teams must have already cleared the Topkok Roadhouse, since Rune and his dogs had the prime stable shelter. It was good luck to have the prime shelter but bad luck he was still running last.

He was glad the roadhouse had fresh water. That meant they likely had food to share with his dogs. He'd use what supply he still had for this rest stop and secure more for the days to come.

After he unhooked each dog from the towline, Rune let them wander inside the dim stable and settle down on their own. He wouldn't tie them to any post. He didn't have to. Besides, if they had to face any unforeseen danger, he didn't want them handicapped. If they needed to take off, he wanted them to be able to do so. They would come back to him when they could. He'd no doubt of it. Using all the time he needed, Rune took great care in removing each dog's harness and placing it next to them.

Farley Smith stepped out of the storm and inside the stable with two buckets of water.

"Here you go, son." He set the water down. "What's the weight on your huskies?" he asked, obviously still curious about the Siberian team.

Rune moved the water buckets to within easy reach of all the dogs. He watched them drink.

"Average weight," he finally answered.

"So what's that?" Farley started to come closer.

"Forty-five to fifty pounds," Rune said, hoping to cut the man off with the truth. No need for the huskies to be disturbed any more than they already were.

Farley Smith burst out laughing.

"Average weight, my Aunt Fanny!" he said and shook his head back and forth. "Son, the huskies here in these parts are much bigger and stronger. You got game to run your Siberian huskies agin 'em, I'll give you that."

"Game's better than nothing," Rune gritted out, more for his own benefit than Farley Smith's. No one needed to remind him how the odds were stacked against them from the start.

"It sure is, son," the now serious road-house owner said. "Listen, when you're all done here, come inside for vittles and a warm bunk. Nothing like food in your stomach and a good rest to get you back in the race," Farley added, sounding concerned, almost fatherly.

"Thanks," Rune mumbled back, with Farley having struck a nerve. It wasn't the time or place to remember family. Rune didn't think they missed him anyway, especially his father. His mother or his sister, either.

Just then Zellie nudged her head under Rune's hand, forcing a pet.

Xander did more than that. He suddenly lifted himself on his hind legs and pushed against Rune with his front paws in play, which set Rune's footing off.

"Hey now," Rune protested with a laugh, grateful for their companionship and loyalty. He didn't know what he'd done to deserve it, but he welcomed it all the same. These dogs felt more like family to him than his own, especially here, especially now. The gods of the ancients didn't need to ask for his help. He'd give it willingly, no questions asked. That's what family should do.

"Time to eat and then rest, you guys," Rune announced, and gave Zellie and

Xander a last pat. "We've got a lot of ground to cover when the weather breaks." He fetched the supply pack from the sled and divided out the dried fish, one going to each dog. The food was gone at once. Rune watched the dogs gobble their portion then settle in sleepy circles, each one, on the straw-covered stable floor. Satisfied the dogs were all right, he headed inside the Topkok Roadhouse, looking forward to a little food and rest himself.

Almost a day lost! Precious hours in the race! The storm finally let up. Rune anxiously harnessed his team then hitched them to the towline. The sun had even come out, so brightly his eyes saw black shadows around every corner. This made him hurry all the more. Glare from the snow or from the sun both blinded, and each caused shadows he didn't want.

Soon he had his team geared up and the sled ready to go. They had to make up lost time. If lucky, he'd go "on by" the other sleds before the day was out. If unlucky . . . He didn't want to think about that.

"Good luck, son." Farley Smith had come outside.

Rune nodded to him and then placed his hands securely on the sled's handlebar.

"Mush!"

Eager and ready, the dogs took off in a heartbeat. Sometimes pedaling, sometimes running alongside, and sometimes placing his feet on both runners, Rune did whatever he could to help add his speed to that of the dogs. Their energy fueled his, and kept him on the path to Candle. They had to pass through five checkpoints before Candle: Timber, Council, Telephone, Haven, and First Chance. Rune went over every inch of the roughly one hundred fifty miles in his head. There were some bad spots coming up. He didn't look forward to the glacial lakes or the "valley of blizzards" they'd have to cross. In spite of the sunshine overhead, it wouldn't last and Rune knew it. They'd hit storms again, soon enough.

When the trail called for it and the dogs could run across open tundra, Rune experienced the true might of the Chukchi dog. They ran smooth, solid, and fast; never veering, never seeming to tire. Rune could feel their muscled strength pump through the sled and through him. They ran as one, *the wolf and the dog.*

He thought of Odin, of the wolf he'd encountered on the beaches of Nome who told him the secret of the runes. In true Viking spirit, Rune felt like a part of the wolf rested within him. The mark at his neck gave him reason to think so. He wasn't any god, but he would heed the gods, since he needed their help every step of the way to Candle and on the return to Nome.

Anya waited in Nome.

He was remembering her bright smile, then her seal-brown eyes and the look of trust she had for him. She was depending on him. He sent a quick kissing sound to Zellie to speed up the sled, when he didn't need to. Zellie and the dogs already ran at top speed, as if they knew Anya was depending on them, too. If they didn't encounter any problems, Rune figured they'd reach Candle in eight to ten hours.

Two hours went by. Then three, then four, and on they ran, and let nothing stand in their way. When the winds picked up speed, so did the team. When snow began to fall again, the dogs dug their paw pads in deeper and kept on. Rune watched each dog as they ran for any sign of injury or fatigue. He was exhausted himself, but he wouldn't give in to it. He couldn't. It would slow the team and handicap their chance to be first across the finish line.

At each checkpoint he asked for any news of the other racers, but no one at Timber, Council, or Telephone had anything to tell him except that the dog drivers had checked on through. At the last stop, the race watcher had reported downed telegraph lines and trouble with communication.

Rune immediately suspected what had brought the lines down, and it wasn't bad weather. In warmer months a lightning storm could down power lines. The winds of winter could also down the lines, but then so could other forces, evil forces never heard or seen before, never dreamed by anyone living on the wild Alaska frontier. If he tried to tell anybody about being pursued by the Midgard serpent over the Norton Sound, they would laugh at him, call him crazy, and tell him he was seeing ghosts. Well, he *was* seeing ghosts. Not long ago he might have laughed at the idea, but not now.

People might accuse him of not having good sense, but he didn't care. Heck, he didn't think most miners and locals in Nome had any sense themselves, the way they only seemed to want gold and more gold, like they had gold dust running through their brains that kept them from thinking straight. They had gold fever. There were lots of ways a man could die. Rune suspected gold fever was one.

Greed clouded people's minds and hardened their hearts. It was true for his mother and his sister, Inga. They woke up greedy and went to bed greedy. Neither would ever be mistaken for having a heart of gold. Funny, he thought, that choice of words. He tried to shrug off the odd turn of his thoughts. More and more, thoughts of his past came back to haunt him. He didn't like the feeling, and he didn't have time for any distractions now. He needed to think about reaching Candle.

"Easy!" he called out to Zellie to slow down, edgy all of a sudden at the feel of the ground beneath, as if the sled traversed ice and not snow.

Zellie took his command immediately, signaling to Magic and Midnight with her clear change in speed. The copper-red and white pair swung the team behind Zellie just enough to keep their rhythm, yet begin to slow. The huskies in the power position ran easily now. Little Wolf had the most trouble slowing. The eager runt stubbornly obeyed. As for Midnight and Xander, they took the force of the change in speed, in muscled stride, and made sure the sled stayed a safe distance from them.

"*Mush!*" Rune called the sudden change, sensing danger beneath them. They had to outrun whatever it was. He had to take the risk, even though the sled's weight and their moves might cause the ice to give way. They must be over one of the glacial lakes he'd been warned about. But he didn't remember any lake between Telephone and Haven? He must have missed it.

Zellie changed her speed to full, and all the dogs followed in kind. They ran as one over the unsure ice. Something thrashed beneath it. Their canine instincts sensed the danger they were in. Still, they didn't slow down, used to the hunt; used to running despite stormy weather and bad conditions. They were born and bred to run. They wouldn't stop until their guardian ordered them to, or until they couldn't run any more. In no time, they'd cleared the frozen lake.

Rune breathed easier.

Finally making it to First Chance, the last stop before Candle, Rune slowed the team to a stop. They had outrun the serpent and anything else that might have tried to chase them down. He didn't know if any shadows followed them. He couldn't see the edges of anything, and believed himself to be snow-blind. Maybe his vision would come back; he couldn't count on it. There wasn't much he could do but rely on Zellie and her guidance and the rest of the team's help. He had the trail fixed in his head — at least he had that, even if he couldn't see it clearly.

"You all right, Rune Johansson?" A man approached.

"Yeah," Rune answered. The man's face was a blur to him.

"Well, you've got near forty miles to Candle. You gonna make it?" the checkpoint watcher asked. "By the way, I'm Hank Bronson."

"Yeah, I'll make it," was all Rune said.

"Sure you don't wanna stop here a spell? You look done in."

Rune bristled at the comment.

"We're not done in, my dogs and me. Have the others gone on by?"

"You mean Allan and Lundgren?"

"Yeah, that's who I mean," Rune said, his back still stiff.

"They headed out of here, Allan afore Lundgren, and likely rested in Candle. They're probably there now, the both of 'em," Hank threw in. "The telegraph is sketchy at best. Don't know for sure."

Rune still couldn't bring his vision into focus. Hank Bronson seemed friendly enough, but Rune didn't have time for anything but leaving First Chance.

"We'll be on our way, Hank. If you can, send back to Nome that our sled is good. Will you do that?" Rune thought of Anya waiting to hear.

"Sure thing, Rune Johansson," Hank assured him.

Rune appreciated that the checkpoint watcher didn't have anything critical to say about his Siberian huskies, and that he didn't call them rats or little wolves. Rune took that as a sign of respect.

"Mush!"

On his command, the dogs set off for Candle, where they would take their much-needed rest. Rune knew he had time to make up, but he wouldn't do it at the expense of the dogs. They had to rest. Glad to have the provisions he picked up in Top-kok, he was anxious to give the dogs a good meal. Luckily, Farley Smith had just had his supplies replenished and could help Rune out. Rune didn't know about race rules. It shouldn't be a disqualifier, giving food when it was needed.

In the distance Rune heard the cry of the wolf, as if it were drawing the sled to the sound. He had the strangest feeling the wolves could somehow sense his predicament, that he couldn't see well. Rune shook his head to help clear it. He was thinking crazy. True, he couldn't command Zellie to "gee" or "haw" with any accuracy, to turn right or left on the trail; but he refused to entertain any more crazy thoughts about wolves guiding him to Candle. Zellie would do that.

Everything rested on her now.

If he lost her . . . all *would be* lost.

CHAPTER FOURTEEN

Anya woke with a start. Her necklace burned against her skin. *Vitya!* She'd dreamed of him and not Rune, and had imagined Vitya in trouble, calling for her, but she couldn't reach him. He drifted farther and farther from her on a jagged ice floe, then suddenly disappeared into a black sea, pulled down into the unknown Deep. She'd called out to him, desperate to hear his voice, but no sounds echoed from beneath the ice

When she awoke, she was glad to discover it was only a dream, but her relief quickly turned to worry. Dreams brought signs. Why would she dream of him now? Vitya was in danger. Her hand went to the pocket of her kerker, to her knife. Separated by the great Bering Sea, they were an ocean apart, she and Vitya, and she could do nothing to help him.

She was worried enough over Rune and

the dogs. Now she had new worries about her forever friend back in her village. Only half awake, she imagined hearing him whisper, *gitengev,* calling her "pretty girl," over the din of noise in the crowded race headquarters.

The race!

She forgot all about her necklace and Vitya.

Jarred fully awake, she rubbed her eyes hard then turned to peer over the liquor casks at the all-important chalkboard, looking for any changes in the marks, trying to see if any names had disappeared. Rune's had been listed at the bottom. Men stood in front of the board. Panicked, she couldn't see anything. As she was about to come out from her hiding place, one man shouted over the rest.

"Telegraph lines are down, all of 'em between here and Candle. The storm brought 'em down, folks," Bartholomew soberly announced.

"How do you know?" someone shouted back.

"You think that Rune Johansson did something?" another asked accusingly.

"Bad luck, those Siberian rats in our race!"

"All right now." Bartholomew spoke loud and clear. "Hold your horses. You know what kind of damage bad storms cause. Not a one of you in this room can deny it. Besides, you think any of the racers left have time for anything but trying to make it back here in one piece?"

Anya froze in the too-warm saloon. Fighting renewed panic she instantly remembered the grotesque snaking whip that crawled out of her nightmares when she was at the mission school, the evil that tried to suffocate the dogs. Its lash snaked and bit, and had left trails of blood. Its monstrous tentacles, not any ordinary storm, had taken down the telegraph lines, she feared, and she clutched her knife hard. She'd been able to do something then, and master the evil. The circling Raven stalked Rune and her dogs still, and wanted their blood! The Raven wouldn't stop until —

Anya couldn't finish her thought. Out of time, her physical body had already begun to disappear into the spirit world.

Exhausted, done in but alive, and without new troubles hindering them in spite of the storm, Rune and his loyal team made it to the remote mining town of Candle, the halfway point in the All Alaska Sweepstakes. Whether Zellie carried them the right way on her own or with the guide of distant howling wolves, Rune didn't know, but he was relieved they had finally arrived at the 204-mile-marker checkpoint. His eyes burned; his vision was poor. He'd slowed the team. *Dammit.*

Maybe he just needed a little rest and his vision would get better. Fuzzy vision or not, he'd go on after this stop. Right now the dogs needed to eat and sleep, especially after all they'd been through so far in the race. Their breed would run until they could run no more, and Rune knew it. He'd moved beyond admiration to a place of awe. Wherever the other racers were on the trail, Rune believed he'd catch up to them, given time. He'd made a promise to Anya and he meant to keep it.

It was the middle of the night, Rune guessed, as far as he could tell. He'd lost track of time since the Topkok Roadhouse. Had one day gone by or two? Had the storm let up yesterday or today, only to return with more force? He couldn't afford any confusion, with the lives of the dogs in his hands. Where was the wisdom he supposedly held in one of his hands? Right now he felt anything but wise, even doubting the secret of the runes. Maybe he didn't carry the sign of the ancient gods. Maybe the gods only existed in his dreams. Some Viking warrior he made!

An uproar from the dogs got his attention.

Rune scanned his surroundings, his eyes strained, but he saw nothing except the dark outline of the few buildings and structures in town. No lanterns shone from any one of them, welcoming him to the checkpoint. It seemed as if no one expected him. Strange, he thought, uneasy over the eerie sensation. He didn't see or hear anything that might have upset his dogs. Snow fell slightly in the dim moonlight, he could tell. He could feel it on his face. The winds had died. At sea he would have thought himself in the eye of the storm. Maybe that's exactly what upset the dogs: *they were.*

The moment he spotted a sled and team of dogs flash by in a blur and heard the crack of a whip, he knew it had to be Frank Lundgren's team leaving the Candle checkpoint. The sound of the punishing whip told him all he needed in order to identify the dog driver. The poor excuse for a man had waited until he was out of Nome to beat his own dogs to a win. Anya had been right to warn Rune about him.

Rune's team tried to take off after Lundgren's team, still raising an uproar.

"Whoa!" Rune yelled his command and

411

was able to dig the snow hook in the ground in time to help him hold back his team. "Whoa!" He knew why all the dogs wanted Frank Lundgren and his leader dog, Brutus. The dogs wanted to be released for the hunt, maybe not to kill, but to circle and stop their prey long enough to best them. Rune could feel their thirst for revenge through the handlebar of the sled, the way they angrily yanked and pulled on their lines. Even the gentle Chukchi dogs had their limits.

"Easy!" he yelled reflexively, when all he wanted to do was release them and follow Frank Lundgren himself. "Easy now," he said again. "We'll catch up soon enough," he promised, and stopped at that.

Zellie and all the dogs finally quieted and began to settle, although they were still restless in their hitched positions.

"Say, what's all this?" A man suddenly appeared next to Rune.

"A race team," Rune answered, as deadpan as he felt.

"Well, I'll be." The man scratched his uncovered head. He looked like he'd just woken up and thrown on his parka for good measure to go outside.

His vision seemed improved, and Rune tried to take the man's measure.

"I thought only two teams was left in this race, son. You must be Rune Johansson. Frank Lundgren said you was not a'coming. He said you done dropped out at Topkok. Telegraph lines went down so's I didn't know different, or I'd of been a'waiting for you."

"Wishful thinking on his part," Rune deadpanned again.

"I'm Buster Upton and damn glad to meet you, son, and your dogs, too." That said, Buster walked up and down the line of Siberian huskies. "They're a good-looking bunch, small but good-looking."

"Where can we bed down?" Rune asked. He didn't feel like making small talk.

"Sure, come on with me. The stable's just yonder and there's a warm bunk for you right next door."

"Thanks, but I'm bedding with my dogs."

"Suit yourself, son," Buster said good-naturedly. "Follow me."

After a four-hour stop, Rune and his team left Candle with Zellie in the lead. Scotty Allan, Rune learned, had left a little before Frank Lundgren's sled. Rune planned to overtake both and go "on by" to a win in Nome. The previous storm must have held all the sleds up, Rune decided, based upon

413

all accounts. Out on the race trail for two days at least, he wasn't sure how he was doing time-wise. The race was run over four days, but four days wouldn't win this — not the way the two sleds in front were running. Confident in his Siberian huskies, Rune didn't doubt he would overtake them before Nome.

A little queasy since he'd left Candle, Rune fought the urge to retch. His head ached and his stomach pained him. It was hard for him to keep his balance, so he held on to the sled's handlebar tighter and did his best not to slip off the runners. This wasn't any time to give in to sickness. A treacherous glacial lake waited for them. So did a steep run through the "valley of blizzards." He needed his wits about him to best help the dogs. They'd slowed down over the last miles without him giving any command.

Dammit!

The food!

The food given to him at the Topkok Roadhouse had something wrong with it, Rune suspected. He and the dogs had eaten the same meat. Tainted food could make you sick. So could food laced with tasteless, odorless arsenic! He thought immediately of Frank Lundgren. What was it Farley

414

Smith had said back at Topkok? "I've got plenty of extra meat for you, just left here, as luck would have it." Rune knew it wasn't luck but poisoned food left by Frank Lundgren, meant to bring down Rune's team.

"Whoa!" he yelled out to the dogs.

They all slowed more then stopped, some of them stumbling.

Rune didn't have to throw the snow hook to keep them stopped. He didn't know how they'd kept running, as they were likely feeling as sick as he was right now. The light of day on his side, Rune moved from the back of the sled to the front of the team, his step faltering. Zellie still stood, but he could see she didn't want to. She looked sick and about to collapse.

"Easy, girl," he whispered and gave her the hand command to lie down. The moment she did, he went up and down the line of dogs to send those that hadn't already, to a lie-down position. Frost and Flowers vomited, then Xander. Rune knew their stomachs all must pain them the same way his did. He didn't think they had enough poison in them to kill, because they'd all be dead by now. But they all had enough arsenic in them to wear them down and lose the race.

It would be hard for Frank Lundgren to escape a murder charge, but then Rune knew it would be hard for anyone to prove the unscrupulous dog driver had anything to do with the incident. Frank Lundgren must have thought they'd eat the bad meat before leaving Topkok, which is why he reported what he did to the race watcher in Candle.

Unsteady on his feet, Rune slowly paced around the dogs, and checked each one repeatedly. Not long afterward, he vomited himself, and fell to his knees near Zellie. She put her paw to him, in silent understanding. He felt a little better for her comforting touch and was able to stand back up. Zellie stood on all fours now, and she looked more recovered than the rest of the team.

"You're a brave girl, you are, and a strong one," Rune praised, rubbing her behind her ears. He thought her the most beautiful dog he'd ever seen, and certainly the most intelligent and steadfast guide.

The winds suddenly picked up. The "valley of blizzards" waited for them. So did a hazardous glacial lake. He worried about hidden crevasses in the steep valley and unnatural holes in the ice. Rune knew they'd lost precious time in the race, and precious more would be lost to the coming storm. Time mattered, every second and minute of it. With his dogs disabled at the moment, only Zellie looked recovered and ready to go. Questioning the wisdom of it, still unsteady from the effects of the arsenic, and still fighting for clear vision, Rune began to unfasten Zellie's hitch to the towline.

"Girl." He knelt in front of her, eye to eye with his valued leader dog. "We don't have any time to lose. I'm going to release you to go on ahead and scout the safest way around the glacier lake and through the valley of blizzards in front of us. We need the fastest path. I know you can find it. I know I'm asking much of you, to do double the work and return for us, but we need you, girl. When we can, the dogs and I will follow your guide and catch up on the trail."

He prayed his tone and manner would somehow trigger the iron will he knew she had within herself. If ever there was a time for the gods to help, it was now: helping Zellie understand what she must do.

Ancient drums of the Chukchi beat out their message.

The Gatekeepers heard.

The wolf heard.

Zellie stared trustingly at Rune, her ears pricked as if she were picking up something in the changed Direction of the arctic winds. Wolves howled from afar. Zellie sniffed the air in sharp, short intakes, then suddenly barked, ready to go.

Only Xander barked in response. His barks turned to howls. Wolves answered in the distance. Still hitched to the towline and weak, Xander couldn't move from his position.

Rune guessed at Xander's upset.

He slipped Zellie out of her harnessing, thinking it the best thing to do. He didn't want anything unknown to catch her up.

"Mush!" he gently commanded the moment she was free.

Zellie took off in a flurry, but hesitated in the distance, stopping and looking back toward Rune and Xander and the rest of the team. Then, in a split second, she'd disappeared.

Xander whimpered and fell down. He put his head on his front paws and stayed that way, his eyes shut.

Rune guessed Xander felt just like he did: lost without Zellie there with them. He prayed again to the gods to help her find her way out and back again.

"Easy. We'll rest for a while, then we'll go, too," Rune said, talking calmly to the dogs as if they understood. They needed to regain enough strength to run despite the arsenic that was probably in their systems. "We'll find Zellie soon enough," he told the dogs as if reassuring old friends. He walked the line of huskies again, and checked each one, giving them the "lie down" command when they tried to stand. Fierce winds blew, ruffling their fur but not their temperaments. The dogs lay silent and unmoving, and would until their guardian commanded them to "mush."

True to prediction, the way ahead for Zellie was no way at all but a web of cracks in the ice across the glacial lake and impasses around crevasses in the steep trail leading to the valley of blizzards. Winds whipped at her back, which took her off course more than once. Heavy snow rained down like ice. Her fur clotted with it, her outer coat almost a frozen sheet of the stuff. Something had caught her back foot and cut it when she'd made her way off and around the glacial lake. Her foot hurt and bled, but she didn't stop.

In her husky head and heart, she knew she had to "mush" back to her guardians. Perhaps Anya's face and Rune's appeared before her. Only the gods would know if such a thing happened. Only the gods were able to understand the ways of the Chukchi dogs when no mortal could.

Zellie's canine instincts pulled her back from the edges of a bottomless crevasse just in time, stopping her fall into the deep, black hole that waited far below. Whimpering, then sniffing hard, she edged away from the crevasse to search another way. Ice surrounded her as if coating every part of the trail, making her unsure of her steps. She didn't see or hear the ravens cawing in angry circles overhead. She couldn't hear anything now but the drums of the ancestors sounding for her to run . . . to run from this place *now!*

Zellie fell then, her bad foot catching another unexpected jag of ice, setting her off her footing and sending her down, down, down into the deadly crevasse hundreds of feet below. There she lay, alone, bleeding, dying. Try as she might, instinctively she wanted to follow the command given her to "mush," but she could not. She couldn't move a muscle in her pained, battered body. Whimpering low, she didn't have the strength left to call to her guardian and the ancestors. Able to keep her eyes open a little, Zellie blinked against the dark cold, taking in quick inspirations, the last moments of her life playing out.

Then she saw the light — at first a glow and then her guardian Spirit.

The seal-brown husky nuzzled Zellie's cold face, licking her, warming her, holding back death long enough to bring some kind of comfort. Then Spirit lay down alongside Zellie, and nestled close.

Zellie didn't whimper anymore. She was able to move her paw over Spirit's, recognizing her forever friend and guardian. With her pain lifted, Zellie closed her eyes a final time. Her last breath came easily.

Spirit lay motionless and watched Zellie's body vanish into the spirit world of the ancestors, into the company of the Gatekeepers. There Zellie would sleep in peace and wait for the rest of the dogs and help pull each one's sled across into heaven. So it had been for centuries past, and so might it be for centuries to come *if* Spirit could prevail. Raising her muzzle heavenward, Spirit howled in mourning over her lost friend and companion, beloved in this world and any other. Her grief echoed through the deadly crevasse, shaking its shadows and walls.

Rune had over a hundred fifty miles to go and no time in which to do it. He worried about the dogs, hoping they'd recovered enough to take to the rugged path. Something had just stirred them up. One moment they were lying down, and the next they got up, raring to go, struggling against their harnesses and fighting their hitches. None of them got sick after their first bout with the arsenic poison. Rune didn't understand their speedy recovery, especially as he still felt bad himself, and his vision still blurred in and out. He'd heard the same cry of the wolf in the distance, thinking maybe the wolves had the dogs stirred. Or maybe it was the worsening storm. Whatever the reason, they weren't excited over Zellie's return. She hadn't yet.

Rune worried about her; she'd been gone so long and not come back. She must have run into trouble. Anxious to get on the trail and find her, he knew they couldn't make it to Nome safely without her as a guide. Even with the sunstone of the Vikings fixed in his brain, he doubted his skills without Zellie's help. Anya waited at the finish line. Anya waited for the safe return of them all. She waited for them to cross first and win. The two teams in front of him already made good headway, he was sure. Those teams couldn't cross first. He couldn't face Anya if they did.

"Mush!" Rune commanded in a roar, want-

ing to be heard over the storm.

Magic and Mushroom didn't hesitate.

Little Wolf yipped as he took off in his power spot behind Flowers.

Xander stayed quiet, every ounce of his muscle and strength driving the sled to a fast start.

Rune held on to the handlebar, pedaling and running with everything in him, and charged into the storm along with his team. They hit the glacial lake all too soon.

"Come haw!" Rune yelled, doing his best to veer the sled left and off the ice before it was too late. The serpent waited beneath the ice, far-reaching, ready to strike. Maybe it didn't lie in wait. Maybe it did. Rune refused to take the chance, even though to cross the lake would be faster and even though it might lose the race for them.

Desperate to spot Zellie, Rune pressed the team on around the jagged edges of the frozen lake, refusing to look over the ice for any breaks where she might have been taken below. If something happened to her he'd have *Hel* to pay, and pay he would. He'd travel to the hottest depths to slay the beast if anything happened to Zellie! *Nine serpents you must slay;* he remembered the ghostly Viking command given him. He must protect all nine of the dogs. If he had to go to

He! nine times, so be it!

Zellie ran up just then.

The dogs didn't need any command from Rune to stop.

Rune hoped he saw right, that Zellie had come back.

Xander barked first in greeting, then the rest — all wagging their tails, obviously happy to see Zellie again.

Rune walked over to her and knelt down.

"My brave girl," he whispered, relieved. "I knew you could do it. I knew you'd come back for us." He took her mask in his hands and gently rubbed behind her ears, never more respectful of her abilities and those of all the Chukchi dogs. Her pretty face and intelligent eyes shone. Strengthened by her, he gave Zellie a last pat, then went to the sled to get her harness. In moments he had her set and ready to lead the team safely around the hazardous, frozen lake then over and down into the steep valley of blizzards, confident in her guidance. The miles ahead didn't seem quite so long to Rune anymore. He wouldn't stop on the race trail because time had run out. It was all up to the heart, skill, and breeding of the Chukchi dogs now, and not him. There was only one command left to give.

"Mush!"

And so they did, into the storm, against all odds.

Scotty Allan and his team crossed the finish line of the 1909 All Alaska Sweepstakes in eighty-two hours, two minutes, and forty-one seconds. They were the first team in. The waiting crowd cheered. The press ran off to spread news of the big win, sending the news by telegraph and telephone where they could, throughout the District of Alaska and the Outside.

Anticipation still ran high among the excited crowd while they stayed to watch for Frank Lundgren's team. He didn't disappoint, coming in at exactly eighty-two hours, eighteen minutes, and forty-two seconds. Another roar from the crowd went up, then died as the jubilant onlookers started to break for home or for the nearest saloon to celebrate their win. The Eskimos didn't leave, but stayed to wait for the return of the third sled, out of respect. The People ran on the race trail. They would not desert the Chukchi dogs.

Albert Fink remained at the finish, trying to decide if he should wait there as president of the Nome Kennel Club, feeling obliged to as a race official. The race start judge stood next to him.

425

"Listen, Albert. I tried to talk the kid out of racing. Those dogs of his can't finish this course in any kind of time, and you know it. Last we knew, he'd made it to Topkok but that's it. I'm sorry to say it, but after the weather dies down, we'll likely have a dead dog driver and nine dead Siberian dogs to find. If there's anything left to find," he finished soberly.

Albert shook his head, in reluctant agreement with the judge. The last thing he wanted was to have even one dead dog, much less Lars Johansson's son! The shipping magnate could help ruin business in Nome if word got out that his son died under the watchful eye of the Nome Kennel Club. Hell, Albert didn't want the kid dead, either. He felt bad, real bad for Rune Johansson and his team. His dog team tried. At least he gave the kid that. Albert would be the one to tell the father. He owed it to the family and to himself, and he felt the full burden of responsibility.

"You coming?" the start judge asked quietly, before he turned to head inside the Board of Trade Saloon.

"Not yet, Cyrus," Albert answered. "I'm going to give the kid a little more time."

Cyrus said nothing else and left Albert standing in the thinned-out crowd.

■ ■ ■ ■

Frank Lundgren couldn't believe he'd lost to Scotty Allan! He hadn't let Scotty "on by" when rules called for it on the trail miles back. How in blazes did Scotty's team get past him? He must have cheated and gone another way! That ten thousand dollars should be *his,* not Scotty's!

So enraged was Frank that he failed to appreciate the fact that when he'd crossed the finish line, the judges had remarked out loud about the whip lashes on his bleeding dogs; he would be disqualified from any win. The rules said no whips. Frank had obviously punished his dogs with a whip for eighty-two hours, eighteen minutes, and forty-two seconds.

Frank was satisfied about one thing. He'd taken care of the upstart kid and his lousy team of rats. They wouldn't cross the finish line in any kind of time that mattered, if they made it at all, he snickered to himself. If they all died on the race trail from something bad they ate, so what? Even if they made it back to Nome, then so what? No one could prove anything against him. He wandered away from his team, leaving Brutus alone for the first time in days. Luckily for Frank's team, concerned dog drivers, experienced in handling the toughest and roughest, saw to his dogs when he would not. First thing was to fetch the vet.

Albert Fink looked in disgust at the sad sight of the injured dogs, vowing never to allow Frank Lundgren to enter any of their sweepstakes again.

The Eskimos saw, too, and vowed never to be a friend to such an excuse for a man.

Others still watched and waited. A few tourists and businessmen with mining interests in the area looked on, too, speculating on how serious the dogs' injuries were and if they'd ever be able to race again. In quiet conversation and looking in the opposite direction, none of them saw the third sled team arrive quietly in Nome.

Just over eighty-three hours since their start, forty minutes behind the second team that returned, Rune and his dogs crossed the finish line, more alive than dead, as many thought they might well be. Shouts of "impossible" and loud "hurrahs" brought some of the men back outside the Board of Trade Saloon. People started gathering at the race finish from all parts of town, shocked to see the "Siberian wolves" finish in such record time! No one but the Eskimos had believed in the smaller huskies.

Everyone had scoffed at Rune and his dogs and placed their bets elsewhere.

One onlooker at the finish slapped Rune on the back, then offered his congratulations.

"Good for you!" another yelled out.

Rune took heart by their reactions to his finish. His team *won*. He searched the crowd for Anya, able to look her in the eye with his win. She wasn't there? He scanned all around but didn't see her and was suddenly worried something might have happened to her while he'd been gone.

Albert Fink put out his hand to Rune.

Rune removed his fur mitt and shook hands, although he was distracted, and still searched the crowd for Anya.

"You did real good, son," Albert praised. "Fact is I'm happy to see you're all right, you and your dogs. I wasn't sure you'd make it, much less finish third in our sweepstakes."

Third!

Rune slid his hand out of Albert Fink's hold, not believing what he'd just heard. It couldn't be. Third wasn't good enough. He needed to be first and win. He'd been defeated after all; some Viking warrior he made. The battle had been lost, and it was his fault. He stopped searching the crowd for Anya, unable to face her yet, and momentarily forgetting his worry that she wasn't at the finish.

A still-shocked Cyrus came outside the saloon to check all of Rune's team, making sure every dog he started with had returned.

"Good on you, son, getting all your dogs back here safe and sound and not a mark on any of 'em," the start judge said.

"Sure thing," Rune answered, glad they all were safe and sound. "I want to rest my dogs now if you don't mind." Then he gave Zellie a quick kissing sound and ran the team past the start judge and the gathered crowd; they left Front Street and headed to a back alleyway, to their rented shelter. That must be where Anya waited. He didn't know how to face her with his loss.

The storm had ended. He should be glad for it. He should be glad the skies were lit and the winds had died down. No shadows lurked. They'd made it through the storm. But it didn't feel like it to him. He was on his way into the eye of another storm, an even worse one, on his way now to give Anya such bad news, that he hadn't won the race. Coming around the last corner toward the stable, he shut his eyes against his upset.

"Rune," Anya greeted him in a soft whisper.

Xander moaned low, his watch-blue eyes were fixed on Anya.

Rune opened his own eyes, flooded with relief to see Anya. Nothing had happened to her! She smiled at him, the prettiest smile on the prettiest girl he'd ever seen. It broke his heart to have to tell her what he must. He needed to get this over with.

"Rune, I have to tell you something." She came closer.

"So do —"

"No," she quickly cut him off. "You must listen to me first." Taking up his hand in hers, she led him away from the team of dogs, which were all at his back now. "Rune, Zellie is gone," she spoke quietly.

Rune held her small hand in both of his. Anya would need him to help her through his bad news. Worries about the race and her bad dreams must haunt her to make her believe the worst about Zellie.

"Anya, she's all righ—"

"Shhhh," Anya whispered and put her fingers to his lips to silence him. "She is not all right. She is gone." To prove her words, Anya gently turned Rune around to face the still-hitched team.

All the Siberian huskies were there; all but

431

Zellie. Rune knelt down and picked up her empty harness, still tied to the leader tug line.

"I don't understand," he said.

"I know. Sometimes I don't, either."

"But she finish—"

"Rune," Anya gently cut him off again. "Zellie is safe now. She's gone from us, but she's safe in a world beyond ours, safe with the gods.

Rune turned the empty harness over in his hands, then looked to Anya.

"You know this?" Rune thought of his ghosts, his gods. He thought of Uppsala, the holy sacrificial place of the Vikings, where death can come. He tried to reason out what Anya was saying, what world she talked about. Had Zellie been a sacrifice to the gods? Was he supposed to accept this? None of this made any sense to him. Zellie *wasn't* safe. She was dead! There was nothing left of her but an empty harness!

"You think she is *safe* now, Anya?"

"I do," Anya answered him. "I know she is safe."

Rune reached out and wiped away the tears trickling down Anya's soft cheeks. He fought his own. He didn't know what to think about all of this, really.

"I know you loved her," he quietly said.

432

"And always will." She tried to speak brightly.

At that moment he imagined Zellie in a better place, a safer place. If Anya believed this, then so would he.

"Anya, I lost the race," he confessed, his hands ashamedly at his sides.

"No, Rune. That's just it. You didn't lose. We didn't lose," she said. "We didn't have to win, after all. Your finish was good enough. You will see."

Good enough for what, he wanted to say, but he refused to stumble out more questions, and tried to think the matter over by himself. He was confused. Anya had said before they had to win and beat the storm, and now she said they didn't. What had changed? What would he see? It didn't make sense.

"Anya, just tell me if the danger is over for you and your dogs," he demanded, almost angry.

"No, it is not. For you, either." She answered Rune as honestly as she could.

"I'm afraid it's just beginning."

GLOSSARY

adin, dva, tri — one, two, three
amarok — wolf
angare — steamship
ar-gammel — years old
baidarka — Chukchi walrus-hide boat
barn — child
bystriy — fast
chu chu — a little
da — yes
da svidanya — goodbye
dobry — good
Engelska — English
ezdovaya — sled
Far — father
gedh — where?
ice floe — flat expanse of floating ice
imiq — water
isen — ice
jente — girl
kanyeshna — of course
kapvik — wolverine

kerker — Chukchi outer fur coverall

kharaso — fine

koddah — Where do we go now?

kukashka — Chukchi inner fur shirt worn beneath kerker

lighter boat — takes passengers and supplies ashore from a large ship

malinkiy — small

mazuma — money

meck — meat

miaso — food

Mor — mother

mukluks — knee-high fur boots

nyet — no

paddy work — shovel work

pengar — money

pingayun — three

polog — fur-lined sleeping box inside tented yaranga of the Chukchi, large enough for family

pozhalujsta — please

privet — hello

rubles — dollars

Russkiy yazyk? — Do you speak Russian?

sekston ar gammel — sixteen years old

shaman — communicates with native spirits — a healer — a holy man or woman

shto — what?

Sibirskiy haskis — Siberian huskies

skepp — ship

436

sledge — sled

sluice — inclined trough, long box, used to recover precious metals during wash in placer mining

sobaka — dogs

staamat — four

talliman — five

tiblit — food

umiak — Eskimo sled

vada — water

vy — you

yaranga — Chukchi home — walrus-hide-covered tent with large center pole

ABOUT THE AUTHOR

A wife, mother, and grandmother living between Colorado and California, **Joanne Sundell** is retired from nursing. To date, she has six published works: *Matchmaker, Matchmaker,* 2006; *A . . . My Name's Amelia,* 2007; *The Parlor House Daughter,* 2008; *Meggie's Remains,* 2009; *Hearts Divided,* 2010 (volume 1 of her series The Quaker and the Confederate); and *Hearts Persuaded,* 2010 (volume 2 of The Quaker and the Confederate).

Arctic Storm is the first book in her new Watch Eyes Trilogy. This arctic adventure series represents a switch for Joanne from historical romance to frontier fiction that has young-adult crossover potential, making it a nice fit for the quickly emerging subgenre, New Adult Fiction, that is helping to bridge the gap between young-adult and adult-reader stages. Joanne has raised and loved Siberian huskies over forty years and believes it's time to tell their story.

She holds membership in Women Writing the West and Western Writers of America.